The

Counselo Jerno, sat in the cabin's lower bunk. There was a book in his lap. Blood from the gash across his throat had poured down his beard and chest, then had pooled across the pages of the book. He looked at me wide-eyed, his expression hurt.

His apprentice and nephew Kemense lay on his side on the floor. There was blood on his stomach, but not much on the planking beneath him. His eyes, too, were open and unblinking.

I stood there and tried to bring my breath under control. Two men with whom I'd shared many a pleasant word lay dead, brought low by a murderer.

Paranoia seized me and I spun around, but no one stood behind me. The killer was long gone.

But not *far* gone, not when the only available land was made up of three sailing vessels crudely lashed together.

I turned, gulping, and raced out to the fresh air, then climbed to the poop deck. "Officer of the deck!" I cried. "Murder! There has been murder!"

Then the first of the howling winds hit me face-on, knocking me down, ripping my cloak from me, tumbling me toward the bulwark. I slammed into the knee-high wooden wall, bruising my already-sore shoulder. I locked my elbow around the nearest rail post.

My stomach lurched as I felt the ship begin to list, as if leaning over to deliberately slide me into the suddenly-hungry sea. And above, even with the sky night-dark, I could see the black clouds rolling toward us like a cavalry.

THE BARD'S TALE SERIES

THUNDER OF THE CAPTAINS

A BARD'S TALE

HOLLY LISLE
AARON ALLSTON

BAEN

THUNDER OF THE CAPTAINS

This is a work of fiction. All the characters and events portrayed in this book are fictional, and any resemblance to real people or incidents is purely coincidental.

A Baen Books Original

The Bard's Tale characters and descriptions are the sole property of Electronic Arts and are used by permission. The Bard's Tale is a registered trademark of Electronic Arts.

Baen Publishing Enterprises
P.O. Box 1403
Riverdale, NY 10471

ISBN: 0-671-87730-5

Cover art by Ken Tunnell

First printing, July 1996

Distributed by Simon & Schuster
1230 Avenue of the Americas
New York, NY 10020

Typeset by Windhaven Press: Editorial Services, Auburn, NH
Printed in the United States of America

Dedication

Heroics in real life tend to be less glamorous, more tedious, and even more painful than those in fiction, yet they are the ones that matter most. For this reason, *Thunder of the Captains* is dedicated to Beckie and Dave, two people to whom fictitious heroes could look for inspiration.

Prologue

Kin Underbridge,
Valet to King Jerno of Lieda

I entered the companionway of *Wave-Breaker*'s poop deck and rapped on our Liedan wizards' door, but there was no answer.

Yet there was light beyond. They'd left a candle or lamp lit. It was a foolish, dangerous thing to do so aboard ship, so either they were within and not answering, or they were gone and damnable fools. I knocked again in case they were sleeping, then pulled the cord to raise the bar on the other side of the door.

There was no weight on the cord; it pulled easily. That meant a wizard had to be still inside, and had disconnected the cord loop from the bar to keep anyone from entering.

Irritated now—a foolish thing to be when about to confront a wizard skilled enough to be the advisor to a king—I pounded again on the door, then gave the pull-cord a frustrated yank.

Its end came clean through the hole in the door.

1

I held its length in my hand, confused. Such cords customarily ended in knots large enough to prevent the end's passage through the hole. But this one ended with a fresh cut; it had not even begun to fray.

Alarmed now, I put my full weight into the door. Though my fighting skills were usually described as "modest," or at best "adequate," I was large and muscular enough to move things when I chose to. After three blows, as my shoulder became sore, I felt the brackets holding the bar in place give way, and with my fourth blow the door slammed open.

Counselor Fahero, chief magical advisor to King Jerno, sat in the cabin's lower bunk. There was a book in his lap. Blood from the gash across his throat had poured down his beard and chest, then had pooled across the pages of the book. He looked at me wide-eyed, his expression hurt.

His apprentice and nephew Kemense lay on his side on the floor. There was blood on his stomach, but not much on the planking beneath him. His eyes, too, were open and unblinking.

I stood there and tried to bring my breath under control. Two men with whom I'd shared many a pleasant word lay dead, brought low by a murderer.

Paranoia seized me and I spun around, but no one stood behind me. The killer was long gone.

But not *far* gone, not when the only available land was made up of three sailing vessels crudely lashed together.

I turned, gulping, and raced out to the fresh air, then climbed to the poop deck. "Officer of the deck!" I cried. "Murder! There has been murder!"

Then the first of the howling winds hit me face-on, knocking me down, ripping my cloak from me, tumbling me toward the bulwark. I slammed into the knee-high wooden wall, bruising my already-sore shoulder. I locked my elbow around the nearest rail post.

My stomach lurched as the ship began to list, as if leaning over to deliberately slide me into the suddenly-hungry sea. And above, even with the sky night-dark, I could see the black clouds rolling toward us like a cavalry.

That is what most people think of when the name Landfall comes up, as if the storm were the start of the whole thing. Of course, it was not. It started with a love-match.

Chapter One

Kin

I often wondered if Princess Thaliara would have let herself be murdered if she'd known what trouble would arise from her death.

I was twelve when it happened, five years younger than she and far below her station.

The Bards said that her golden beauty would wrench a sigh from the gods. The only daughter of Lady Empress dar Kothia of Terosalle, she was to be married to Jernin, "Little Jerno," eldest recognized son of King Jerno of Lieda. Jernin himself was a favorite subject of singers and painters; he was two handspans taller than his father and had inherited the prominent nose and dark, predatory beauty of his mother the queen.

It must be understood that King Jerno and the Lady Empress could barely stand one another. They merely followed the grand tradition of antagonism between Lieda and Terosalle that went back for centuries. But their children met during Jernin's state visit of the year before. Love hit them like a rock from a catapult, and they spent the next year apart sighing when they should have been breathing.

Their love turned out to be a great convenience, though. King Jerno and the Empress could use the marriage as an excuse to rob one another blind through new treaties of peace and mutual affection. The Bards were mad for the marriage—brave, handsome son and clever, beautiful daughter, a union of kingdoms as well as of princes, and so forth. So sticky-sweet were the songs written in anticipation of the event that I took rotten fruit with me wherever I went. When I heard a minstrel pluck up the notes that grew more hateful every day, I pelted him with decayed apples from a position of concealment—a risky proposition, because some of the singers might be Bards instead of mere minstrels, but I felt it had to be done.

While I was improving my throwing arm, a delegation of King Jerno's officials left Lieda and began the difficult mountain crossing along the Fadornal Track, the best-maintained trade route to Terosalle. Their leader was Buyan, a rising star in the Liedan army and, it is said, an unrecognized son of King Jerno. Certainly his mother was once a mistress of the king's, and it was no secret that King Jerno lavished praise upon him that he withheld from other captains just as skilled.

Buyan's task was to conduct Princess Thaliara to her new home. This way, all the luckless hordes of Lieda might gaze upon her and be reminded of how far short we fell of ever knowing her beauty and grace.

That, of course, is when the trouble began.

Some time after Buyan's departure, a courier in the dress of Terosalle's army came to the capital bearing a letter. I have never seen the document itself—Jerno may have destroyed it, or may have kept it in his quarters; he never told me. But its gist became common knowledge in the streets and pubs and soldiers' barracks of the city: "Thank you for sending your son;

we will kill him if you do not send us his weight in gold. By the way, we are keeping my daughter here; do you imagine we'd ever let her be fouled by the touch of a Liedan prince?"

Those words were, of course, an invitation to war. But Jerno was anxious about the safety of his favorite captain. And he was keenly aware that Empress dar Kothia's reputation for trustworthiness exceeded his own—whose did not? So he sent the ransom. Once Buyan was back, he could launch his fleets and armies to avenge the insult.

But Buyan never came back. Instead, vengeful Terosai armies came thundering across the mountains. Their captured soldiers made the preposterous claim that King Jerno had kidnapped Princess Thaliara, taken the Empress' gold, and killed the girl. Buyan and Thaliara were never seen again.

Suddenly all Lieda mobilized for war. As the son of a decorated officer, I would be expected to follow in the family tradition. But I was only twelve, and it would be another two or three years before I would have to fight; perhaps the war would be over by then.

My brother Tan went off to war. The army sent back his possessions a month later.

My father surprised me then.

First, he cried. He did this alone, where neither my mother nor the children could see him, but we heard it through his study door. Father crying; it was only reasonable that next the sun would shine blue and the gods would complain of the aches of age.

Second, he took me aside for a private conference— man to man. It was the first time he had ever invoked that magic phrase with me, and I glowed inside.

"Kin," he said. "You would begin training in sword and armor in two years. But I think you should begin now."

"Yes, Father." Pride within me warred with the

knowledge that I had no desire to follow Tan's path, no wish to make my parents cry.

"But your mother says you are very quick with your letters. And quick of the ear. You impressed old General Saralar with your manner."

"Yes, Father." Now would come the admonishment that letters and other learning, though useful, were not manly; I needed to learn to read, but only well enough to understand military dispatches.

"Good. I want you to study hard." His gaze dropped as his words betrayed one of the tenets by which he had lived his life. "Kin, I think this war will be long and difficult. I want my boys to be everywhere. Some in the army. Some . . . elsewhere. Do you understand?"

"Yes, Father." Of course I didn't. What I did understand was that I would begin training with the sword two years younger than any of my brothers, and that I might not have to go into the army anyway. The war had taken my brother away, but it had given me two wishes in return. With the mind of a child, I thought that perhaps the war was not so bad after all.

"Good." He gave me a quick embrace and sent me away.

A month later he was gone, too. In spite of his game leg, injured about the time I was born, they accepted his return to service and promoted him. The war was already eating its way into the supplies of Lieda's skilled commanders, and many retired veterans were returning to the life of the soldier.

Two years later, the War of the Princess showed sign of abating. Merchants on both sides grumbled; when not at war, Lieda and Terosalle were one another's chief trading partners, and this protracted unpleasantness was a great impediment to trade. Commanders of opposing forces dined together in their tents when not ordering their soldiers against one another. Advisors to the respective crowns recommended overtures of peace.

Prince Jernin, the brideless groom, was now two and twenty. The First Fleet, under his command, was set upon by combined naval forces of the Terosai. They outmanned him nearly three to one, but his force did so much damage to their navy that the battle is accounted a tremendous victory for Lieda.

Still, Prince Jernin's body was pierced by four crossbow quarrels and washed up on shore a week later, so pasty and bloated that he finally did resemble his father. It suddenly mattered not at all whether the nations' leaders and traders were tired of the war; King Jerno's hatred blazed up like a city set on fire, and then so did the war.

Soon after, my father made one of his occasional visits home. He got drunk and sat up all night in his study. I heard his glass clinking and silently crept in to see what he was about.

He heard me, but gave no sign for a long moment. Then he set his goblet down and said, "Your mother tells me you are learning the tongue of Terosalle."

"Yes, Father." I trembled, lest that be seen as a betrayal—collaboration with the enemy. But I was fourteen now, the traditional time when a boy begins the training of his manhood; it was time for me to demonstrate I was becoming a man. "I have the ear for it. It is something I want to do." I tried to make my voice firm, but not defiant.

"Good." He turned to look at me. I was struck by the fact that his expression, which always seemed so judgmental, now only looked solemn. "You can't learn your enemy's mind unless you know his tongue. You can't . . . learn to distinguish his truth from his lies."

"I don't understand."

"Nor do I," he said. He drained his goblet and refilled it with the harsh whisky of the south. "It is as though two wars are being fought. Ours is fought because they insulted us, took the King's favorite captain, and killed him in spite of the ransom. And theirs is fought because . . . because we stole their princess, and demanded ransom for her, and slew her when it was delivered."

"But we didn't!"

"No."

"What does it mean?"

"One of three things. Either they are lying . . . which I can no longer completely believe. They speak with such anger and conviction. Or we are lying . . . which I do not believe. It would not profit us to do what they said we did.

"Or it means something else. I am not sure what. But I feel that lies are at the heart of the war, and we will never cut through those lies while the war goes on."

"Why do you not tell someone?"

He laughed and reached over to tousle my hair. "You heard about Prince Jernin?"

"I've heard about little else these last few weeks."

"Do you think, even if I could find proof for what I believe, the King would suddenly find his anger cooled?"

"No."

"Well, then." His smile was melancholy. "Go to bed, Kin. The quiet hours of the night are for old men with ghosts wandering their memories."

I grew tall—taller than my father, a source of some pride for both of us. But I also grew blocky and clumsy, inheriting the build of my oxlike uncle, Tesker.

My sister Fara married a merchant captain from the southern parts of Lieda. She sent glowing letters of a life scarcely touched by the war.

My youngest brother, named after Uncle Tesker,

went into the navy as a cabin boy. Suddenly I was the only child left at home.

By then I understood what my father had done. Many of his friends were doing the same thing: Sending their sons and daughters into different provinces, into different professions, sometimes into different families. As the cream of Lieda's youth died in the mountains and on the oceans between the two countries, far-sighted parents did this to ensure that some of their children would survive.

When I had sixteen winters, my father arranged for me to be sent away, too. Not far—not even out of Bekalli, the capital—but still beyond a border as forbidding as the mountains between nations. I was sent into the royal citadel, as appointed companion to Prince Balaquin.

Balaquin was Jerno's second recognized son. From the start he favored his father, being rather less than average height and tending toward corpulence, with no talent for war. However, he was earnest, intelligent, and responsible. He was two years my senior, and needed a companion who shared his love of matters of the intellect but could still defend him in times of trouble. I do not know how my appointment was arranged, but my father was now a hero of two wars; it is not surprising that the court administrators might wish to accommodate him.

I was his companion for three years. I never had to draw a knife in his defense, though I once had to hit a drunken army captain in the face; I was fortunate enough to knock the wretch unconscious, which gave me a wholly-undeserved reputation as a skillful brawler. Mostly, I accompanied Balaquin to the tutors who instructed him in building and engineering.

This was the seventh year of the war, when the fighting was at its ebb and there were whispered rumors that ennui might finally bring peace. Balaquin led a detachment of King's Engineers into the mountainous border between Lieda and Terosalle, to a little-used alternate trail that split off from the Western Trade Route and then rejoined with it a few leagues later, to oversee the expansion of a road-straddling fortress. I went with him.

On this narrow, half-forgotten mountain trail, we— a plump prince, a companion not yet at the formal age of manhood, and a detachment of engineers—ran headlong into an elite unit of Terosai infantry, the spearpoint of a massive new invasion.

Balaquin retreated before them. He dispatched me back to the lowlands to summon help. Then he began to use his engineers to delay and harry the Terosai.

They built deadfalls. They began avalanches. They undermined bridges. When they were too short on materials or manpower to do anything, they spent a few minutes and lengths of rope to disguise perfectly sound stretches of roadway to seem treacherous and deadly. Terosai scouts minced and danced around the supposed dangers and lost precious hours trying fruitlessly to disarm them.

Balaquin's engineers slowed the advance to a crawl and broke the point off the Terosai spear. But when I brought the Liedan reinforcements back along the mountain trail, we found Balaquin and his remaining men frozen to death in a high mountain cave. They'd crept there for shelter and died of weakness and cold.

King Jerno's hatred of the enemy grew into an all-consuming firestorm. That was when he instituted the new punishments for captured Terosai—the laws we call the "measures" when we dare to speak of them at all, the same ones the Terosai refer to as the "atrocities."

Of a sudden, prisoner exchanges stopped even between the nobles. From one day to the next, the songs about glorious fights between knights and captains of two nations disappeared. Suddenly, if court minstrels were to be believed, we Liedans were game-keepers and the Terosai were diseased animals needing extermination.

The King's youngest son was Tarno. Him I knew well; I taught him to read and write. He inherited his father's fair hair and ready smile, but in his case the hair reflected sunlight instead of gold and the smile always matched what was in his eyes. Tarno learned to play the flute because he thought all knights and princes should be tainted by civilized arts. He thought no warrior could be as worthy as a minstrel. In his youthful admiration of heroes of the past, he never realized that he had the skill to be a master at both professions.

In the twelfth year of the war, Lieda's great sailor, Captain Russtin Kohugh, who'd taught Prince Jernin how to sail and fight on the sea, captured a Terosai ship of the line. Amongst the passengers was Ilyada dar Tothian, niece of Lieda's Empress.

And with the predictable perversity that afflicts the line of King Jerno, young Prince Tarno met and fell in love with her.

Tarno wrote a letter—a dissertation, actually—to his father to describe compelling reasons why she must be released and he must marry her. The war could end, the two nations could send examiners to one another's lands to see if both sides were telling the truth about Captain Buyan and Princess Thaliara, and everyone could be happy. It was a good letter; thank the Gods the ing never learned that I helped Tarno compose it.

We were certain that it, and others to follow it, would convince the King. We had time; the girl was not slated for execution for weeks, and Jerno, if seasoned and prepared over enough time, could deny nothing to his last child.

But King Jerno read the letter and, assuming that Ilyada was exerting an unhealthy influence on his son, had the girl impaled that very day. He chose to forego the usual additional tortures in order to ensure that she died before Tarno could interfere.

The Prince took the news well. He sat down and wrote another letter to his father, all by himself. This one, in curiously mild tones, explained that the King had erred and that no good could come of it. He sealed it with his ring and, oddly, asked me to have someone I disliked deliver it to the King. Tarno was so unpracticed with deception that I forgot he could do it at all. I did as I was told.

While I was gone about that errand, the Prince climbed the two hundred steps to the top of the palace's bell-tower, renowned in song and fable for its architectural beauty. He stepped off its summit and dashed his brains out on the pave-stones a hundred feet below.

That was it, Landfall's true beginning, not the storm everyone thinks of. The beginning was Tarno's thinking-meat leaking redly out on summer-warm stones while birds circled and eyed it hungrily. Scarcely a romantic image, but history does not always unfold as if composed by a Bard.

With Tarno's death, King Jerno's hatred vanished like a candle flame in the wind.

I saw him look for it. Once his son's body was cleaned for viewing and mourning and he-looks-like-he's-only-sleeping, the King moved among his courtiers, accepting their condolences and searching their faces for some sign of the rage that had sustained him for so many years.

He never found it.

He did not even kill Ardith Netter, the man who brought him the Prince's last letter. I had to do that myself, months later.

Jerno spent a proper moon buried in grief. Then he sent for Sheroit dar Bontine, the diplomat without a country, the negotiator renowned in song, and commanded him to end this war.

I was happy. I had not yet learned that men renowned in song tended to get the people around them killed.

Now, years after the fact, I take quill in hand to remember the desperate times that followed Sheroit's great success. I am aided in my memory by the chronicles of Halleyne dar Dero, who kept a journal as the events were unfolding. I have mixed portions of her account with my own.

Chapter Two

Kin

Legends say that at Hanuman's Point, giants trying to escape the anger of the gods fled eastward and noticed too late that they'd splashed out into the sea; they turned to stare in puzzlement back at the land, at their cousins following them, and it is then the gods turned them into stone. Thus it is the Point consists of a spine of thickly-clustered hills and mountains that reaches the eastern shore and turns into a knobby, stony finger of land stretching some miles out into the sea. There are also mountains farther out, underneath the waves; they occasionally gut ships the way giants of the oceans were supposed to.

Hard winds whip up these seas, and even where there are not submerged hills, reefs are thick beneath the choppy water. Pirates love these waters, traversing them in shallow-bottomed galleys, hiding their stolen goods in the numberless caves lining the shores and dotting the stony crest of hills, preying on the merchantmen who carry on trade between north and south in happier times. And shipwrecks lie thick on the bottom, not only from pirate attacks, but from the long and noble tradition of Liedan and Terosai ships battering one another to pieces in these border waters.

It is a place of war, death, and misery, featureless gray-green sea to the east, bleak stone to the west. Why come here to negotiate peace? Perhaps because no one would wish to be distracted by scenic beauty; better to stare into the face of the hated enemy than to gaze out at the land and sea.

I turned away from the rail, hugging my cloak tight against the cold, wet Liedan wind that the sun now rising above the sea would not begin to warm for hours, and stumbled my way back to the quarter-deck, ignoring the knowing smiles of the sailors.

Every morning it had been the same: "Look in the aft hold, Kin. I think they're there." "Saw 'em in the brig, chained tight as you please, just yesterday morn."

"Saw what?"

"Yer sea legs."

I never found them. I just smiled for the sailors, at least when my rebelling stomach would let me, and played the fool. After a couple of weeks of this, they decided that I'd borne my drubbing in good grace and they left off the sea-leg jokes.

King Jerno occupied what was normally the captain's cabin. By every standard of a man-of-war such as this, the cabin was comfortable, having ample room for one man, his bed, a desk and chair and cabinet, and with a bank of windows against the stern that he might look out over the water and enjoy fresh breezes; but this cabin was not scaled to a man of the King's size. When I entered he was already awake, his dressers and bodyservants helping him up into a sitting position, his eyes bleary, the great whalelike expanse of his skin a blotchy pink from sleep.

He glared at me as I entered. His voice was deceptively quiet. "My young Lord Underbridge."

"Majesty." The four-poster bed he'd had moved in took up almost the entire cabin, making it necessary for me to walk sideways between it and the far wall to get to the armoire he had installed for this voyage.

"You were not here when I awoke. You should always be on hand, to see to my comfort."

"I was seeing to your comfort." The armoire was divided into numberless slots each holding two or three ensembles; it bulged with the garments he'd brought. I had to guess the identity of each ensemble within from the narrow span of color it presented. "Your comfort for the day. It is cold now, so for the morning you should wear a fine, heavy cloak. But there are no clouds, and Captain Kohugh tells me that midday will be sweltering." I drew my finger across the impenetrable wall of clothing. "I recommend the blue silks." I tried to insert my fingers around the garments in question, but the clothes were packed in too tightly for me to get a grip on them.

With the aid of one dresser on each leg, the King swung around and planted his feet on the deck. "I will wear the gold brocade."

"And by midday you will be in the hell of royal discomfort." I saw one of the dressers suppress a cringe; none of the King's other personal servants could speak with quite that amount of honesty to His Majesty.

He chose to ignore the undue familiarity of my remark. He made one effort to stand, and failed; he sank back into the feathery mattress and began resting for his next attempt. "Did you see what she wore yesterday?"

"I did." I tried again, bracing myself against the armoire frame with one hand and hauling on the blue silks with the other; the garments emerged the distance of a handspan. "Two-tiered green the colors of seaweed and vomit. Enough gold jewelry to sink the tub she sailed in on. The light coming off her was sufficient to blind her scribe."

"I cannot let her outshine me, Kin."

"Your Majesty, quite naturally concerned with the respect that is due his office, failed to notice that the Empress was not spectacular, but merely a spectacle." I hauled again, and the cubicle finally yielded up the clothes I wanted. "She sweated all through the day— her color choice concealed it. But I heard one of her own sailors say she looked like something dragged up by the anchor."

He laughed, quivering the point on his little beard. This was his low, rumbling laugh, the real one, and it shook the bed so that the headposts rapped against the wall.

The cabin door opened and Ardith Netter, his messenger, peered in suspiciously. Doubtless he'd thought the King was banging on the wall to get his attention. I waved him away and he closed the door again, obviously relieved that he would not yet have to work. I handed the packet of clothing to one of the dressers.

The King quieted, summoning his energy, and made another attempt. This time he came upright, and though he wavered for a moment, he kept to his feet. "Well, then. See to your duties, Kin. It's sad, though. I imagine that she has learned her lesson— for a day or so, anyway. She will dress for the weather."

"Well . . ." I edged back around to the door. "If Your Majesty wishes, I will arrange it so that she dresses even more uncomfortably than yesterday."

The King's eyes seemed to gleam in the candlelight. "Can you do this?"

"I think so. I have amazing powers, you know."

"You need them. You're no good as a valet." He

indulgently waved me out. "Do this for me, Kin, and I will give you a rich reward."

"It is done." I retreated and closed the door behind me.

Ardith Netter stood in the companionway, waiting, frowning at the prospect of the new day and the effort it might cost him. "What's his complaint?"

"No complaint. In fact, he said there will be no messages to the Empress or Dar Bontine. You are off duty until the meeting convenes." He smiled in self-appreciation, and I leaned forward to make the killing stroke: "Oh, and we are in for a treat today."

"How so?"

"I heard His Majesty say that he wanted to wear the gold brocade. I imagine that he intends to show that foreign shrew just how a civilized ruler dresses."

He tried to keep his face from lighting up. "Well, that's interesting. Thanks for the word, Kin. I'm off for a walk about the deck." He gave me a knowing smile. "If I see your sea legs—"

"You'll send them to me. Yes, yes. Thank you." Ardith was always one joke behind everyone else.

I watched him leave and gave him a couple of minutes to get clear. It had taken me a week to find out that the inevitable leak in our secrecy had sprung first through Ardith; I now had his petty treachery timed very well. Long before the sun cleared the top of the mountains of Hanuman's Point, the Empress would know just what His Majesty had chosen to wear. Of course, I had to arrange for Ardith to escape his duties and any further chance to see His Majesty before the daily gathering began; else he'd be able to correct his mistake.

After today, even Ardith might suspect that I was on to him. But there was every sign that today would be the last meeting, with treaties signed today or tomorrow.

Halleyne, Personal Scribe to Lia, Majeste of Terosalle

Herself asked me once again about the time I spent working on my decorative borders. "Every free moment you have," she said, in the Shrill Voice, the one that could etch glass, "doing your calligraphy in your little book. It is not normal. Why do you not find yourself a lad?"

Because I do not want to see him die by your order? No, I did not say this. Instead, I said, "I think the gods fated my life to be devoted to scholarly pursuits."

She smiled at me and I knew I'd made the correct answer. And, greatly daring, I showed her the page I was working on, this very page, with its elaborate border of knotwork and rondels and hatchwork marks contained within a frame tinted green by my own hand, and she admired its complexity without ever realizing that these words, my true thoughts, were represented by the nonsense symbols.

This was in the Hour of Receiving Intimates. Herself sat, her tiny body wrapped in a glorious green dressing-gown of silk from distant Chatharre, and waited for those on whom she'd bestowed special visiting privileges to arrive.

Of course, aboard ship almost no one had such privileges. It was not like court; here in the waters off the east coast, with our flagship (the imperiously-named *Thunderer*), the Liedan flagship *Wave-Breaker*, and Sheroit dar Bontine's ridiculous barge all lashed together, Herself had almost no intimates. Only dar Bontine, and he arrived even as I was showing off the artwork that would result in my death if ever deciphered.

I suppose I should describe Sheroit dar Bontine. He is tall and lean as a fencepost, but walks with an agreeable stoop, the better to avoid smacking his head on doorjambs or towering over those he stands beside. His features are actually quite homely, his skin worn by weathering, his chin receding; but he wears a dark, graying beard to cover some shortcomings and a cultured air to cover the rest, and the ladies fawn over him. One need only shave him and put him in a farmer's clothes to make him look like a village idiot. I am fascinated by the effort and deliberation he has put into making himself what he is.

After all appropriate introductions from the doorguard (who has been unhappily pressed into service as a herald), dar Bontine settled into the visitor's chair, stationed almost knee-to-knee with the Queen's chair, and flew straight to the point. "Today, Most High Lady, must be about blame." His voice was a cultured smoothness with no trace of accent; I was reminded that he also spoke Liedan with native skill.

Herself nodded sagely. "Yes, of course. The Liedans must acknowledge the blame for this war, for the death of my beloved Thaliara. Are you getting all this, dear?"

"I am, thank you, Majesty," I said. Herself speaks at an affected, measured pace so that I, with quill and ink, might capture and immortalize every one of her words.

She continued, "They must take the blame and eat it, and choke on it. That is the price they fated themselves to pay when they sued for peace."

Dar Bontine took a moment to respond. The Liedans had not, of course, sued for peace; they had merely sent dar Bontine, the great negotiator from the borderlands where all the unpleasantness began, to suggest that such a thing was possible.

"Yes, Majesty. But something does bother me. Who won the War of the Banners?"

"Why, we did, of course. Nearly two centuries past."

"You say 'we' though you were not born at the time."

"Yes. It is a victory shared by all Terosai, living and dead."

"Who was responsible for the massacre of all the women and children and teachers at the Tainer Fortress six months ago?"

Her mouth twisted as though she'd bitten into a lime. "General Faschett. Who may find himself punished once this war is done and I no longer need his services."

"Ah. But, of course, since you are Most High Lady Empress of the Realm, everything done by your officers is ultimately laid at your door."

I scratched an imaginary itch to cover the smile I could not restrain. Trust Dar Bontine to phrase it in such a manner that she knew the blame was hers and yet could avoid accepting responsibility.

"I do not see your point."

He looked apologetic. "Majesty, if Jerno is to accept personal responsibility for your daughter's death, by the terms of equity we have followed during all these days of negotiation, he will be able to insist that you accept personal responsibility for the Tanier Fortress matter."

She shrugged indifferently. "No one in the fortress was of noble blood. It is scarcely the same."

"Of course not. But you will recall that the treaty document is to be bespoken before the gods so they will bear witness to its terms."

It took her a moment to understand. She leaned forward. "I would be telling the gods to blame me for that accident."

"Yes, Majesty."

"Some of the gods don't acknowledge the difference between noble and common blood. They might take action."

"Yes, Majesty."

Herself paled. "They might curse me. Strip me of my youth and beauty."

Too late, I thought.

"And your charm," he added helpfully.

Too late by a lifetime, I thought.

Once again taking my life in my hands, I whispered, in a voice just loud enough for her to hear, "It is a trap."

She fixed me with a glare. "What do you mean?"

"King Jerno is doomed to an afterlife of misery and despair," I explained, "for all he has done during this war. But if he can persuade you to accept blame for actions offensive in the eyes of the gods—"

"He can drag me down with him." She turned back to dar Bontine and seized his hands. "Sheroit, you are my true friend. You look after me when I am surrounded by enemies and incompetents. We must rid the treaty of the terms of blame."

His face turned sad. "Such a shame. Jerno will be able to get away without admitting his guilt. It will be difficult, though. He was most emphatic about having those terms in the treaty."

"Oh, offer him a concession. Something he cannot turn down for fear of offending the noblemen who support him. What can we give him that we do not want?"

"Tanier Fortress, perhaps? No civilized Terosai would garrison there anyway; it stinks of the Liedans who built it."

"Not much of a loss. Yes." She squeezed his hands before releasing them. "Let us do this, Sheroit. I command it."

He rose. "I am always well guided by your wise counsel. I will begin arrangements now. By your leave."

She gave him the little flick of the fingers that meant she'd granted dismissal from the royal presence, and he left. She began to preen, certain that she'd just shown great generosity and demonstrated superior wisdom to the great negotiator of the age.

"What will the bucket of fat be wearing today?" Her voice was too casual.

"My man in his service says he will be a mountain of gold brocade. A futile attempt to outshine you."

"We will ensure that it is futile. Today will be the blood-red gown with the train and all the jewelry I can carry. Sunlight may illuminate him, but it will make me glow and sparkle like a goddess."

Kin

Well after dawn, the two treaty parties convened for the endless rituals of statecraft.

Most mornings, the trick lay in forcing the other side to be first to the ship's rail. The first party ready, obviously, had to wait for the pleasure of the second, who thereby won a minor victory.

King Jerno, magnanimous in the greater victory he anticipated, gave up that point and emerged first from his cabin, joined by his scribes, his advisors, and me, his valet. Together we moved to the rail that faced the Terosai flagship across dar Bontine's barge.

The barge, of course, was a joke. Barely seaworthy, it was a river vessel designed for comfort and grandeur. The teak of the desk was polished to a high sheen. The rails were of imported mahogany carved by master woodcraftsmen of, it is said, faraway Althea. Bright silken awnings kept the heat of the sun at bay while servitors armed with paper fans kept air fresh in the face of the negotiators. Other servants stood by to bring drinks chilled, it is said, by magic, to the participants in the treaty. As a mere bodyservant, I had never sampled one.

On the barge, under the main awning, Sheroit dar Bontine stood at the head of the table; he would not sit until both rulers were seated.

We waited at the rail, near the ramp descending to dar Bontine's gleaming deck, a mere minute; then the so-called Empress emerged.

Red spurted from the door to the quarterdeck and I imagined for a moment that the Terosai ship had been injured, but the redness resolved itself into the tiny slip of their Queen. I smiled; she had gone for the bait like a hungry cod and now carried enough velvet and gold nearly to double her slight weight. She, too, was surrounded by scribes and sycophants who made a processional of her short trip to her ship's rail.

I heard King Jerno chuckle again. He was wrapped up in a floor-length green wool cloak that concealed his choice of dress; he would not reveal himself until both parties were on the deck of the barge and no escape was possible.

The flags of greeting were raised and the Queen's herald began immediately, stealing a point from our own herald, who flushed red as he realized his mistake. "Announcing the Gloriana Majeste of Terosalle," the Terosai herald called, "Most High Lady Empress of the Realm, Lia dar Kothia Surdosti, beloved of gods, chosen of the people, shelterer of outcasts, benefactor of arts, most-praised of rulers . . ." While the litany went on, the Terosai descended their ramp and reached the barge deck, moving in a stately fashion to the chairs surrounding the table beneath the central awning. The Queen sat; her courtiers remained standing.

Their herald finished. Ours opened his mouth, but King Jerno whispered, "Quiet, you. On a day like this, you get only one error. Kin, announce me. The short way."

Our herald's flush deepened and he silently retreated. I called out, "Announcing King Jerno Byriver, Cenpaydon of Lieda, who travels today without the baggage of titles the better to spare his audience any boredom."

The crew of our flagship laughed, as did several of the sailors aboard the barge. As we descended the ramp and took our place opposite the Terosai contingent, I saw the Queen's face redden until it was nearly the color of her gown.

Then King Jerno, with a dramatic gesture, cast his cloak off, nearly burying me in its folds. He stood in his elegantly understated blue silk, nodded to the Queen, and seated himself.

The Queen stayed scarlet as she realized she'd been had. She glared murder at the junior scribe at her left, a tiny woman nearly lost in the folds of the more cumbersome form of Terosai robe. The scribe gulped, spoke a few words to the queen—and then glared straight at me, an expression that promised an ugly fate if I ever found myself under her hand.

I kept the surprise from my face. This little woman, to whom I confess I'd paid almost no attention in the days of negotiation, had worked out in a matter of moments who was responsible for her mistress's bad choice of dress. That meant she was Ardith Netter's contact among the Terosai, and meant either that Ardith had told her from whom he got his information or that she'd discovered that fact elsewhere. Either way, she bore watching.

I folded the King's cloak and handed it off to the now stiff-faced Ardith, who would carry it back up to the cabin. I took my place behind the King and to the left, beside the royal bodyguard; one disadvantage to the role of valet is that one seldom has the opportunity to sit.

Sheroit dar Bontine took his chair, then stared gravely between the two rulers. "I remind Your Majesties that we might be able to conclude matters today. We are very close. And the Lady Empress has just moved us a step closer, provided that you, King Jerno, can match her bountiful generosity. Queen Lia has moved to strike the provisions of blame from our treaty, and to return to Lieda the region of Tanier Fortress . . . provided that you agree to allow a council of her advisors access to the officers and records of Lieda, the better to determine the final fate of her murdered daughter."

I saw the Queen nodding a little during the first part of dar Bontine's statement, then a little startlement appeared in her eyes during the second. She hadn't been privy to all dar Bontine was going to say, then. Interesting.

The king, not waiting for his advisors to whisper to him, cleared his throat. "I am not averse to such an inquiry, provided it is equitable. I would wish for my own counselors to have similar access to the officers and records of Terosai, the better to clear up mysteries that afflict us as well."

"Not unreasonable," the diplomat said. "But if it is offered on both sides, then it is scarcely compensation for what the Queen has offered, and the Liedans must offer something else on the matter of blame and Tanier Fortress. The fortress is a valuable strategic site in disputed territories . . . worth, perhaps, fishing rights to the Nesmass Reefs, in the far west?"

The King pursed his lips and leaned over so that his advisors could have his ear . . . and the day's races were off in earnest.

Chapter Three

Halleyne

Today has been both successful and disastrous. If I am very lucky, Herself will overlook the latter and revel in the former. But I am never very lucky.

It started when the Liedan king's oversized lout of a valet baited his daily hook with false information. I had not hitherto realized that it was a hook. The King chose to dress comfortably; I was led to believe he would dress lavishly; the Queen chose to match him in glamour, and she suffered through the longest, hottest day of the treaty negotiations in sweat and barely-suppressed rage.

Still, the negotiations went well. We won the village of Allynvy, pushing our western seaside borders north to that point. It may have been that King Jerno so enjoyed the spectacle of Herself roasting under the sun that he was inclined to be generous.

By midafternoon, all terms had been agreed upon in principle. Sheroit dar Bontine looked as merry as I've ever seen him. But more trouble struck when that damned valet of King Jerno's whispered in the King's ear again. Jerno smiled as though he'd just won the war while no one was looking, and he said, "Since the hour is late and the scribes will need some time to draw up finished drafts of the treaty, I think the Queen and I ought to retire to our respective cabins to bathe and rest. I am made exceedingly tired by the rigors of statecraft."

Before I or anyone else could advise her, the Queen retorted, "The King may retire if he is feeling weak, but We are inclined to remain above deck and enjoy the weather and companionship."

The King nodded as if in regret. He stayed, and beamed at the broiling queen during the hours it took dar Bontine's scribes to finish copying the treaties. Hours in which the heat of the day was greatest. Hours in which the air became still, offering not one bit of wind to provide relief. I arranged for the light meal of the afternoon to be brought out, and for the Queen's to include drinks cooled by young Teuper's magical ices.

During all that time, the Queen sat upright, posture perfect and shoulders stiff, a pose that promised dire retribution for any slight, real or imagined. All I had to do was make one slip of protocol to find myself punished again. I said nothing except when addressed, and when not in observance of my duties I imagined the world's greatest storm sweeping Herself overboard and marooning her on a small rocky isle with one tree and only that oversized Liedan valet to keep her company.

As the sun began to set, servants lit oil lamps, and shortly thereafter dar Bontine's scribes presented us with the freshly-penned copies of the treaty.

Each of the royals' scribes read each of the five copies—one for each ruler, one for each nation's senatorial body, one for dar Bontine—and confirmed that they were identical in wording to the original. Then, finally, with the sun vanishing beyond the western horizon, the rulers set their names to the documents.

Cheering broke out among the sailors and witnesses, and in the darkness beyond the ring of light cast by the lanterns I saw winesacks already being handed about—even between Terosai and Liedans. I could hear as the word moved to the sailors aboard the ships, a ripple of laughter and cheering and singing that spread out from the treaty table.

King Jerno smiled broadly for his scribes and assistants, promising them proper rewards and entertainments upon their return home; but the Queen sat still as a spider, her hands folded before her, a cold smile on her lips as she no doubt contemplated the fates that would befall everyone who annoyed her today.

Finally dar Bontine arose. "My friends," he said, "we are witness today to one of the great efforts of statecraft of the modern world."

It's nothing but a treaty between two nations tired of killing each other, I thought, but that sentiment would not have been appreciated.

"Our reward is the peace and prosperity we will enjoy—perhaps to the end of our days," he continued. "But it need not be our only reward. I know that our royal participants need some time to retire to their quarters and contemplate what they have accomplished today—"

To bathe, I amended.

"—but in two hours' time, the decks of my own mighty fighting-vessel—" He waited through the laughter that arose at his self-deprecating description "—will be thick with food and drink and good company. Return and celebrate our mutual victory."

There was much cheering, and the royals soon parted. Herself strode away, showing great vigor considering the physical demands made upon her by the day's events. She was surrounded by her ladies-in-waiting, one of whom, young Jiarna, gave me a sympathetic smile before she was swept away.

I waited until the Queen had had time to reach her cabin, then I went belowdecks, dodging the ship's sailors as they trotted hither and thither on errands or just to spread the gossip of the day. I soon found the little cabin assigned to the doctor and knocked.

The rough voice from beyond the door called, "Go to hell."

I opened it and peered in.

Maydellan Ha was an oddity in the Terosai court. The Queen preferred to surround Herself with tall, handsome, charming men. Maydellan was none of these. He was a dwarf—a *real* dwarf, from the mountain city of Rakkatar, famed for its engineers, not one of these oddly-formed humans who join theatrical troupes and spend their lives portraying dwarves—with a face that looked as though it had been run over by a hay-wagon and never healed properly. A thick brown mustache and beard, untrimmed, concealed his lower face. He dressed in plain brown garments that often had old bloodstains, or stains of even less reputable substances, still visible on them.

He peered at me through his spectacles, over the thick book he'd been squinting at; smoke from his pipe drifted past my face. "Oh, it's you. What is it, Halleyne?"

"*She* has been under the sun's rays all day and must be near collapse."

"I know. Sometimes she is the stupidest creature within three days' walk, snails included."

"Can you do anything?"

"I already have. There's a drink waiting for her by her bath. It will replenish healthful agents that she has lost . . . and perhaps calm her."

"Thank you, doctor."

"Don't slam the door."

My next stop was at the officers' cabin that had been given over to the Queen's two wizards—one senior, one junior, as prescribed by the earlier treaty that had brought about this meeting in the first place. I knocked.

There was no answer, just a rustling noise from beyond. The hair on the nape of my neck stood; unexplained noises from a wizard's chamber often promised danger at best. With some trepidation, I called, "Dar Delerio?"

Another moment of silence, then a young man's voice: "No, it's Teuper. Stay at anchor a moment."

"Very well." *Stay at anchor*, indeed. The young man snatched up nautical terms as though they were dropped coins—in the hope, I thought, that they would make him a real sailor.

The door opened a moment later and Teuper dar Hiaro stood within. He was tall, slim, with fair skin and dark hair, handsome enough to please the Queen and not yet twenty; it was said he was quite a favorite of the ladies-in-waiting. "Did you need the senior wizard? He's not about."

"No, you. The Queen has become overheated during the day's negotiations; I thought you might make sure to keep ices near at hand for her during the night's celebrations."

An expression of disappointment crossed his face. "Halleyne, think of what you are saying. *Night's celebrations.* I might have other things to do. Drink. Toast. Dance. You know, there are women aboard. Yourself included. I thought perhaps you might dance with me."

"Teuper—you know I can't."

"Perhaps when the Queen has retired for the evening. She will quit long before the celebrations do. She won't see you."

"One of her sets of eyes will, and will whisper into her ear in the morning." I had no defense from my own words and I felt bitterness swell up in me.

He looked at me in sympathy. "Halleyne. You mar

yourself with makeup and unsuitable clothing. You live a lie, and every day you walk on the edge of her displeasure. Why don't you leave her service? I could row you to shore under cover of darkness. We could travel overland to Lieda. You speak their language like a native. You could be free of her."

That took me a step back. I could not keep the surprise out of my voice: "That would shame my family."

"Because you left the Queen's service? Or because you ran off with a penniless wizard-apprentice?" He leaned close and caught my hands in his. "Your family should be ashamed already. For selling you into service to convenience themselves. Shame them back. Show them they can't treat you that way."

"I—" Surprise had closed my voice down to nearly a squeak. "Teuper, what are you offering me?"

He shrugged. "Good times. Good company. Protection for the trip to Lieda. Beyond that—who knows?"

"I'm surprised you did not ask Jiarna. She's new and pretty enough that the Queen is already glowering at her."

"She wouldn't go."

I snatched my hands back. "You're a rat, Teuper. A ship's rat." I struggled to get my voice back under control. "Ice for the Queen."

"I'll create a block of it and have it at hand in a bowl beside her. With a servant and a hammer to break her off pieces whenever she wants. While I dance."

"That . . . will suffice." I turned and left him, heard his chuckle follow me as I fled.

I dared not go to the Queen's quarters, did not wish to go to the cramped cabin assigned to too many scribes, and the deck was full of sailors only too happy to enjoy my company no matter how badly I made myself up, so I descended the gold-carpeted ramp to dar Bontine's barge. Servants were setting up tables to be laden with food and drink; I could see dar Bontine sitting on his chair, his feet incongruously up on the treaty table, but the placement of his chair was such that I could not see his face.

He, at least, would be an island of intellect and calm. I headed toward him. Hearing my footsteps, he looked back at me over the top of his chair.

Not dar Bontine. It was the ridiculous thick-bodied valet of King Jerno. "Oh, it's you," I said.

"And not the master negotiator of the world," he said amiably. "Come, we're at peace now. Officially. Sworn before the gods. Can't you forgive me a little stratagem?"

"I doubt it." But I took my own chair. Even this lout would be better company than the Queen now, and I could sit. "Why are you at his chair?"

"I've always wanted to know what it would be like to take the seat of power and put my feet up. I've already tried King Jerno's chair, and your own Queen's. You should try it."

"Thank you, no. You're not a very good valet, you know."

An expression of dismay crossed his face. "Is it that pathetically obvious?"

"More than pathetically. Why does he keep you on?"

He paused before replying. I knew the answer; his father was a general. But his expression became a little melancholy, and he said, "Because I knew two of his sons better than he did."

"Oh." All King Jerno's known sons were dead, I knew, just as the Queen's daughter was. My next question, if I were to continue making a duel out of conversation, should have been, *You used to be their bodyguard, then?* But an honest regret in the man's expression stilled my tongue.

So I sit here, ignoring him, while I bring my journal up to date and work on my decorative borders, and wish to the greater gods that the Queen will be in a better mood when she emerges for the feast.

Kin

The feast preparations were fast and polished. I wondered how often dar Bontine's servants had practiced them. They brought out great quantities of roast fowl and lamb (borne on sun-platters, gold-washed serving dishes ensorcelled to keep warm whatever was placed upon them), kegs of beer and half a rack's worth of wine bottles, huge entire cheeses, aromatic sauces, platters of bread, and more. These they set out on the table where the Terosai scribe and I sat, working around us without comment.

My mouth watered. The King, I thought, would feast well tonight.

Soldiers crowded the rails of their respective ships; they would not descend before the royals did. Their own tables, being filled with meaner but still hearty fare, were set up at the bow. The Queen would not emerge from her quarters before King Jerno did, and King Jerno would not emerge until I told him the feast was almost ready. Startling to realize that it was I who held the power to forestall this feast almost indefinitely.

To be sure, I caught Sheroit dar Bontine's attention as he rushed by on one of his preparation errands. I shrugged a question; he nodded. Yes, it was time.

The Terosai scribe—I recalled her name at last: Halleyne—was still working mightily away at her colorful volume full of borders. Something about the way she laid down the curious hatchwork designs was odd. "Lady Halleyne."

She looked up.

"Here is a gift, with no tricks. I go now to tell King Jerno that the feast is ready. I will tell him your Queen rushes to reach the food first, that she might be able to take all of the lamb dar Bontine has pronounced the best. All you need do is tell the Queen that he is dejected by all he has lost in the treaty and will not even play his game of making her wait."

She smiled. It looked like a genuine smile. "I will tell her something. I see our rulers are not too far apart in their habits of statecraft."

"If statecraft is the word for it. Tell me something."

"Yes?"

"Your manner when you compose those designs is that of a scribe and not an artist. Is that a form of writing?"

She paled. It was obvious even in the torchlight. She rose, catching her book up to her breast, and left in a rush, saying nothing more.

Chapter Four

Halleyne

It is now days since the events I relate, but this is the first opportunity I have had to set ink to page since they transpired.

The storm hit—no, I get ahead of myself.

On the night of the signing, before the storm, when I found Herself, she had bathed and dressed. She now sat in her favorite chair while Jiarna finished her makeup. She smiled as I entered, and I knew no random punishment would be forthcoming tonight.

I told Herself what that oafish but too-clever-by-far Liedan valet said about King Jerno. "Then we must hurry," was her answer. "Up, up, up!" She roused her ladies-in-waiting and marched out the door, leaving them to catch up and form up around her. I trailed along behind.

As we reached the railing, the sailors and officers not ordered to remain aboard gathered behind us, and we descended well in advance of King Jerno's party, which was only just emerging from the quarterdeck. Jerno hurried to catch up, but we reached the table well

41

before he did, and Herself was already having slices of lamb from the leg I had randomly declared the most choice by the time he arrived. He did seem briefly annoyed, but was all smiles when the Queen bothered to look up at him.

The feast went well. The King and Queen stood a half-dozen feet apart, close enough to exchange pleasantries whenever the situation demanded, far enough apart to ignore one another the rest of the time. Sailors and soldiers exchanged stories of their valor and mishaps during the war. There was no animosity shown between the fighting men of the two nations; some even demonstrated great respect for the other's officers and noted fighters, especially the Liedan captain Russtin Kohugh and our own Admiral Lesto dar Ostaferian.

Dar Bontine's musicians poured out music as though it were wine from a bottomless bottle. Sailors danced their sea-jigs, while during the court dances the women aboard were much sought-out as partners. I declined to dance, as did any of the Queen's ladies-in-waiting who realized that to fall under her eye while being appealing to a man was not the best way to remain in Herself's confidence or affections.

"Can I ask you a question?" The words boomed into my ear, spoken by someone standing behind me. I started, then whirled on the speaker.

It was the valet Kin Underbridge. I tensed, lest he ask me again about the writing in my journal. But he looked around the assembly instead and asked, "Where are the wizards?"

I looked as well. There were scores of celebrants on the decks, but wizards are usually distinctive; I think they dress to be recognized as mages so when they dress differently no one will notice them. "I do not see them. Ours or yours."

"I saw your apprentice wizard a while ago; he danced

the first dance with your Lady Jiarna. But he is gone and she is still here."

"Meaning he has not persuaded her to dance with him below decks," I said. "Well, perhaps they are all huddled together, conspiring to do wizardly things. Mages are like that."

"Exquisitely boring, you mean."

In spite of myself, I smiled. "Go tell them that. I want to see on how many legs you walk on when you return."

"I will! They need some relief from ponderous matters." He gave me a bow of minimally appropriate courtesy and left.

His words made me curious. I listed in my mind all the women from the Terosai crew and all the ones I could remember from the Liedan ship and dar Bontine's barge. Not all the women were present—some had to be on duty still on the sailing-vessels—but all the ones who had struck me as likely targets for young Teuper's interests were still within sight. Had he settled for a plainer partner and retired below decks with her? It did not seem like him; to my knowledge, he never looked beyond glowing face or shapely form. Nor had he ever shown sign of appreciating the company of handsome men for that sort of sport.

I diverted myself for a bit with music—something lyrical and merry, not a tune for dancing. The Queen's favorite Bard-apprentice, Shallia dar Kantrin, accompanied herself on the lute as she sang "Banner Year."

A good choice. They say it was composed by a Terosai Bard in celebration of the victory over Lieda in the War of the Banners. But the song is about all the units coming home with their war-banners held high, and what became of the banners in the months to come, as mothers made them into swaddling-shirts, and barkeeps used their tatters to mop up spilled beer.

It was a song of the end of war. Shallia, with her strong, sweet voice so broad of range, with her captivating dark looks and cheery manner, made both the song and the audience her own. She looked aside at me during the lyric about the strips of bright cloth cut to decorate a luthier's carry-case, and we both smiled at the secret we shared. Then the song was done and she stood to receive the applause of her audience.

Kin Underbridge had by now been gone for some minutes. Then I thought I heard him shouting from a distance—the voice was his, and though I could not make out all the words, I recognized "Murder." Many of us turned to look, straining to spot him through the darkness beyond the barge's rails.

That is when the storm struck.

It was like nothing I had ever seen or heard before. The first wind pushed me up against the dining-table; I struck hard enough to lose all breath and hung there, helpless, with others pinned to the table-length to either side of me. The wind tore free the canopy above us and hurled it to wrap around the *Wave-Breaker*'s main mast. Half or more of the celebrants on the barge's deck were thrown from their feet and flung toward the barge rail; I saw a half-dozen roll over the rail and into the sea.

The roaring of the wind overrode all other sound. I turned and looked for the Queen—safe, pinned between two of her bodyguards who stood more or less upright against the wind—and then for Admiral dar Ostaferion.

He stood at an odd angle, holding on to the corner of the barge's quarterdeck, battered by wind, his hand clutching at his throat. His cape trailed behind him, straining as if struggling to be free. It took me a moment to realize the thing had to be strangling him. He managed to undo its catch and the cloak flew away, lost instantly in the distance beyond the Liedan ship.

Then he began screaming, words that were lost to me, and motioning toward the *Thunderer*. Many of his sailors were already in motion, walking bent over or even crawling toward the gangway that led up to the upper deck.

The *Thunderer* was already listing, its empty masts leaning toward the barge. The barge's port side was lashed to the *Thunderer*'s starboard, and the barge's starboard side to *Wave-Breaker*'s port. I could feel the barge's starboard side rise as *Wave-Breaker* began listing.

I pushed off from the table and managed to get my arms on the belt of one of the Queen's large bodyguards. I think he scarcely felt me as he hustled the Queen toward the gangway. The lot of us, bent over in the face of the wind, pushed as hard as we could to reach the barge rail, but it took us a long minute to reach it.

The Queen and her guard got their hands on the gangway rail. Then the rain struck, big drops blown so hard that they drove us to our knees; my head rang as if struck by the blows of a child with a hammer.

Above the shriek of the winds, I could hear cries of pain or fear, and then a new sound—cracking, ringing noises, one after another.

I crawled forward and got my knees onto the gangway. As I watched, a black snake, its length lost in the distance, whipped through the air and severed the head of the guard I'd been holding. His body slumped over the rail, tumbling into the ocean.

No, it was not a snake; I heard another crack and saw another snake uncoil. The lines that held the three ships lashed together were snapping and then whipping through the air with great force. Through the rain I dimly saw sailors aboard the *Thunderer* hacking at the still-intact ropes with hatchets. I prayed they'd strike down any snake that meant me harm before it struck; then I prayed they wouldn't cut free the gangway ropes before we were aboard.

Kin

I was almost hurled over the rail twice before I could descend to the main deck. Then the rain struck and made me nearly blind.

Carpenters had already sprung into action, chopping away to separate *Wave-Breaker* from the ridiculous barge that could bear her to her doom if it foundered. I stationed myself beside the near end of the gangway and began dragging people up on deck as they reached its summit. They were helped along by the great wind at their backs. So the Terosai fleeing for their own ship had to climb against the wind. I wished them luck.

Captain Kohugh was among the first back on board. Relief flooded me like the warmth from a fine brandy. Half the world's gods couldn't do more than Kohugh to ensure our safety in a storm. He slapped me on the shoulder for the hand up and allowed the wind to push him beyond my sight.

The twelfth man to board was the King. Even with the wind to his back he was a load to haul; I struggled with his arm as his feet slipped on the rain-washed gangway. Then he was up, leaning backwards against the wall of wind and rain.

He leaned close to my ear. "Get me to my cabin."

I gestured to one of his bodyguards to take my place at the rail, then shouldered some of the load of the King's weight and aided him toward the quarterdeck. We were listing badly by this time, but Jerno's great mass helped us cope with the slipperiness of the deck.

Once we were inside, the King lay on his bed and roared and fretted until I had a lamp lit and he could see again. He was a sight: His clothes hung sopping like badly-wrung laundry on a line, rain had taken the oil and curl out of his hair and plastered it against his face, and his eyes stared wide and frightened. I doubted that I looked much better.

Even here, the roar of wind outside forced him to shout. "This is a storm sent from hell."

"I should go back on deck, sire. Help get people aboard."

"Sent by that bitch Queen Lia to destroy us, I'm sure . . . You'll do no such thing. You will stay here with me and attend to my needs as usual." He fixed me with a royal scowl. "Honestly, Kin, sometimes I think you anger me deliberately, as though you wish me to discharge you."

I opened my mouth to respond. The words, *I did not think that helping to save your subjects from death by drowning would anger Your Majesty* waited there like arrows to be launched; but I dared not say them. "Majesty, Fahero Solune and his nephew have been murdered."

He sat upright, as straight as he could manage with the ship at such a tilt. "You lie. Who could murder a wizard like Solune?"

"Someone he trusted, I imagine."

"That was what you were on about just before the wind struck, wasn't it? Look in the companionway and bring in one of my bodyguards."

I obeyed, but there was no one standing outside his door. Not far down the companionway, the hatch to the outside swung slamming open and shut, letting heavy rain in with each swing, and I could see lightning flashing in the near distance. I trotted to the door and dogged it shut, then returned to the side of the King. "Your guards are gone, Majesty. I imagine Captain

Kohugh has pressed them into service for the moment. He may be short of hands."

"He *cannot* press royal guards into service."

"Technically, Majesty, by the laws of the sea, he can." I affected a look of sympathy to soothe his injured pride.

"Then you certainly may not leave my side. You have been a bodyguard, and there is a murderer aboard. The royal person must not be left unguarded."

For once, the King was right. I would have to wait until relieved by one of the guards. Even then, the King might not release me; who knew who the murderer was? I swore to myself.

Then I did so again as the ship heeled and listed sharply to starboard. The King's bed slid a foot and crashed into the cabin wall, tumbling Jerno up against the bare wood planks of the wall. "What is happening?" he roared.

I managed to keep my feet by hanging onto the bed post even as it moved. "We are free of the barge," I said. I tried to gauge more from the motion of the deck beneath my feet. "I think we are moving. I would guess that we are either turning into the wind or trying to run before it, from what the captain has said to me about storms." A blast of lightning punctuated my last word; the bolt itself, blinding-white, must have struck near the stern of the ship, it glared so fiercely through the windows at the rear of the cabin.

"I agree," he said, in haste. "I will let him pursue this course of action so long as it remains the right one. Now, shutter those windows and bring me some wine, would you?"

"Of course, Majesty." I sighed, resigning myself to the care of a large baby I desperately wished I could spank.

↪   ↪   ↪

Halleyne

Herself made us cluster around her as though we were kittens and she were the mother cat, but we were there to soothe, not to be soothed. As the *Thunderer* rolled and pitched, the god whose nickname the ship bore hurled lightning, bolt after bolt, each one causing the Queen to jump and cry out.

Shallia struck up a tune on her lute. She sang a child's song of Bleilan the Fox, in the time before he learned he was the god of cleverness, when he was trapped on a log as a turbulent river carried it toward doom over a crashing falls.

Queen Lia snapped, "Damn it, child, if you were a full Bard you'd know how inappropriate that is. As if you could ever become a full Bard."

"It's appropriate, Majeste," Shallia said, as assertive as she ever became. "Please listen. You'll see." She started in again, and it was true; all of us, the Queen included were soothed by the familiar melody and lyrics we knew from childhood.

When it was done, and before Shallia could start another, the Queen asked, "How is it that Kiaran dar Delerio did not inform us of the storm's approach?"

We looked at one another and did not answer. Any answer we gave would make her angrier, and all of us liked the aged wizard. His great skill lay in detection of trouble to come, which is why the Queen chose to keep him close; but he had not the power to save himself if she chose to punish him.

"Well, We will have to find out," she said. "Bring him here." She looked between us and waited a moment. When she spoke again, her voice held an impatient edge: "Must I choose the messenger of my wish?"

"No, Majeste," I said, and stood, despite the rolling of the floor. "I will find him."

Fortunately, I did not have to step out into the wailing weather; a ladderlike set of stairs within the quarterdeck gave me access down to the cabin assigned the wizards. I passed rushing sailors with frightened faces, which did little to inspire my confidence.

No one answered my knock at the wizards' cabin. The door yielded to my push.

The cabin beyond was empty. In the light from the lamp in the passageway, I could see that the bedding was rolled up and tied carefully upon the bunks—tied *to* the bunks, else it would be on the floor with the chairs, which slid slowly back and forth as the ship pitched. The wizards' belongings, their chests of clothes, their books, their packs of ritual ingredients, were all gone.

I stood frozen, clutching the doorway for support, as it dawned upon me that kindly Kiaran dar Delerio and his apprentice must have sensed the storm coming and abandoned us to it.

Abandoned us, perhaps, to die.

I returned to the Queen's cabins. I did not have to pretend to be grave as I told Herself what I had found.

She sat a mere moment, her face flushing dark even in the dim lamplight, then screamed. Her ear-splitting cry would have summoned all the sailors on the ship had they not been busy with more pressing matters. She lashed out and struck poor Jiarna beneath the eye, tumbling her to the deck, then stood over on unsteady feet and kicked at the girl's ribs as though Jiarna were responsible for all her woes instead of another random target. The rest of us dared not interfere.

She kept kicking until her anger was spent. Jiarna had been still for several moments when the Queen recovered. The Queen clutched the back of Shallia's chair for support, and, in a surprisingly clear and pleasant tone, announced, "We will, of course, ride out this storm with Our customary grace, then return home and purge the family dar Delerio from all the clan rolls of Our land. Now get that wretched girl out of Our sight."

Shallia and I leaped to obey, grateful for any chance to escape the royal presence. Between us, we lifted the pale, semiconscious girl and carried her from the cabin, down to the leaky, foul-smelling officers' storeroom that had been given over to the Queen's ladies-in-waiting. Jiarna moaned as we moved her and was still moaning when I brought the doctor to her. But she was conscious, and her eyes pleaded with us—as though we could protect her from the storm or the Queen should either wish to harm her more.

Kin

It was a near thing with King Jerno and the wine. He drank one bottle and then another, enough to sooth his frayed nerves. I worried that in either fear or seasickness he would bring the wine up again, giving me a mess to contend with in these cramped quarters. Instead, he lay back and began snoring, oblivious to the lightning-cracks and the grinding, snapping noises coming from the ship herself.

I checked the passageway again. Wonder of wonders, this time I found a guard, massive Viriat Axer, on duty. He gulped as he saw me—not, I realized, from fear, but from seasickness. "The King sleeps," I told him. "Enter if you hear any thumping; he may have fallen from his bed. Otherwise let him be."

He nodded, still gulping. I imagined that his expression was not too different from my own as I pulled my cloak tight around me and left the quarterdeck.

The wind caught and tore at me, driving rain into my face like sling-stones, as I struggled to close the door.

I was reminded of old legends of winds that were like men, living things with angers and passions and great powers. In that moment, I believed the stories, believed with all my heart that evil spirits assailed us and intended to throw me personally into an uncaring sea.

I literally crawled to the ladderway down and made it to the main deck. Things were much better there. The poop deck and quarterdeck seemed to serve as a wall against the wind, which did little more than spray increasingly-cold rain on us from unexpected directions.

I saw sailors buttoned into cloaks of oiled wool moving about their business, running when the wind followed, battering their way along when the wind was in their face. I do not know how, but they had managed to rig sails on the foremast and bowsprit. We now ran before the wind, bobbing and weaving like a drunken duellist, but under control.

The sky overhead was a black mass regularly illuminated by flashes of lightning. The *Thunderer* was nowhere to be seen.

And standing below the main mast was Captain Kohugh, relaying orders fore-and-aft with the arm signals used by Liedan sailors. He rolled as the ship did, standing in his drenched dress shirt, unmindful of the soaking rain and thunder-cracks, intent on the featureless enemy that threatened to sink his ship.

I made my way to him and shouted into his ear, "Can I help?"

He smiled his enigmatic elf-smile. "Keep the King from distracting us to death with damned-fool orders."

"I already have, for the next few hours anyway. And I will be at his side to keep him from yours afterwards."

"Then we will ride this storm out. I've survived worse storms in worse vessels."

"Be careful if you go astern, though. The wind is twelve times worse back at the quarterdeck than it is here."

He gave me an odd look, as though he only half-believed me, then waved me back to the stern and turned to peer through the rain at the officer at the bow.

I unclasped my cloak and draped it around him. His hands absently reached up to pull it around him and fasten the brooch. Then I did as I was bid, walking and reeling my way back toward the quarterdeck. My heart was much lighter; if the famous Captain Kohugh said we would survive this storm, we would.

I heard another crack of thunder, then realized it was no such thing. No flash of light accompanied it. But ahead, the mizzenmast leaned forward and swung down at me.

I leaped away from the falling pole. My feet slipped out from under me and suddenly-howling winds hurled me toward the rail. The impact smashed the bulwark half-out and my legs stretched out over raging water; I got my arms wrapped around the railing, praying to the gods that it, too, would not give way. Then I saw the ruined mast strike.

Its midpoint smashed into the quarterdeck, staving it in above the door to the officers' quarters. Farther forward, the remainder of the mast ripped into the main deck, shattering the longboat lashed astern of the mainmast.

And one of the bare yards of the mizzenmast tore through Captain Kohugh, spearing him as a careful fisherman would spear a fish.

I do not know whether it was fear for my own life or the blow struck to the captain that gave me strength, but suddenly I found it easy to struggle up from my precarious position. I pulled myself upon the deck, then half-crawled, half-slid my way to the fallen captain.

He lay facedown on the deck, blood on his mouth, his eyes wide and staring.

As I reached him, he looked at me. It shocked me;

I'd thought him already dead, and now it was as though he had returned from death to speak.

"Your cloak," he said; his voice was a rasp.

"Yes?"

"It's bad luck."

His eyes closed. Sailors clustered around us and stared down at the naval legend that had come to its end.

Chapter Five

Halleyne

In a child's nightmare, he is pursued by howling monsters. The ground is treacherous and he cannot flee. Familiar faces are distorted and alien.

So it was that we rode a child's nightmare for day after entire day. Our howling monsters were the winds, screaming gusts that relentlessly drove the ship on before them, snapping spars and sweeping crewmen over the rail, hurling blinding rain into the faces of the sailors.

Or so it was reported to us. We stayed belowdecks. Shallia and I took turns tending the now feverish and unconscious Jiarna. In her rare moments of wakefulness, we tried to spoon-feed her as the deck dipped and swayed so nauseatingly that we ourselves could not bear to eat.

Maydellan Ha came as often as he could. The injured and dying lay all over the ship, most suffering broken bones from bad falls; a fall through a hatch into the hold had crushed one man's head, and he lingered near death, taking much of the doctor's attention.

Still, I preferred to be caught in the midst of a nightmare to tending the Queen. Anger at what she'd done to Jiarna burned in me. I cooled her brow with a damp cloth and told Shallia, "She should have fought back."

Shallia looked surprised. "Not against the Empress."

"Against anyone! She is failing, Shallia. She may die. Is it our duty to stand up nobly and be killed just to satisfy a moment's pique?"

"Kingship and queenship settle on those chosen by the gods," she said, though not with the conviction of the Queen's most ardent courtiers. "So, by law, yes. But more importantly, the worst that can happen to her now is that she will perish—"

"It does not need to be any worse than that!"

"—but if she fought back, her entire family might die. True?"

I sighed in vexation. "True. But you do not have a family to endanger. If the Queen tried to do this to you, would you strike her back?"

She shook her head. "The gods gave me the gift of song, and the gods gave me a queen who is no gift. There is balance in this. I will try to make something of my life and the gods will choose the time of my death."

"The gods may choose, but I will try to dicker with them."

That earned me a smile.

Then, as I recall it, I closed my eyes for a moment. When I opened them, the sun was overhead burning down at me and I ached as though trampled by horses.

Kin

I felt the ship heel as the wind shifted, and thought, is the storm over? Can we return home now?

We came about for several long moments. I breathed easier.

Deep in the belly of the ship, timbers shrieked. The *Wave-Breaker's* wooden bones began to shudder and grind—their noise enough to wake the King from his wine-induced slumbers. Then the bow rose a little before us, and the King's bed moved toward me. I realized the cabin floor had begun to bend and twist. I scrambled from the chair I had occupied, but not fast enough; the floor sagged further, and the bed, bolted to the bucking floor, pinned my legs to the wall.

The King roared, "What's happening, Kin?"

I struggled to free my legs. "A moment, sire."

The ship's shuddering ceased, but she began listing rapidly to port. I heard voices raised out on deck, and that was a change: for voices to carry, the wind must have died. I couldn't make out what they were shouting.

As the ship listed farther, the cabin floor unbuckled for an instant; with one last heave, I pulled my legs free. It was another few moments to drag the King from his bed, for half-besotted and half-afraid, he refused to rise. I assisted him from the cabin, into darkness.

Since the storm began, we had had nothing but darkness; still, this was distinctly a nighttime darkness. Though clouds scudded low and rain struck our faces, these were not so heavy that they could have concealed the sun.

Sailors stood on deck, a few. Some ran along the port rail, looking down at the hull. Several others hauled ropes to hoist the ship's boat. I made my way down to that crew, and saw to my relief that it was being bossed by Jenina Morlin, the ship's second mate. "What's happening?" I asked her.

She gave me a scornful look. She was a woman of drive and accomplishment, having risen to the position of naval officer in spite of her low birth, and she accorded only minimal courtesy to those who acquired status without working as hard as she had. Such as me. "Underbridge! Still alive?"

"Except for my knees."

"Not you, halfwit. The King."

I believe I glared. "Still alive, and demanding to know what's happening."

"Tell him the good news. Land only two or three arrow-flights to port."

"Wonderful!" The thought of land underfoot—solid, unmoving ground—was overwhelming.

She grinned with malice. "Oh, and bad news too. Reef gutted us. King can go down with the ship or roll that fat gut of his into the ship's boat. We're not waiting for him."

"Yes, you are."

"Care to test me? Take your time, then."

I gave her another glare and sprinted back to the King, who leaned against the remains of a mast near the door to his cabin. I heard Jenina's laughter follow me, and then the cries of "Abandon ship!" began. Began again, I should say; that must have been what they were calling before.

Contrary as the King sometimes was, all I had to say was, "We're sinking." It was no secret that he'd had a nightmare of drowning ever since the body of his son Jernin washed ashore. We reached the rail long before we were in danger of being left behind and clambered down into the pitching ship's boat with far too many other survivors.

We did not have to climb far. *Wave-Breaker* was sinking fast. As we pushed off from her side and began rowing against the heavy sea, crewmen continued to spill up from below decks. Some clustered at the rail; others leaped into the sea to follow the ship's boat toward land.

Though I had no skill with it, I pulled an oar with the sailors. The promised land did not immediately rise into view, so I tried to emulate the rhythm of the more accomplished oarsmen and thereby settle my mind— thinking of nothing but the wood under my hands and the occasional directions of Jenina Morlin and Daneeth Po, the sailor she'd tapped as her temporary second-in-command.

Then, a century or so later, sailors began spilling out over the little boat's sides, standing up in water that was only waist-deep, and pushing the boat for all they were worth in an effort to beach her. It was still so dark that we'd reached the shore before I realized it; even now I could barely discern the outlines of a rise before us. Belatedly, I joined the sailors at their employ, for the King would not and his weight would make their task more difficult.

We beached the boat. I helped the King out, and at his frantic demand for shelter we dragged the boat from the beach and turned it over that he might lie beneath it. He passed out almost immediately, looking oddly peaceful and childlike with water runoff trickling through his hair. I returned to the beach and helped swimmers drag themselves up above the tide-mark whenever I spied them. Others, Jenina Morlin among them, did the same.

A few steps down the beach, I tripped over a swimmer who'd collapsed half in the water; waves threatened to drag him back out to sea. I took his arm and hauled; he was not entirely unconscious, for he managed to get up and take a couple of off-balance steps before his legs gave way. I lowered him as gently as I could to the sand; at least now he stood little chance of being taken by the ever-hungry sea god.

Then I realized by his clothes, which when dry would have been more flowing than my own, that the man was Terosai.

"How did you come to be aboard *Wave-Breaker*?"
I asked in his own language, but he was too exhausted
to answer, or pretended to be. Sudden suspicion filled
me, for someone had to have killed the Liedan wizards, and a Terosai stowaway was as likely a suspect
as any. But I let him lie for the time being and continued down the beach.

A dozen steps farther, I tripped over another body.
I cursed him and the darkness, then got a look at who
had caused me to fall.

An unconscious woman in Terosai dress.

Halleyne

I came to wakefulness in a patch of shade cast by
a tall, branchless leaning tree; beyond its leaves high
above I could see the sun. Near me lay other men and
women of the *Thunderer*, some still as death, others
gasping or moaning from injury. The doctor, Maydellan
Ha, knelt over one of them with his back to me.

I called his name, my voice a croak. He turned and
smiled over me. "Ah, the lady dar Dero is awake.
Would you like something to eat?"

"Yes, please."

"Well, as soon as you find something, you can eat
it. In the meantime, drink this." He tilted a cup of cool
water to my lips; I drank deeply, suddenly aware of the
magnitude of my thirst.

He took the bowl away before I could empty it.
"Now, hold still and move."

"Which?"

"Lie there and move your limbs. Tell me if anything
hurts."

I did and felt pain throughout, especially in my arms
and shoulders. "Everything hurts."

"But nothing made you scream. I think you came

through it in good condition. Better than the *Thunderer*, at any rate. I prescribe rest until you can move, then you can get to work—there's much to be done."

"By your manner, I'd say you were a wagon driver before you became a doctor." I turned my head to see farther down the beach, where Terosai men and women carryied goods—broken barrels, bits of wood, masses of sandy cloth, oars—to place them on a central pile. It looked oddly like a funeral bier. "What happened to us?"

"We sailed, we broke up on a reef, we swam, some of us still live." He shrugged. "Shallia dar Kantrin says you were asleep when we hit the reef and unconscious thereafter. She managed to haul you ashore."

"Where is she?"

He paused and looked glum. "Burying Lady Jiarna." He rose, looked among the half-dozen or so of us lying in the shade. "I'm going to tend my other patients. Should any of you die before I return, I'll make you regret it."

One of the injured, a sailor whose name I remembered as Sepeter, whose arm now lay bound in a sling, grumbled, "But you can die anywhere, doctor. You have my leave to do it. So long as it's soon."

The dwarf grinned at him and strode off down the beach, past the pile of recovered goods.

After a while I was able to sit up, despite the pain in my abdomen, and draw back until I could lean up against the bole of the tree. I thought about Jiarna, and cried a bit. Then I took stock.

We seemed to be situated on a headland narrowing the access to a bay. Ahead of me across the water, a few minutes' walk if it were dry land, was the opposite headland; the bay was fair-sized and very pretty, surrounded by white sands. Even at its far end I could see the occasional antlike dot of someone walking; we were obviously very industrious this morning.

I still had my scribe's pouch. It was customarily tied off to my belt, so that I'd always be able to record the Queen's words. The quill-pens were ruined by water. My stoppered vials of ink had survived well. And the books, though bloated and warped with seawater so that the artistic virtues of my decorative borders were ruined, were still readable. Professionally at least, I was intact.

At last I was able to confront that which I feared. "Sepeter," I said, "what became of the Queen?"

The sailor kept his eyes closed but snorted. "Herself is in charge. And you've angered her, girl, by not being on duty to record her words."

I stood. My legs shook with the effort, but everything seemed to work and all the pain was bearable. My scarf was half-dry; grimacing, I pulled it about my hair, then tugged it forward so as little of my face as possible would show. That and posture gave me the manner of an older woman. "Do you know where we are?"

"North end of the bay."

"I mean, which land?"

"Dry land."

"Thank you for your help, Sepeter." I left him and the other wounded and made my shaky way along the beach.

I passed the bier of rescued goods. A few dozen steps past, I came across a group of men sitting in a circle and talking intently; one was Sheroit dar Bontine and another was Admiral dar Ostaferion. They took no note of my passage. A little farther still, and I ran across the Terosai junior wizard. "Teuper!"

His clothes were a sandy, matted mass; he carried a coil of rope and a belaying pin. He gave me a distracted little nod and made to pass me by, but I seized him by the arm. "Teuper, what became of Kiaran dar Delerio?"

He grimaced and finally looked at me. "I don't think I want to say."

"Why didn't he warn us of the oncoming storm? That sort of divination is his speciality."

"I think . . ." He took a long breath. "I think, Halleyne, that he fled its approach and left us to suffer it. I had been looking for him for some time when the winds struck. I was in dar Bontine's company—you can ask him."

What a curious thing to say. "I don't doubt you."

"Well, the Queen does. Thinks because she did not see me before the storm hit, because I couldn't predict it like my master, that I neglected my duty and am *personally* responsible for marooning us here."

"Why would dar Delerio do this to us?"

"Doubtless someone paid him enough to make it worth his while." He shrugged. "That was no natural storm, Halleyne. Take it from one who knows. It was an attack, a spell of great power. I could feel its energy. Perhaps it was a Liedan trick to destroy us, but they failed to get clear of it in time. I have to return to dar Bontine." He gave me a little bow and continued toward the sitting group.

I passed another group of the injured; Maydellan Ha was tending them. Beyond was a line of a dozen bodies laid out on the sand, their clothes sandy and tattered, their shoes and belts—and, I noticed, finger-rings and other jewelry—missing. Some were Liedan bodies.

Finally, nearly halfway around the bay, I found the Queen. She stood in strange company. It surprised me less to see King Jerno among them than it would had I not seen Liedan bodies on the beach, but it still jarred me to find that both ships had washed up on the same shore.

With the Queen were Shallia, pressed into duty as a scribe, scratching away at a slate with chalk, and two of the royal bodyguards. With King Jerno were his hopeless valet, the messenger Ardith Netter whose services I had used one time too often, and a huge man who was the King's chief bodyguard.

They were all squared off as though the Queen and King were fencers during the mocking, taunting minutes before a match and the others were their unhappy seconds. As I joined them, the Queen snatched the slate and chalk from Shallia's hands and pressed them into mine, all without breaking the pace of her harangue.

"It is clear," the Queen said, in shrill tones that allowed for no disagreement, "that you are in no position to dictate terms. You have lost your wizard counselors, your doctor, your captain, all your senior officers—I doubt that there's one among you who can use a sextant or build a raft that would withstand a bathtub's waves. I might be persuaded to share Terosai resources with you, but make no mistake: I am in command."

The slate bore a lot of cramped writing, which I scanned. Most of it seemed to be snippets of conversation. It took me a moment to realize that Shallia, rather than try to record this entire exchange, had been taking down interesting turns of phrase of the Queen's, "touches" in the verbal match they were playing. "Should have nailed a sail to your head and lashed a rudder to your vast royal fundament; we might have come through the storm safely then," stands out in my memory.

The King smiled as if dealing with a slow-witted niece. He shook his head. "You are in command of your Terosai, certainly, at least for as long as they will endure you. But let us leave off exaggeration. You have no spell-weaver worth worrying about. Lady Shallia there is a beauteous and talented Bard-in-training—" I could not repress a wince, for Shallia had just been added again to the list of women the Queen would find time to punish, "—but is not a full Bard. Young Teuper is too busy sniffing around the ladies to have acquired any substantial skill at wizardcraft. Your doctor, if he is to be true to his oaths, will not hesitate to treat Liedans as well as Terosai; I have no fear of your ill favor on that count. And though there is no doubt that your admiral is a seaman of renown and ability, we have manpower you lack; we outnumber you three to two, and have a surviving ship's boat besides." He spread his palms in a gesture of reasonableness. "I would be more than happy to cooperate, but as a fellow sovereign, not a subject."

"Then you will cooperate by returning to us all goods from the *Thunderer* your subjects recover. Hand them over to my quartermaster."

"Certainly. We will trade them for all the Liedan goods your subjects find."

"We'll take them now."

"At my convenience."

"Tell your crew of thieves to stop stealing from the bodies of our dead. It is profane."

The King snorted. "As though your workers hadn't rifled the bodies of our dead as they found them."

Her voice became a hiss. "You will learn to comply or there will be unpleasantness again between us."

His laugh, the genuine joviality of it, surprised the Queen. "So much for lasting peace." He leaned close, towering over the Queen. "Attack if you will, and we will kill you until you decide again to try for peace. Or you can send dar Bontine to negotiate for you, and we will maintain the accord we signed two days ago."

His valet stage-whispered, "Three."

"Three days ago," the King amended. "Time slips by when you're on a pleasant ocean voyage. Good day to you, Lia." He turned his back on her and strode away with his bodyguard in tow.

That, plus the use of her familiar name, was a double

insult. Herself stood there, mouth agape, for a long moment as she flushed. Then she spun, seized Shallia's arm, and began dragging her back the way I'd come, paying me no mind. "Come along, girl. You need to learn a lesson about the way you parade yourself before foreign dignitaries." Her bodyguards accompanied her, and of a sudden I was alone.

Almost. Kin Underbridge lingered at the rear of King Jerno's party, then stopped and came back my way. His face seemed troubled. "Lady Halleyne, might I ask a question?"

"If you feel you must."

"Well, I'm not enough of a flatterer to tell a lady who's been dragged through raging seas and had her clothes ruined by waves and rigors that she's been made beautiful by the experience—"

"Please get to the point." I looked after Shallia and the Queen. Perhaps I could come up with a distraction for Herself, allowing Shallia a temporary escape.

"How did your nose get unbent?"

"What?" I looked up at him.

He leaned closer, an unconscious imitation of the King's gesture of intimidation, and peered into my face. "Your nose has become straight, and you've lost the lines of years from the corners of your eyes—"

I swore in a very unladylike fashion and looked around. The Queen was too far away to have heard.

I ran toward the beach's edge, toward the foliage beyond and the ordinary soil it concealed, as fast as my waterlogged skirts would allow.

And that cursed valet followed, still talking. "The Queen is well known for her beauty. Every song from Terosai makes the claim that she is the most beauteous of her court. Is that by law?"

"Be quiet." I plunged into the brush, was held up for a moment by a bush grabbing at my garments, and freed myself with an angry yank. I bent and frantically dug at the soil. I saw with gratitude that it was rich and black.

"So it seems that a very pretty young woman, in order to survive the Terosai court, would do well to mar her beauty. Just enough."

I rubbed mud on one cheek and my forehead, two blotches that would divert the Queen's eye until I had a chance to repair my makeup. If I could find something to repair it with. Perhaps I could burn some wood for dark ash or find some ocher. "Are you happy now?" I asked. "You have pried open one of my secrets. All you have to do is present it the right way to the Queen to see my head come off. Is that what you want?"

"Not at all."

"Then what do you want? What buys your silence?"

He looked surprised. "I don't want anything."

"Oh, I have seen enough of these affairs of state to know that there is no gift without counter-gift, no present unaccompanied by a demand for gratitude."

"Well, if you put it that way, I already have my reward."

"Which is?"

"Confirmation. That I was seeing what I thought I was seeing."

"Well, that is all you will have of me." I can only hope that I kept from my face the bitter disappointment I felt, disappointment that my secret had fallen into the hands of an enemy. "You might use that knowledge to hurt me, but I will never let you use it to wrest secrets or concessions from me."

He smiled at me again, an expression I was beginning to think of as infuriatingly superior, and left me without another word.

Chapter Six

Kin

And so began our exile on the Landfall Islands.

During the first two days, we were all too injured, tired, or dispirited to press disputes with the Terosai. To be sure, there were fistfights and one inconclusive knife-fight between sailors, but the nobles and officers remained civil with one another and punished the fighters.

The Liedans numbered fifty-one; the Terosai, thirty-four. Half their number were women; a third of ours were, and all of our women were sailors, while many of theirs were ladies-in-waiting. All in all, more than a hundred and fifty from the two ships must have perished. More than thirty bodies washed up on shore in the days after the wreck.

The night the reef gutted the *Wave-Breaker*, the skies began to clear; just before dawn, Jenina Morlin took a rough reading of the stars. She told us that as far as she could tell we were well off the sea trade routes and much farther south than she had ever sailed—probably near the great sheets of ice that covered the polar latitudes. We were not, she thought, farther south than the most distant parts of Terosalle, but almost no one lived in those desolate reaches.

And the air was colder here than even it had been at the site of our negotiations. The sun did not much warm us by noon of the first day.

In the company of Second Mate Jenina, senior surviving officer of the *Wave-Breaker*, I reported all this to the King. "We must consider that we are likely to be stranded here for some time," I said. "Search ships are not likely to get this far before the bad weather sets in, and already winter presses."

He glared at me. "How long?"

"Who can say? If we had a priest, we could ask the gods." None of the priests had made it ashore, though. "But we have to consider that we may be wintering here. We need to make plans, and fast. Marshal resources. Organize our work."

He gave me an irritable look. "So draw up a plan, Kin. Present it to me."

Thus I became the architect of our community on the island.

While I was about that task, and though we had recently come to peace and would now profit from a little civility and cooperation between the two groups, the Liedans and Terosai managed to find a new conflict and begin fighting, of all things, over names.

Shortly after noon of the first day, we found fresh water inland on Fishtail Island. The stream ran down from high in the central hills, pouring over a pretty little waterfall, flowing as a broad creek to the north, and broadening into a small, crystal-clear lake before it ran downhill again and emptied into the sea on the north shore.

The messenger Ardith Netter, foraging inland, found the creek and quickly traced it to waterfall and lake. And, being Ardith Netter, he named this divine gift immediately in such a way as to curry favor. The waterfall became Jerno's Curtain. The creek was Jernin River. The broader body of water became King Lake. Ardith returned to the beach full of himself and puffed up with accomplishment. Still noting our supplies and resources, and awaiting word from the sailors I'd sent a-scouting, I merely shook my head and stayed away from those who celebrated the discovery of water.

The next day, we breakfasted on dried meat that the *Wave-Breaker's* cook had brought off the ship with him. He had one kettle, too, and so we built a fire and warmed the stuff in water, making it a sort of jerky stew that was both unappetizing and difficult to eat.

Sheroit dar Bontine joined us. "Warm food! You're far better off than the poor Terosai," he said.

"Have some," said the King, pointing to the dregs left in our kettle.

"Ah, no. I've already broken my fast. A word, Majesty? In private?"

In private meant with a scribe present, and, as the most useless lettered person available, I joined them.

Dar Bontine uncharacteristically came directly to the point. "I come in the hope of averting additional dispute between the two great rulers," he said. "The Queen is unhappy that your sailors are wandering hither and yon naming every tree and rock they set their eyes upon. She considers it an inconsiderate effort to give every square handspan a Liedan name and therefore deny her any commemoration she and her people deserve."

The King snorted his amusement. "Since our unwilling arrival here, I have yet to go to the effort to be inconsiderate to the Queen. So her opinion, as ever based on fallacy, is wrong."

Dar Bontine gave a little nod of sympathy. "Still, considering that these names are only of consequence until we are able to leave these islands, and the Terosai and Liedans must live in close proximity until then, it would be well to encourage peace. Her proposal does just that, in fact. She recommends formation of a naming committee, which will be responsible for making maps and proposing names. The names would be balanced in number between matters of Liedan and Terosai concern. When you and the Queen can agree on the names, they will be so registered; when you disagree, I cast a vote to break the tie."

"This is reasonable. But it would be a concession. Especially since these industrious mapmakers will be rowing about in *my* boat from island to island. What does the Queen offer to make this deal worthwhile?"

"Knowledge. It is known to the Terosai that the most knowledgeable Liedan sailors are dead, while the Terosai admiral, Lesto dar Ostaferion, is in admirable health. He has retained a complete set of navigational instruments, has fixed our position very precisely by the stars, and is the son of a shipmaker. He can direct work-crews to the construction of a boat fit to carry our united peoples from this island."

The King smiled. I knew why; he didn't care about the names and knew he was giving up nothing. "I accept. How many people has the Queen prematurely appointed to the Terosai portion of the naming committee?"

"Two. Lady Shallia for naming and the wizard's apprentice, Teuper, for mapmaking."

"Her Bard-apprentice and her wizard-apprentice. Both her so-called mages. What on earth have these two done to earn her disfavor, that she banishes them to work among the Liedans?"

Dar Bontine smiled. "They have done only good deeds, and thus are being honored in this way." His lie was impeccably told; I suppressed a snort of derision.

"Very well. Unlike the Queen, I will demonstrate

that I can abandon a certain amount of physical comfort to advance relations between our kingdoms." He fixed me with his stare. "Kin has a good hand and a fair sense of proportion, so I will make him a mapmaker." He turned to survey the others gathered in the little glade that, with a recovered blanket strung overhead to act as a marker and provide additional shade, served him as a throne room. He settled on his surviving dresser, Nerrin Axer, younger brother of his favorite bodyguard. "Nerrin here is quick of wit, and he will be my namer. It is done. When will we meet the Terosai admiral?"

Halleyne

It is late in the evening of the second night since we were shipwrecked. Earlier, before twilight, we held a meeting of both Liedans and Terosai, which Shallia (with her usual brevity) had begun to call "the two tribes." This took place on the broadest, smoothest curve of beach on the bay.

Sheroit dar Bontine conducted matters, yielding the floor—the sand, in this case—first to one side and then the other, carefully timing matters so that neither of the tribes was shorted. But truly, both tribes gathered to hear the words of Admiral dar Ostaferion.

His words did not hearten us. "We know that this is a small island, two hours' walk along its longest axis, and there are several other islands within view, none very large.

"We are well away from Feyndala. In three days of riding out the storm, we traveled much farther than three days of good sailing would have carried us. In addition, we are well off the trade routes, and the direct course back to Feyndala carries us against ocean streams. For these reasons, I would not give an expedition much chance of reaching our home in the *Wave-Breaker*'s boat, even if the great Captain Kohugh were still alive to captain it." The Liedans murmured at this compliment, one sailor's acknowledgement of an enemy's skill in a time when such remarks were not often forthcoming.

"Nor is that all the bad news. Winter is close upon us. We are as far south as the southernmost tip of Terosalle, so we can expect harsh weather. We must act swiftly if we are to survive. We must search out the islands' bounty and harvest it. Fish seems to be plentiful in the bay, and I have seen melthues frolicking out in the waters beyond the headlands." That was good news; the seal-like beasts were edible and yielded up thick fur that was warm against the cold. But it occurred to me that the melthues of Terosalle migrated in winter; we might have to act quickly to profit from their presence.

"But matters are not hopeless," the admiral continued. "This island seems well supplied with hardwood and softwood. Over the winter, I will design us a vessel that can carry us back to our homes. We will begin building in the spring. We may lose a year in these distant waters, but we will lose little more . . . if we are industrious and efficient."

"A year?" That shriek was the Queen; she strode forward to stand nose-to-nose, or perhaps nose-to-sternum is more precise, with her admiral. "If I am gone for a year, then the treacherous Liedans will renew war and move against Terosalle."

Dar Bontine broke in: "King Jerno's regent will not be foolish enough to do so, for he knows that Jerno's absence will doom his armies to confusion, despair, and defeat. Which is precisely why your own ministers will refrain from taking advantage of Lieda's temporary disarray; without you, they will not dare wage war. Majeste, we need to be thinking of ourselves for the moment, not our nations, which will survive in our absence."

Within minutes, the attention of the gathering shifted from dar Ostaferion's long-range plans to items of more immediate attention. Sheroit dar Bontine, Lesto dar Ostaferion (speaking for the Queen), and Kin Underbridge (speaking for the King) answered questions as fast as they arose, and I heard surprisingly little discrepancy among their answers. Perhaps this was because they did not consult the rulers, which would have allowed for new disputes to brew up, before answering.

What were we to eat? Dar Ostaferion pointed out that sailors had already caught fish, and predicted that these waters would be rich enough to sustain us; Kin said that the Liedan scouts had spotted animals on the island, and they might add to our supply of food.

What part of the island was now Terosalle's, and what part was Lieda's? Kin Underbridge said, with fair diplomacy, that should the two nations choose to live apart, the matter of who owned what would be decided in negotiations to which only the two rulers and their advisors would be party; for now, anyone caught fighting over disputed sites or resources would be beaten by a royal bodyguard of the appropriate nation.

If a Liedan committed a crime against a Terosai, under which law was the offender to be tried? Dar Ostaferion replied, "Dar Bontine's Law," an answer that brought some chuckles.

What shelter would we make? Kin Underbridge drew designs in the sand and explained. For now, we would make lean-tos of some sail that had washed or blown ashore. Before anyone asked, he proposed to divide it into eight shares, three going to the Terosai and five to the Liedans, reflecting the proportions of our population. (The Queen demanded a half-and-half split but dar Bontine soothed her while the discussion continued.) Then, since many of the two ships' carpenters had survived, we would build long houses, large single-room huts made of the native woods, each one housing eight or ten of us. This would mean there were not too many buildings to construct, no more than ten, and they should be easier to keep warm in than larger dwellings or smaller ones made for fewer inhabitants.

Someone asked why the Terosai could not have use of the Liedan ship's boat. Dar Ostaferion fielded that one: "This I have discussed with His Majesty. He says he will reasonably grant use of the boat to us when they are not utilizing it." This was not reassuring to the Terosai, but it was true that if we were to maintain peace the Terosai could no more demand the use of the boat than the Liedans could demand the use of the Terosai admiral.

And so forth, and so on. Once I realized that open warfare would not break out tonight, the gathering became dull. I crept off, back to the portion of the beach and forest inland where we Terosai had been building temporary shelters.

I found Shallia beneath the overhang she had constructed. She did not hear my approach, for I have learned to walk quietly through my association with the Queen, and I discovered her bent over her ruined, water-warped lute. As I watched, her expression went from sadness to resigned mockery; she strummed a silent chord on the water-stretched strings. "Here is a song in praise of shipwrecks," she said to an invisible audience, and strummed harder, making a horrid jangling noise.

Then she spotted me and her expression changed to one of surprise and embarrassment. She set her instrument aside.

I moved forward and sat beside her. "We have been so busy I have not had a chance to thank you," I said. "For bringing me to safety."

She shrugged cheerfully. "I couldn't let my best student drown."

"Your best student?"

"Yes."

I hugged her. "Thank the gods I'm your only student, then. Else I would not have been best and I would have perished."

She smiled. "Keep it in mind. In case I begin to conduct a formal class. You might actually have to improve. Well, we won't be practicing on my lute, or yours—I haven't even seen yours among the wreckage. But perhaps we can make new ones; I made mine, after all. At the very least, we can carve woodwinds."

"Just think, an idyll on a distant isle so that we might relax and do nothing but sing and play."

She laughed. "True, we'll have to seize every moment we have. We have one now, while all those barrel-heads argue the fate of the universe. And since the only instruments we have available are our voices—"

"Softened by dehydration, seawater, and screaming—"

"—we will sing tonight. Shall we try 'Banner Year?'" She ignored my sigh and sketched the beat, and we sang while the rulers and officers and opinionated lower ranks decided how life would be organized on these islands.

Kin

The first snow fell the next day. It did not last long, and the snow vanished almost as soon as it touched down, but it was a sign of things to come.

I found being chief mapmaker for the Liedans a pleasant enough assignment. Teuper dar Hiaro and I got along well; we were men first, and never zealots defending our respective nations. We had first access to the ship's boat, though Viriat Axer squatted in its lee at all times when it rested on the ground in order to protect it from theft; the King had a fear that some Terosai sailor would steal it and sail off to oblivion.

Our usual tactic was to row to one of the nearby islands, walk and sketch it individually, then get together and compare our renditions. We compromised on discrepancies and walked together to explore areas we had both neglected. By this means we drew maps that would not delight real cartographers but were certainly enough for fourscore castaways.

The island upon which we had landed was small; one could walk its circumference between dawn and noon. It turned out to be roughly triangular, like a fishtail with a bite taken out of it, the bite being the bay onto which most of the survivors had washed or landed; for this reason, and rather than have any of the islands reflect the interests of one kingdom or another, the namers called the place Fishtail Island. Inland, Fishtail rose to hills covered in rich greenery; we could not fault the island for luxuriant growth. The men who buried those who'd died during the shipwreck said the soil was rich, and that a few feet down they reached a thick layer of white ash.

Fishtail was one of the three larger islands of the little group. It lay southwest. Northeast was a larger island, all rocks and hills, with a larger southern bay and a broad, deep, rocky shore. On that bay, the melthues clustered in their hundreds and thousands, already preparing their young pups for the great migrations that would come with the onset of winter, not long off. We found no fresh water on the place, and other than the melthues, little life. The namers called the rocky place Hopeless Island.

Southeast of Hopeless, directly opposite a broad stretch of water from Fishtail, was an island roughly twice the size of Fishtail. Longer north-south than east-west, with a narrowing constriction of land toward the southern end, on the map we made it looked a little like the triangular head of a tortoise. Shallia and Nerrin called it Turtlehead Island. Turtlehead was not so green as Fishtail, but liveable, and had its own fresh water, a lake on the eastern side, opposite from the Fishtail Island facing.

Fishtail was separated from Hopeless by a strait that took a handful of minutes to row across on the *Wave-Breaker*'s boat. Hopeless, in turn, was set apart from Turtlehead by a strait narrow enough that a good archer could fire an arrow across it, but the waters between were treacherous with speedy current, so it was safer to row across a wider stretch of water and avoid the strait.

There were other islands as well, most of them little more than sandy rocks close in to the three large islands. One, due south of Fishtail, was home to countless seabirds (so thick was it that the sailors called it the island of the damned birds, and Damnbirds Island it became).

We saw no sign of large animals on the islands, but there were smaller ones, and (after another round of discussions between the rulers) they, too fell under the power of the mighty naming committee. Mits, the nuisancy jumping mice of eastern lands, we already knew by reputation, and trebbies, too; those were prolific, scampering rodents that weren't too bad if roasted properly. But there were a couple of beasts we did not know.

One, a fast, wooly, knee-high creature with split hooves and a miniature rack of horns, became the gulbuk, after the Liedan sailor Gulbuk; both had the same sort of shaggy, wooly beard on their chins. And Gulbuk the sailor, if he tried, could manage to look nearly as intelligent as the creatures named for him.

The gulbuks were not numerous on Fishtail Island, but we saw quite a few on Turtlehead.

We also found a sinuous, sneaky rodent that pounced upon the mits and trebbies. This creature reminded us of a snake with legs and oily fur, and experimentation showed that it tasted bad no matter how prepared. We ended up calling it a kafarra, after the famed Dresten Kafarra, a detested cousin of the King—a conceit that greatly amused Jerno.

Perhaps the Queen would have objected to two animals being named after Liedans, but we made sure it reached her ears that the second, nasty one was named for a member of the Liedan royal family, and afterwards she was quite happy with the naming choice.

All in all, this would not have been a bad place to spend a well-provisioned spring. Arriving here without resources just before the onset of winter, though, made for a daunting prospect.

While we determined the scope of the lands in which we'd found ourselves and inventoried our resources, and as the snowfalls became more thick and frequent, the rulers played at determining the fate of those lands. For warmth and convenience, the two tribes moved inland to the river. We Liedans settled on the west bank, where the hills were higher and would provide a little better cover from the blasting cold of southern winds; the Terosai stayed on the east, with ready access to the bay and the earliest encampments.

The river was duly renamed the Jernin-and-Thaliara, which the Terosai called Thaliara-and-Jernin. The waterfall, Jerno's Curtain, became Gloriana Falls, and it was I who pointed out to Sheroit dar Bontine that he could tell the Queen that the falls were more important than the lake because they stood higher and were more beautiful. King Lake retained its original name, and thus Ardith Netter became the one person, other than the naming committee and the sailors who'd given

Damnbirds Island its name, to have contributed to the map.

It was sad but inevitable that the two tribes wasted time and resources in duplicating officers and organizers. Both sides had to have someone in charge of building shelters, someone organizing melthue hunts, someone in charge of gathering nuts, someone in charge of fishing, an "army commander" (chief bodyguard, in both cases), a "navy commander" (their dar Ostaferion and our Jenina Morlin—giving the Terosai a clear advantage in naval knowledge), and on, and on.

It was Jenina who pointed out a problem resulting from all this. One night in camp, she joined me at the campfire which was unofficially for officers trying to stay out of earshot of the King. Mealtime was done, and I, a late arrival, had some of the dregs of the fish stew and was sitting alone. Jenina sat next to me, snowflakes graying her hair, and said without preamble, "Too many. One for one."

"One for one what?" I was half-starved from the day's work and ravenously devouring my stew before it all leaked out. I had made myself a crude bowl from a cut-up leather jerkin I'd found on the beach. I was no leatherworker, and Sheroit dar Bontine, who knew that skill, was too busy doing more critical work like making boots to help me with my project. I had not done a good job, and so I had to rush or watch my meal dribble out.

"One of us for one of them. Not Liedan and Terosai." She drank her own stew from a proper cup; like many Liedan sailors, she always had a tin cup on a cord tied to her belt, so that she not miss out when water was being ladled out. "Officer and commoner. Commanders and doers."

"Everyone works, Jenina." I gulped down another mouthful and made a face about the amount of stew straining through the bowl and dribbling into my lap.

"Not true. Some of those Terosai ladies-in-waiting just wait, or whatever it is they do. Their queen says it would lessen her dignity for her ladies to do labor. Kill them all, I say, and feed them to the damnbirds."

"Jenina!"

"And even with those who work, not everyone does work worth having. You, for example. The maps are good enough. Now it's just knowing where every twig is so they can name it. You could be fishing. Trapping melthues or smoking their meat. Putting something in our larders for the winter."

"True. But if all of us whose time is being wasted were to stop, there'd be war. And then everybody would have plenty to eat. Everybody left, that is."

She gave me a nasty smile. "The way I count it, there's one person bringing in food for one person not. We'll starve if we can't put that second group to productive work. Or get rid of them."

"That's our King you're talking about," I said, joking.

I'd finished my soggy bowlful of stew before I realized she wasn't answering. I glanced at her. She looked as though she were waiting for me to continue that thought. "What are you suggesting?"

"That you listen. Listen to the sailors and common men, not just to that king of yours." She rose. "You know, you might be worthwhile if you'd learn to row against the current once in a while." Then she left.

I did as she suggested. On the occasions when I was in camp, not wandering around the uncharted portions of our new home, I'd occasionally join in with the fishermen and shelter-builders at their labors. I found myself talking to angry men and women.

At first, they were shocked that I would deign to help them. Among the "uppers"—by their definition, anyone who didn't have to do hard physical labor—Jenina was the only other one who would help. The rest, including bodyguards, bodyservants, scribes, and advisors, kept their hands clean. And they constituted half the number of the shipwrecked Liedans.

The "lowers" complained about endless toil, bad weather, harsh words, bad commanders, boils, bunions, rickets, missing their children, missing their lovers, sand in their shoes, and thousands of other things. But the tone of their complaints changed, becoming quieter, more intense, when they spoke of the uppers who did no work and yet got the first of the shelters while winds became colder.

On our long walks, I talked about this with Teuper. "It's the same on the Terosai side of the river," he admitted, nearly two weeks into our exile. "Worse, maybe. At least your King doesn't beat people who displease him. Does he?"

"No . . . I think he's saving up his beatings. Not wasting resources until we get home. There will probably be a mass beating then. But even by his own standards he has been quite calm since arriving here. More like an indulgent uncle with a short temper."

"You're lucky."

We were on Hopeless Island, crunching across an unmelting layer of snow, cutting westward across the eastern headland, the arm of land that pointed to Turtlehead. We'd had to wait to cross to the island, for when we arrived where the boat was normally beached it was gone—Admiral dar Ostaferion had requested passage to Hopeless to look at the lumber there, and had been rowed across. We'd already lost part of the day and were walking fast.

But no sooner had we topped a rise that overlooked one of the broad stony beaches seething with melthues than Teuper pointed, asking, "What's that?"

"What's what?" The creatures crawled all over the stones, playing, teaching their young, swimming, beaching themselves, fighting—by biting with their sharp teeth or slapping with their flippers. I saw nothing odd in their actions. They had not yet reacted to our presence; we stood some twenty yards away, with the wind blowing our scent to the north, so the short-sighted creatures had probably not detected us yet.

"There, over there." He pointed until I saw it, a spot of snow-flecked green in amongst the gray stones and black and brown melthues.

"Seaweed or algae, perhaps." But, curious, we moved toward it.

As we neared the edge of the sea of melthues, the nearer ones saw or smelled us and made their barking noise of alarm. They moved away in their odd rocking-crawling motion, but not at a pace that suggested they thought they were in mortal danger; they simply advanced before us and filled in behind us, staying clear.

The green mass was a woolen cloak. A man lay beneath it, his right arm and legs protruding. I drew the cloak aside.

It was Admiral dar Ostaferion. He looked as though he were asleep, his hair rumpled, his expression oddly comfortable as he lay upon the rocks.

Teuper touched his cheek with the back of his hand. "Cold. I think he's dead."

"He may be cold and alive. Sometimes cold slows the heart."

He put both hands on the admiral's shoulder and rolled the older man onto his back. I began to bend over to look dar Ostaferion in the face.

Then it happened, a blur of green and red stabbing up from the ground at Teuper.

Without thought, I struck at the thing, catching it with my forearm, and hurled it away, then drew my knife. The green thing landed a couple of feet away— a serpent. It curled and struck again, this time at me. I slid back a half-pace, watched the snake miss me by a hand's breadth, and stabbed at it.

My knife entered its head and pinned it . . . to dar Ostaferion's shoulder, the blade penetrating a handspan into the admiral. I cursed at the injury I might have done the old man, but paid attention exclusively to the snake for the moment.

It was a beauty. About four feet long, in brilliant green, with a pattern of diamond shapes in blood-red down its back. It writhed in its death-throes, its skull sheared through by my dagger, then finally settled to stillness. Satisfied that it could not free itself, I looked at the damage I had done dar Ostaferion.

No damage. I pulled the knife free, with the snake still impaled upon it, and set it aside, then pulled the admiral's tunic from his shoulder. A little of the snake's blood spotted his skin, but the wound I'd made was clean; no blood welled up from it. He had been dead for some time, though not for as much as a day; I'd seen him that morning.

I belatedly realized that Teuper was cursing and had been for some time. I looked up at him; he was pallid, staring at the snake. "It's dead," I told him.

"Where did it come from?"

"It was under the body." I looked at the place from which the snake had struck. It was a hole in the sand. "This was a burrowing snake."

"There may be more, then."

"True." I pulled the dead thing from my blade and handed it to Teuper, who took it reluctantly. While he was distracted, I wiped the blade clean in the sand and sheathed it. Then, with his help, I pulled dar Ostaferion up to a sitting position and was eventually able to get him up over my shoulder in a rescuer's carry.

It was hard work, and we had to keep our pace slow as we walked along the melthue-covered beach, but it was not as bad as it could have been; dar Ostaferion had been an old man and was the lighter for it. Teuper, still carrying the dead snake (I insisted he do so), kept his eyes open for more burrow-holes. He thought he spotted one or two and we kept well clear of them.

"Where did that knife come from?" he asked.

"It's mine."

"I gathered that. But I did not see your sheath."

"I'm no longer a bodyguard, so I do not have to advertise that I'm armed. But I do remember a trick or two."

"Yes, you do. That was nicely struck. Even if it did perforate the old admiral."

Not knowing whether that was a compliment or a jibe, I chose not to respond.

We reached a stretch of shore well away from the main population of melthues and lay the body down there. Then Teuper sprinted off to bring Viriat and the boat.

Chapter Seven

Halleyne

The Admiral dar Ostaferion's death has put every-one in a sorrowful mood.

It is not just that we admired him. We did; his disciplined leadership and wisdom meant much to Terosalle during the war. I have known heroes—I put his name among them without reservation.

But of all of us—and the Queen made sure to ask about this in the days since the Admiral died—Lesto dar Ostaferion was the only one with extensive ship-building experience. Others here could build a raft or small boat, but did not have the engineering skill to plan a ship that stood a good chance of making the crossing back to the continent Feyndala.

So as much as we mourn him, we mourn our loss, the loss of our best chance to effect our own return home. Even the Liedans are saddened.

And then there is the matter of the snakes. Since Teuper and and Kin warned us of them, the melthue hunters have seen two or three on Hopeless Island.

Maydellan Ha made a daring trip to capture one of the things; Kin made a pole for him with a loop of cord at one end that might be drawn closed. But so far the doctor has not been able to find another to capture.

In all this sorrow and absorption, though, I see one face that is mostly happy: Shallia dar Kantrin.

I think the shipwreck has been harder on her than she lets on. As part of the Queen's court, we are together much of the day, and sleep under the same lean-to; we will share a hut with the ladies-in-waiting when it is built. So I know that most days she awakens disoriented, crying "Mother!" and then not remembering why—a curious thing for a woman who never knew her mother.

But most of the time she seems more than content. This is not her putting on a happy face for benefit of those she should be cheering; she practically glows with happiness. When we are together in private and she teaches me to play the woodwinds we have carved together, she cannot be induced to perform sad songs, only bright ones. I ask her about it and she only says, "I will tell you soon."

Her pervasive cheerfulness has roughened the nerves of Herself, as well. The Queen, already inclined to punish Shallia for attracting the King's eye several days past, now makes an effort to catch her on every little mistake or imagined offense and beat her on whim. Today was the worst; Shallia bumped into the Queen and the Queen sent her out for three lashes at the hands of one of the sailors. Though greatly pained by the blows, Shallia bore them in such good spirits that the Queen had her lashed still further for insolence.

Kin

I was fascinated to find myself under suspicion of murder. I had, after all, put my knife into Lesto dar

Ostaferion. Even though the wound was shallow, even though it did not bleed, even though Doctor Ha maintained before the Terosai that a viper's poison had brought the admiral low, many of them believed that I was somehow responsible for the beloved sailor's death.

. Teuper perhaps did not help my case by describing how I produced my knife "with magical speed" and slew the serpent, causing the knife to disappear immediately after. Suddenly I was not only a murderer, but a cunning and magical murderer as well. For a while I stayed away from the Terosai, and made sure my bedding was free of serpents that might have been placed there by some vengeful admirer of the admiral's.

Instead, I spent my time among the workingmen of the Liedans. When I had hours to spare, I helped them build shelters and smokehouses, and encouraged others of the courtiers to do likewise; some, particularly the bodyguards and bodyservants, did. I think this helped stem the tide of resentment Jenina had warned me of.

Soon after the death of dar Ostaferion, hard winter rode its ugly omens across our lives. The birds of Damnbirds Island rose in their masses and headed northward. The last leaves blew from the trees, and snow that fell no longer melted away. We woke in the morning to find thin sheets of ice on our drinking water; we huddled closer to garner what warmth we could from each other. Too, we watched the melthues with interest, but their numbers on the rocky beaches did not seem to thin; I found myself hoping they were of some undiscovered type that wintered in the cold lands.

One particular day, more than a week after the admiral's death, Viriat Axer and I set out to meet Teuper at the site where we beached our longboat. Teuper was not yet there when we arrived, but another

Terosai stood shivering in her layers of thin silk: Lady Shallia, their Bard-in-training. She fidgeted near the boat guard who had relieved Axer; she seemed grateful to see us. "Lord Underbridge."

I was cold and not in the best of moods. "I'm supposed to be greeted as Lord Assassin Underbridge."

She smiled. "I forgot. I wish to make a request of you. I would like to have an audience with the King. At his earliest convenience."

"*The* King."

"Yes."

"Not *your* King."

She hesitated, so I pressed on: "I thought it was by your Queen's order that King Jerno was never to be referred to as 'the King.' Though other forms were acceptable. 'Your King. The king those Liedans deserve. That bloated simulacrum of a king.'"

My words were obviously no challenge to her; she held her smile without strain. "Might I arrange such an audience?"

"I should think so. Viriat, let us conduct her to the King's hut." I glanced at the bodyguard and was arrested by what I saw: A singular lack of curiosity. Normally, such a request would have Viriat furiously pondering its meaning. He demonstrated no such effort now. That meant he knew already.

I gestured for Lady Shallia to precede us while I wondered what that meant.

An hour later, the Bardling had her audience.

The King held such audiences in his "throne room." As had Queen Lia, he'd insisted on having a hut of his very own, one he wouldn't have to share. But he'd gone a step further. His hut had been built north of a steep hillside, one which some of the men had climbed and decided was in no danger of producing rockslides. Between the hut and the lowest slope of the hill was a large, flat glade, which the King was having walled in as an open-air thronal chamber; it was nearly half-walled now. Eventually it was to have a roof, but for now the walls were all the symbol he needed.

The King sat on the rough wooden chair that served him as a throne; it was set on a small mound of earth that he might have some altitude on his subjects. I stood awkwardly at his right, Viriat at his left—awkward because the slope of the mound made footing tricky.

As soon as she was brought before the King and recognized, Shallia knelt before him in proper fashion for a visitor and said, "Majesty, I come to beg a favor of you."

"Beg away." The King's expression was one of puzzlement. The Queen would never let one of her subjects come before him in this fashion.

"I wish to come live among the Liedans."

The King cleared his throat, something he did to stall while thinking. "My lady, I cannot have one among us who has two royal allegiances, two kingdoms to be loyal to."

She shook her head earnestly. "I wish to renounce my former kingdom, knowing that I will leave it forever and make an enemy of its ruler, in order to be a Liedan."

Jerno cleared his throat again. "Will you swear allegiance, before the gods, to the throne of Lieda?"

"I will."

"Will you be my Bard? Gods know we could use a real musician among us."

She smiled. "I will."

"Well, then." The King did not speak for long moments, and the smile faded from Shallia's face. The King looked between me and Viriat before addressing her again. "Why do you do this? Answer honestly, girl. Is it because of the way you are punished?"

"No, Majesty. I do not deny the Queen her right to

make such punishment." She flushed just a little. "I wish to marry."

"A Liedan."

"Yes."

"Whom?"

"Nerrin Axer."

The King and I both looked at Viriat Axer, who merely shrugged. I grinned at him. That explained everything. His brother and Lady Shallia, thrown together in the ludicrous "naming committee," had fallen in love. Viriat already knew this when he and I met Shallia. Perhaps he had suggested the rendezvous, knowing that I could arrange her an audience.

Jerno returned his attention to the Bard. "You wish to be married soon?"

"We do."

"We have no priests on the island. But I, as king of a great people, may perform the ceremony. In fact, I would be delighted to marry you."

She smiled a brilliant smile.

He made her take the oath of allegiance. Interestingly, though he had no proof of her royal standing, he had her take the oath of a noblewoman. Then he allowed her to return to the Terosai encampment, in Viriat's protective company, to pack her goods and make her goodbyes; it was anyone's guess whether the Queen would ever allow a Terosai subject to talk to her again.

"Kin." The King's manner was sober, but not depressed or lost as it had so often been in recent days.

"Majesty."

"Odd that a foreign Bard would be able to show me the truth."

"What truth, Majesty?"

He gave me a contemplative look. "When my last son died, I lost all need to live. When we were shipwrecked here, I was half-convinced that we would be here forever, trapped in conflict with those Terosai, doomed to watch our numbers diminish as our hatred built, until only annihilation would result. The day Admiral dar Ostaferion died, I was completely convinced of it.

"But look at that! The girl finds love. The girl plans a future. Effortlessly, she lives, and shows others how to live." He breathed a great sigh. "I need to follow her lead. I must have heirs, that Lieda not shake itself to pieces in wars of succession when I finally die. I must have a loving wife, that I be constantly reminded of the virtues of living."

I felt my stomach sink. "And what of Queen Elowar?" The King's wife still lived; she, in fact, would be assuming the reins of Lieda even now.

"She can bear me no more sons, Kin, and she does not love me. So here is what I will do, and it will be a mercy to both of us." He began counting off items on his fingers. "First, I will declare the foundation of a new kingdom. Since my family name is Byriver, and it is beside a river we now live, my portions of these Landfall Islands will be known as the Kingdom of Byriver. I am King; there is no Queen.

"Second, I will choose a wife from among my subjects, and she will be Queen of Byriver.

"Third, when we return home, I will grant Queen Elowar a divorce by royal decree, and visit on her titles and land to allow her to live lavishly. Unfortunately, I will also have to pay monstrous bribes to certain members of her family to enable them to forget what they will doubtless perceive as insult.

"And fourth, I will proclaim my Queen of Byriver the queen over Lieda as well.

"All proper protocols will be met, and the children of my new Queen will be heirs to the throne of Lieda."

"Majesty, I think that would be a mistake. It would make an enemy of Elowar—no money you can give her will replace the throne you will take away.

Besides, you can declare the children of mistresses to be heirs."

"Perhaps I do not want a woman who would be content to be a mistress. You can go now, Kin." He was not angry with me; he was lost in thought.

I left with the sinking feeling still in full force. Nothing good could come of the King's plan.

Halleyne

Where I sit, against a tree a few yards from but out of sight of the Queen's hut, I can still hear her shrieking. She received word a little while ago of Shallia's defection. I am still half in a state of shock over it.

I was returning from an errand—asking Maydellan Ha if he'd had any progress in his vague plans to fabricate more paper from the pulp of native trees, which he had not—when I saw Shallia and one of the Liedan bodyguards under the lean-to she and I used for shelter. When I came up to them, I saw that she was packing her few possessions in a blanket. Her face was shining. The Liedan came on guard and watched me as though I were a potential assassin, and Shallia noticed me.

"Halleyne! I'm so glad you're here." She rose to give me a quick embrace, then returned to her business.

And then she explained what that business was. Leaving to marry.

"You didn't tell me about Nerrin," I protested.

"I'm sorry, sweet. It was sudden, and I dared not tell you."

Her words were like a slap. "Whyever not?"

"Oh, no." She embraced me. "Not because of *you*, Halleyne. But whenever I wanted to tell you, I felt the ears."

"Ears?"

She gestured at the trees around us. "Ears nearby. Listening to me. And more, I think, to you."

"You're making no sense."

"I know." She looked apologetic. "Ears hover about us here, and I dream of sluggish spirits waiting to awaken, and there is something far, far below that sleeps even more deeply. But the things I feel don't become words very easily. I'll have to keep trying."

"Queen Lia—she will be so angry. We won't be able to sing together." I must have sounded broken-hearted; I was.

"Come with me, then."

"My family would suffer for my actions."

"Then we will find a way to get together. We will have to be even more circumspect. That is all." She kissed my cheek and was gone.

Duty required me to go tell the Queen. Instead, I found Sheroit dar Bontine where he was working on his tiny hut—built back at Landfall Point, the beach where most of us washed ashore, so that by the placement of his hut he would not have to declare allegiance to either nation—and told him. Told him what it could mean. "She will forbid us to deal with the Liedans. She will make the river a wartime border. If Shallia is treated well, more Terosai will defect . . ."

"I will make everything well," he said, in his kindliest tone, and that is the only relief I have had of the situation.

He was right; he could fix everything. I do not know how he did it.

He let the Queen rave and rant for a couple of hours, then visited her in her shack. She shrieked for a while longer, probably sobbing on his shoulder, and then quieted. All I could hear was the occasional rumble of dar Bontine's voice.

When he emerged to leave, he waved cheerily at those of us standing within view of the hut. One of the

Queen's ladies waited a few moments more before entering, and she and the Queen emerged, all smiles, minutes later.

The Queen laid down no new declarations. In fact, she rescinded some of the old ones, privately telling her confidants that it behooved us all to cooperate here, suggesting that we treat the island as one community, with Queen and King brought in only to administer justice on the subjects beholden to them.

Later, dar Bontine said that it was my words that had given him the key to her decision. "More Terosai will defect," he said. "That one phrase put terror in her. It was not hard to make her understand that in six months' time the island could consist of herself, myself, and Liedans—no Terosai to serve her. You think very well, even in the extremes of emotion, Halleyne; perhaps you should consider diplomatic service."

"I am in diplomatic service," I assured him. "I simply make it look like scribe's work."

Dar Bontine laughed; he does not laugh often, but when he does, he laughs well.

Kin

The next day, the King did declare his portions of Fishtail Island to be the Kingdom of Byriver. Within hours, the Queen had declared the rest of the island to be the Kingdom of Tarrene, a word meaning "Empress" in the older form of the Terosai tongue.

The winds grew colder, our huts grew more numerous and sturdier, and our efforts to catch and smoke the meat of the melthues and fish became more strenuous. Winter was hard on us.

A week after Shallia's defection, it came time for her wedding to Nerrin Axer. She had spent her time well, composing songs in praise of the King but wandering much among the commoners to dispense music and cheer. She told us to call her Shallia Kantrin, ridding herself of the Terosai "dar," which means "clan," and adapting herself as fast as she could to Liedan customs. In spite of her odd ways, in spite of the distress she projected when she awoke, calling out for her mother every morning, she quickly became beloved of the Liedans.

The ceremony was to be conducted in the throne room. In attendance were Shallia and Nerrin, the King, all the nobles of the Liedan retinue, Jenina Morlin (as the head of our pathetic navy), Sheroit dar Bontine . . . We were surprised at the arrival of a Terosai retinue, led by the Queen and including her noble followers and her scribe. The Queen was cultivated and charming, and approached the couple before the ceremony to give them a gift: A gold chain she had worn during the shipwreck, a chain of sufficient length that it could be used for the binding portion of the marriage ceremony. Shallia contained her surprise and sweetly thanked the Terosai ruler.

Then, as the feast of fish cakes, fruits, nuts, and freshly-roasted melthue was being laid out, it was time for the ceremony.

King Jerno stood before the assembly, not yet calling the happy couple forward, and addressed us all: "It is often the unpleasant duty of rulers to decree harm. Wars. Sentences of execution. Sentences of exile. These are the unfortunate duties of those who wear the crown. But sometimes we are privileged to give gifts to the deserving. This I plan to do today, twice.

"Kin Underbridge, valet to the King, step forward."

It took me a moment to respond. I knew I had no part in these proceedings. But I did as he had bidden me. He commanded me to kneel, and I did so.

"Kin, in these last few years you have shown loyalty and wisdom beyond your years, and I have been long in rewarding it. As king of Lieda and Byriver, it is my pleasure to bestow upon you the title, rank and privilege of Great Judge of both nations. You now may adjudge disputes and crimes of the highest order, confirm agreements and the severing of ties between any parties beholden to my throne. You have the same rights and protections under the law as any greater landowner. With this title comes a stipend in accord with your new status—though we must wait for our return before I am obliged to give it to you." That drew some laughs.

I knelt there in a state of shock. Only when I heard more laughter from the assembly did I remember that I was obliged to respond. Then did I realize I could not summon up one word of a reply that was correct in protocol. I managed, "Thank you, Majesty," to a chorus of smothered laughs.

"Stand then, Judge Underbridge. Stand." He drew me to his side. "And now, for the other great gift." He smiled down at the happy couple. "This first marriage on Landfall is of great consequence. It reminds us that no matter our circumstances, we can rise above hardship. It reminds us that, just as a Liedan and a Terosai wed this day, our two lands can live in peace.

"Since this is such a momentous union, we must not fail to make of it everything we can. So plans must change to accommodate the needs of nations." He made a regretful bow toward the couple.

He stood down off the royal mound and turned to face me. "Judge Underbridge, as your king, I charge you: Marry me this day to the Lady Shallia Kantrin."

Chapter Eight

Kin

I remember how quiet everything became, as if an
nseen blanket had descended and smothered all
ound.

I'm told that this didn't happen, that furious whis-
ering immediately broke out among the assembly, that
ar Bontine had a sudden coughing fit, that the bride-
room Nerrin Axer began making a wheezing sound
 he tried to extract words of protest. I heard none
f it; perhaps my hearing contracted as a man's sight
metimes contracts when he is injured. All I could see
as the good cheer on the King's face and the shock
n Shallia's.

I finally said, "Majesty, I do not understand."

He remained patient. "Today I will be marrying the
ady Shallia."

"Ah. Then I do understand." How to refuse him?
ow to delay matters? "Majesty, I have never con-
ucted such a ceremony. Perhaps we could step aside
r a moment so you could instruct me."

"Surely you have attended wedding ceremonies."

"Yes, but they have all gone right out of my head."

He sighed and nodded assent, and the two of us drew back through the door into the royal hut. As soon as the door was shut, I heard the assembly break out into loud conversation.

"Majesty, I think this is a mistake."

"And now, at last, you have the absolute, throne-granted right to tell me so. Never again need you fear that your loose tongue will cost you your head."

"Yes, thank you, Majesty." I somehow had to pass by the shield of his beaming, affable face and get to the thoughts beyond. "But if you marry the lady against her will, you will make her unhappy."

"Kin, it is my right to insist on this wedding."

"Of course it is; you are King. But should you? Should you do this knowing that it will bring the lady grief?"

"The grief will pass, shortly. She will come to respect me and enjoy her status. She will love our children. I do not pretend to be certain that she will love me; that is for the gods to decide."

"And Nerrin Axer?"

"I feel sympathy for the boy, but his needs cannot stand paramount over the needs of Lieda. I will give him a captain's commission in the army; his future will be set; the commission will bring him the attention of many ladies seeking husbands of rank. In time, he will realize that his life is the better for it."

"But—"

"Kin, I have decreed this wedding. You are obliged to obey and conduct it. Now, do you need instruction in the ceremony?"

And there it was, balanced on the edge of a sword. My duty on one side, every bit of common sense on the other, and me feeling the cut in the middle.

Halleyne

Riotous noise erupted as soon as the King and his new judge quit the ridiculous, dirt-floored throne room. Everyone began talking except Nerrin Axer, who began shouting, and the Queen, who began laughing so hard she could not control herself.

The King's bodyguards moved into place beside the doors into the throne room. All except for Viriat Axer, who pressed to the front of the crowd to stand beside his brother. Viriat looked perplexed and angry, though his emotions were merely a dim reflection of his brother's. Shallia looked lost and hurt; I made to move toward her, but the Queen's hand closed about my wrist and I was obliged to stay with the Terosai party.

It was not long before the King and Kin emerged. The new judge looked pained; the King's good cheer had not wavered. I counted that a bad sign. Kin stood before the throne, the King at the bottom of the mound.

King Jerno gestured to Shallia. "Come, girl, stand beside me." His face wore an expression of kind sympathy. "As your king, I command it. You swore allegiance to me. You must obey."

She wavered. Nerrin Axer beside her made a sudden lunge toward the King, but his brother seized him. I could not tell whether Viriat was doing his duty and protecting the King, or protecting his brother from the other bodyguards; perhaps he did not know. His own expression of dismay was eloquent.

Shallia composed herself and moved forward to stand beside the King. She bowed her head.

Kin sighed and began the ceremony. I barely recognized it; it was short and unsentimental. "The gods look upon us and bless us. Jerno Byriver, King of

Lieda, Cenpeydon, do you consent to be wed to this lady?"

"Yes."

"Shallia Kantrin, noblewoman, do you consent to be wed to this lord?"

She hesitated and cast one last look over her shoulder. It was a pleading look, directed at the Queen, but it did nothing but set the Queen off on a second gale of laughter. Shallia turned forward again. "Yes." Her voice was faint.

"No! All the gods damn you, Jerno—" That was Nerrin, struggling to free himself from his brother's grip. The King looked over, made a flicking motion with his hand, and Viriat began to drag his brother toward the main door. The guard on that portal came forward to assist him.

"By my right as Judge of Byriver, under the eyes of the gods, I declare the union of marriage between Jerno and Shallia. Let happiness find them." Kin had omitted any preface, the tying together of wrists with a cord or chain, pleas to specific gods for specific blessings, and any sort of blessing on behalf of any children that might come from this union. But in every significant particular the wedding was correct and legal.

"I will kill you—" Nerrin again, just before the two bodyguards got him through the door and outside.

The King turned and waved a hand at the assembly. He did not wait for the applause he knew probably would not come. "And now, the feast begins. Enjoy yourselves." He took his new bride by the shoulders and led her forward through the door to his hut.

And that was Shallia's wedding.

I was obliged to stay beside the Queen at the start of the feast. She was in such a good mood she could not conceive of her handmaidens and courtiers missing any of it. We walked the crude, hastily-made tables (which would later be worked into the walls of huts), grazed on the food, and chatted dismally with the other guests. Then the Queen's attention was diverted by dar Bontine; they talked and I was able to slip away.

If I went back to the Terosai camp, they would ask me how the wedding went, and I did not want to give anyone the answer. I headed along the trail back to the beach and wandered along it, sand and coldness slipping instantly into my increasingly tattered slippers. I would have to ask dar Bontine for shoes.

And there he was, sitting up against a tree, wrapped in his cloak against the harsh winds: Kin, the new judge of two nations. He ignored me, and as I came upon him anger swelled up in me.

"Why did you do that?"

"I thought they made a handsome couple."

"You aren't funny."

"Here." His hands emerged from beneath the folds of his cloak. They were empty; but he folded them together and separated them, and in one hand he held a short knife with a wicked, narrow blade. This he offered me. "You want to kill me? Stab away."

"I won't let you escape punishment just by dying. Why did you agree to it? How could you doom Shallia that way?"

He glared and tucked the knife away. "It has to do with duty."

"Duty to the King, your so-generous patron."

"To the King? You're deluded. The king is an idiot, bloated, short-sighted, selfish, vainglorious, feeble-minded cretin whose sole virtue is that he is twice as good as your Queen."

He was nearly shouting, and I found myself trying to shush him.

"And I'll tell you this, Halleyne dar Dero, if you ever tell the King I said any of this—" He paused, and an old expression crossed his face. "If you do that, I swear by the gods that I will admit the truth of it. There. All you have to do is tell it to the King to see my head come off." He turned from me and stared out over the water. "Now we are even."

"Why did you perform the ceremony?"

He heaved a sigh. "If I refused, he would make someone else a judge and the ceremony would be performed anyway. Probably your friend Ardith Netter. But mostly, if I refused and we did return home, my family would fall out of favor. My father would be sent off to fight battle after useless battle until he fell. New taxes would descend on our estate and my mother would be driven from her home. It was duty to my family, Halleyne."

"Oh." The anger that had visited me left just as abruptly. I moved to the tree and sat, my back to it, beside Kin.

"And besides . . . If I remain a judge in the King's favor, perhaps I can do something."

"Do what?"

"Persuade the King to give her up. Recently—until today, anyway—he has been showing some odd little signs of decency. Perhaps I can find a way to appeal to them. And of all the Liedans present, I am now second highest in rank. I must be able to use that to some good effect."

"Queen Lia will make every effort to turn this situation to her advantage."

"I know. But I don't know how she will approach it."

"Nor do it." I thought over what I meant to say next and the enormity of what I was considering took the breath from my lungs. It was long moments before I could speak again. "But I will find out, and I will tell you."

He turned to look at me. "She could kill you for such a betrayal of confidence."

"She doesn't need that much reason. She could kick me to death for spilling soup. No, I'm going to become the perfect scribe and confidant, joining with her in all her little plots. Only then can I work against the ones that are most damaging. Where will we meet?"

"What?"

"I'm not suggesting a romantic liaison, you oaf. I want to know what the King is doing. You want to know what the Queen is doing. We both want to free Shallia from this mockery of a marriage. We must, well, conspire. You know the island better than I; you've left your footprints all over it. Where will we meet?"

He told me of a little glade he'd found, a few dozen steps west of a notable evergreen on the bank of the Thaliara-and-Jernin, so surrounded by underbrush that one could not approach it without a great crashing sound unless he knew the way the foliage lay. It is there we will meet; it is there we will commit treason against both our rulers.

Kin

The day after the wedding was appropriately funereal. It dawned windy and cold, with the sky sheeted in clouds the gray of granite.

Upon waking, the King proclaimed a royal holiday. Reminded—by me—that a day of rest might doom some of us to death in the bleakest part of winter, he amended himself to say that it was a royal day of forgiveness, with all prisoners released and all crimes forgotten. Reminded—again by me—that we had no prisoners or criminal concerns pending, he fretted a moment and proclaimed a royal pardon for Nerrin Axer, who was clearly guilty of treason for his death threats of the day before. I dutifully made the proclamation at morning breakfast before the main body of men and women went to work.

Then I found Nerrin Axer. It took some time; instead

of helping build a smokehouse, his assigned duty, he was off in the woods, practicing with a crudely-made bow and arrows. He fired wobbly shafts at a target that was a mound of mud with a royal crown crudely shaped from mud at its summit. I watched him for a while, waiting until his entire sheaf of pitiful shafts had been fired before approaching.

I stepped on a twig, startling him, and when he saw me he glowered. "We might hunt melthues more successfully with bows," he said.

"Nerrin, please. I'm not stupid."

He pulled a shaft free of the target and nocked it; I stopped where I was and continued, "Nor am I here to attack you, or betray your intentions to the King. Kill him or don't; it's all the same to me."

Puzzled, he lowered the bow. "I'll kill you, too, once the King is dead."

"As you wish." I walked up to his target and broke the mud crown from its top. "But your chances improve if you disguise your intentions better. No one seeing this is going to believe you wish to hunt melthues." I began working the mud into a crude melthue head.

"It does not bother you that I will kill the King?"

"No. Come on, give me some help, you started this. Do the flippers."

Accustomed to obedience, he set the weapons aside and gathered up some of the mud. "It does not bother you that I will kill you?"

"Not much. What bothers me is that you will kill Shallia."

He straightened. There was murder in his expression. "How dare you say that? You have hurt her; the King has hurt her. I never have."

"Are you sure she loves you?"

"She gave up everything she knew for me. Yes, she loves me. And I her."

"Even now, do you think she has hope?"

"Of course. We both live. Anything could happen."

"If the King dies, what will happen?"

"We will be married—"

"Who will be suspected of the murder? Which one person, among the nearly hundred men and women on the island, said he would kill the King?"

He glared again but did not answer.

"Correct. You. Those loyal to the King will come and get you for killing the King, and perhaps for killing me, and execute you. What will happen to Shallia then?"

"We could steal the boat and flee."

"Neither of you a sailor? Noble of you to be willing to drown your lady-love. So, as I was saying, the loyalists kill you. What happens to Shallia then?"

He looked away. "I do not know."

"Well, either she gets over your death and finds another lover—"

"Shut up."

"Or she does not, and loses all hope, and pines away, and dies. Which outcome do you prefer?"

"I said shut up!" He made as though to strike me, but I grabbed his arm and slammed him into his preposterous mud target. It gave way under his weight and he slowly fell backwards across its ruin.

As he struggled to free himself, I continued. "Nerrin, I want you to understand, and I want you to say it back to me. If you kill the King, you die, and Shallia may die. If you can think of any other outcome, I'd like to hear it."

He stood and looked ready to strike at me again, but held himself in check. Finally he allowed, "Perhaps I should wait until we have all returned to Lieda. Then Shallia and I could run away."

"Well, you're thinking better, if not well. Lieda it is, then. I wanted to ask you something else. Do you think the King a good man?"

He brushed mud from himself. "He is a vomitous mass."

"And the Terosai queen? A model of virtue and nobility?"

"You make me laugh."

"I'll bet you my knife against your bow that within the week Queen Lia will find a way to talk to you. She will suggest ways you might be avenged on the King. Perhaps she will talk about hiding you among her Terosai. But mark me, Nerrin: She wants only to satisfy herself. To score blows against the King. You'd be a weapon for her to use and discard. You know she hates Shallia; yet she will say she has realized she was wrong and wants only to help her. Don't be fooled; she will discard Shallia too. Then she will have another laugh and you will both be dead."

"She does hate Shallia, so she will never talk to me."

"My knife against your bow."

"Done." Rising, he gave me his muddy hand in the traditional confirmation of a wager. "Even if you win, I'll have both weapons when I kill you."

"See? Already you are thinking with more hopefulness."

Chapter Nine

Kin

During the next several weeks, ice crusted thick on the banks of the river, then sheeted over entirely. It crept north from Duckhead Point and joined ice growing south from Hopeless Island. But the melthues still had not left, and we began to feel more hopeful that we would have enough food to survive the season.

Since, as Judge, I now had administrative duties, I appointed Raldan Cosmith, a handsome, clever young sailor, as Nerrin Axer's replacement on the "naming committee," and Ardith Netter as mine. I was certain that Teuper, a level-headed man, could keep an eye on Ardith and keep him from getting into too much trouble.

Between us, Halleyne and I worked out the means by which we could coordinate the decisions of our respective rulers. It was simple and consistent.

An example of how it worked: The naming committee, no longer exploring very much because of the cold, turned its attention to the trees and animals. The question of the poisonous snake that killed Admiral dar Ostaferion came up. The snakes themselves were of little concern to us now, because it seemed that they were remaining in their burrows through the cold weather; but the question of what to name them became a political matter. Name it for Terosai and the Queen would take issue; name it for Liedans and the King would object.

Halleyne and I used the occasion to test our skill in manipulating the royals.

Halleyne, in normal conversation, said to the Queen, "I hear King Jerno wants to name the viper after himself, since it is beautiful, and is dangerous when roused."

The Queen spat back, "Him? Beautiful and dangerous? Preposterous."

I, speaking with the King, said, "Herself thinks the new snake should be named after you, since it is poisonous and reptilian." After which I had to endure an extended period of the King's grumblings about his Terosai counterpart.

Naturally, the snake was named the Gloriana viper, after Herself, and both rulers were well satisfied.

Another example. Halleyne wanted to visit Shallia to learn music. Shallia was not welcome east of the river; Halleyne could only travel west of the river when in the Queen's company, by the Queen's decree.

I went to the King and said, "Herself is at it again."

"Oh, what now?"

"She wants to forbid all Liedans from coming across to her side of the island—"

"We'll not be denied the beaches and the fishing there!"

"—and also intends to demand that your lady-wife teach one of her handmaidens so the Terosai will have a minstrel, however poor."

"Demand! Her demands will gain her nothing."

Meanwhile, Halleyne, while working with the Queen, said, "I hear that the King is gloating."

"About what?"

"About the fact that the Liedans have the only skilled singer on the island. It is said he plans to order that bitch Shallia—" I had to insist that Halleyne use that phrasing, which she did not care for, but it had its effect, convincing the Queen that Halleyne no longer cared for the Bardling "—never again to play before a Terosai, so we will be denied music. And she is never again to teach a Terosai."

"I was not aware that she had taught anyone. She is an apprentice; she had no apprentice."

"Well . . . she taught me a little. Before she betrayed you and sneaked away. It is said she feels she owes no more debt to the Terosai and thus does not object to the King's new decree."

"Well, we will see about that."

So it was that the Queen sent Sheroit dar Bontine to demand that Shallia teach Lady Halleyne all she could of musicianship. The King, seeing this as the first of two unreasonable demands, made a counteroffer: Halleyne and any other pupils Shallia cared to teach could learn from her at any time if a truly open border existed between the two nations. Dar Bontine returned the next day to say that the Queen had no objections to a decree declaring the border open. Since Shallia was only too happy to have Halleyne as a regular visitor, the king believed he had scored against the Queen and gotten something for nothing. Since the King had instantly backed away from what the Queen had thought was a position important to him, the Queen believed she had scored against him. Both rulers were happy. Halleyne could visit Shallia at will, and both of them were the happier for it.

Halleyne and I could legitimately trade visits and thus abandon our chilly glade, and that was a cheerful prospect as well. More and more, I found myself thinking of our visits with happy anticipation, and it was not long before I had to admit that it was her presence and not just the opportunity for gainful conspiracy that affected me so. Increasingly, I found myself wishing to move past the protective wall of her measured caution, wishing I could persuade her to speak her mind and laugh freely, never worrying about anticipated punishments from her Queen.

Too, I thought that these visits might just save Shallia's life.

The first few days after the wedding were worst. She did not emerge from the King's hut at all the first day, and when she did the second she was so silent and withdrawn she seemed to be a priestess of the goddess of gloom. She walked where the King steered her, ate what was placed before her, and replied briefly to questions put to her; otherwise she did nothing.

On the third day, I heard her playing some sort of wind instrument from inside the King's hut; her tones were beautiful and pure, but painfully melancholy, so poignant that they could drive an unhappy lover to suicide . . . and she was an unhappy lover.

But on the fourth day, the King broke the news to her that Halleyne would be coming to study with her, if she wished, and she managed a genuine smile. And though her misery at her condition, that of prisoner and wife, did not change, it was now forgotten during Halleyne's visits.

Not long after my conversation with Nerrin by his mud target, I emerged from my hut—my new hut, all my own, for the King had insisted that the judge over all Byriver be given one in size only slightly smaller than his—to find a crude bow propped up against my door. Honest soul that he is, Nerrin had acknowledged that I'd won the bet. I hoped it also meant he was having nothing to do with the Queen's plans.

Halleyne

We are hard in the grip of winter. We are also in the grip of strangeness.

First, of course, there is Shallia. Kin says that she no longer awakens calling for her long-dead mother, which I suppose is good. But her new role in life oppresses her. When we are together, sometimes she must put down her instrument and sit there crying, as I hold her and try to persuade her that things will improve.

Since she seems in the grip of more than unhappiness, I once asked, "Is there any chance you are with child?"

She shook her head. "I am not. I have made sure of it."

"Made sure of—how?"

"Bardic training. Female Bards on the road choose not to be saddled with children at inconvenient times. A simple spell and conception is prevented for a moon at a time." She dashed tears from her eyes. "I will never bear his child. He will never know why. It is one punishment I can visit on him."

Last night was better; her mood stayed nearly happy throughout the evening. In my lessons with Shallia, played on her newly-finished lute (no substitute for her old one, alas, but we can pick out a melody on it), something odd happened.

We were in King Jerno's dwelling—that is what Shallia calls it, for she will not acknowledge it as her own home. The King himself was out in the throne room, supervising the winter storage of the ship's boat; Kin had finally persuaded him that if we left it out on the beach with a guard all through the winter, we would have a ruined boat and a stone-frozen guard.

I was singing a refrain from "The Saga of Melthue," the story of the sea-goddess for whom the creatures were named. We'd been at it a long time, with Shallia correcting my chords, showing me how to accommodate my vocal range to a song that tended to stray a little outside it.

It was then we heard the bump at the foot of the outer door, as if someone had laid a heavy sack against it. I rose to open it . . . and outside were three melthues, staring intently up at me, rearing up in a peaceable fashion as if to be more eye to eye with me.

"Shallia, do you see this?"

"I do."

"What should I do?"

"Shoo them away before some fool of a Liedan sees and decides to eat them. It would be rude of you to have called them to their deaths."

"I called them?" I turned on her, and she was staring at me with an expression to match the melthues'.

"You did." She flicked her hands at the melthues, a gesture of annoyance. "Get out now. Shoo. Halleyne, play something annoying. Your version of 'Amongst the Petal Blossoms.'"

"I'll get you for that." But I did as I was told, and as soon as the sound of chords I had not quite mastered assailed their ears, the melthues made sounds like misplayed horns and turned away from the door, awkwardly crawling away.

"What do you mean, I called them?"

"You did. You were singing of them. They heard and came." Her expression was worried, but she rose and hugged me. "Halleyne, you have it. A touch of magic, of the summoning voice. A shame you didn't know this years ago. You might have been a Bard's or wizard's apprentice now, safe and free back in Terosalle."

"No! Better for me to be here. Maybe something can be made of it. If I can summon fish, we might not go hungry. If I can summon—" I grabbed greedily at the thought. "If I can summon a wind—"

"Don't say it. That's a tricky casting. It's said the winds sometimes turn on and kill those who call them."

"Then sometimes they don't."

I slept little that night, thinking about what had happened.

The next day, I walked with Kin among the craggy hills south of the encampments—a place where few came, other than the hunters of the increasingly rare gulbuks. I was halfway through telling him the story when I realized that I truly trusted him. Why else reveal this advantage I suddenly possessed?

Perhaps a little distracted, I finished my story. We walked in silence a while; then he asked, "Is a wind, then, a living thing that can be called, like a melthue?"

"It is said so. Some are spirits, with their own sort of life. Shallia says that the world is filled with spirits that only the magically adept can see or feel."

"It would be worth trying. But only if we could first find a way to strike at the wind, should it prove disagreeable."

I looked up and saw the naked man at the top of the next hill. "Who is that?"

He looked and squinted. "That's Teuper."

"He looks cold."

"I would be, too, standing nude on a hilltop where the wind blows ice from the south."

We climbed to where Teuper stood. He stared off to the southeast, only the vaguest light of intelligence in his eyes. He was so cold that his feet and hands were blue, and parts of him were so shrivelled that they could be barely seen.

His clothes were strewn down the northeast slope of the hill. I gathered them while Kin took off his cloak and wrapped it around the freezing man. Kin picked him up over his shoulder, then carried him down tricky slopes all the way to the Liedan encampment.

And those were my two strange days.

Kin

Maydellan Ha proclaimed Teuper to be as sound as any man could be after standing naked in dangerous cold for some extended time. He prescribed that Teuper be swaddled in blankets and fed warm broth whenever he could be persuaded to eat; I put Teuper in my own hut and assigned Gulbuk the sailor to that task.

The next morning, Teuper awoke seemingly none the worse for his experience. When I asked, he could not remember how he had come to be naked atop the hill, but thanked me profusely for saving his life. Then he dressed and returned to the Terosai, where doubtless the Queen would want an explanation.

I pitched in then with the meat-smoking crew. In the circular smoking-huts, fire-tenders made sure the fire below smoldered; above, I and the other meat-hangers lay sliced meat—melthue, fish, and even a little gulbuk—out on crude wooden racks.

It seemed to me to be another quiet workday; since the wedding, the other men and women spoke little to me. It took me some time to notice, and when I did, I could not seem to catch their eye.

I waited until we'd finished work in one smokehouse, and lagged behind as the others left. When all but one had departed, I called his name: "Daneeth."

He spared me a quick glance. "Judge Underbridge?"

"No, when I have fish oil all over my hands, I'm just Kin."

He almost smiled. "Kin, then . . . sir."

"I seem to quell conversation in my presence, Daneeth. Is my new rank so intimidating?"

"No, sir."

"Then why?"

He struggled with his answer, doubtless straining it through the net of his discretion. "Nerrin Axer's one of us, you know. Common. Good man."

"I know."

"Ain't fair, Himself having everything good."

Himself. It was the first time I'd heard that precise usage. "You're talking about the King and Shallia."

"All the lads liked her. Nerrin won her. Whoosh, like a hawk, Himself carries her off. What's next?"

"And I'm greeted with silence now because I was part of that?"

He answered with silence.

"Daneeth, anyone in my position would have had to marry them."

"Or kill, or die, or run, or collapse foaming at the mouth, or do a dozen other things. Anything to keep from doing it."

"And someone else would have wed them."

He nodded. "Someone I wouldn't mind so much crushing under my hands. I used to think well of you." He turned and left.

That was the first sign I had of the sudden change wrought on the Liedans by the marriage. After that, I could get nothing more than monosyllabic replies to questions put to the workingmen.

Viriat Axer resigned from the King's guard. When Jerno told him he was not free to resign, Viriat said, in a cold, dead tone, "I am no longer certain that I am capable of protecting Your Majesty." Jerno was convinced. I assigned Viriat to the hunters.

That left Garris Bricker the only official bodyguard of the King. I asked if he shared Viriat's concerns, and he said no, and seemed sure of it. I assigned no other bodyguard to the King; I could find no one, even among the survivors who were of low nobility, who did not speak of resentment against the King.

I told all this to Halleyne. She said, "Things are no different among the Terosai. Herself is given to fits of laughter whenever Shallia's troubles are mentioned. Some of the common-born are murmuring that perhaps our Queen is not sound of mind."

During that winter, I sometimes longed for the war that had just ended, for by comparison it had been a simpler and saner time.

Halleyne

Earlier today, King Jerno was elsewhere on the island, huddled with Sheroit dar Bontine in the negotiator's hut. Shallia finds his absences welcome and usually asked Kin to ask me over, as was the case today.

"I think," she told me, "that we should try an experiment. Make sure that the other night's affair of the melthues was not an accident—that it was your doing. I want you to sing to a friendly spirit and try to draw him to you. With enough practice, perhaps you *can* learn to speak to the ear of a friendly wind."

So we spent time selecting the proper music, in this case "The Story of Dayam," the tale of the first man, who received gifts from the gods presented him by their messenger-spirits. It's a children's song in which are recounted all the traits that give man mastery over animals.

I played it a couple of times through, refamiliarizing myself with the chords and lyrics. I went through a set of Shallia's Bardic breathing exercises, the ones meant to calm the mind and bring it to a receptive and meditative state suitable to the practice of Bardic magic. Then I returned to the lute and the music.

Again and again I played "The Story of Dayam," each time wishing my music would reach the ears of friendly souls. Between each iteration, Shallia absently corrected my mistakes and suggested other improvements—though this was an experiment in magic, she could not abandon her responsibilities as a musician.

As the night deepened, as I became more and more familiar with the melody, I was able to concentrate less on performance and more on the intent of the song. I thought of the spirits whose story it recounted. I thought of what we needed from a spirit to escape this island: A wind to our back on the dangerous ship's boat trip home, or certain knowledge of our location taken to the minds of captains back home, or knowledge brought to us, like that which Lesto dar Ostaferion possessed, of the building of sturdy ships.

And finally I felt a response to my query, as if all along I'd been singing to a sleeping audience and suddenly one distant pair of eyes opened. I sensed the interest behind the eyes, the willingness to aid, and I tried to lure them closer.

When the song ended, Shallia began a new set of suggestions, but I shook my head at her and immediately launched into it again.

And the distant eyes, sensed but not truly seen, began to move closer.

Shallia must have understood what had happened. She did not interrupt when I finished the song once more and immediately began it again. She filled a cup for me and made me drink brief sips between choruses so that my throat would not grow too hoarse. And all the while, I sensed that helpful watcher moving closer and closer, until I could almost hear its heavy footsteps coming through camp to our door.

Then I did hear them, a slow, heavy pace, one step for every four beats of my heart. As I heard its approach my heart began to race and the spirit's pace increased.

And I sang all the while, so Shallia did not hear that heavy tread until it was mere feet from the door to Jerno's hut.

She looked up and asked, "What is that smell?"

I smelled it too, a sick, half-sweet scent of rot. And yet the presence I felt approaching bore no ill will—I was sure of it.

The King's door crashed open as though hit by a battering ram and a man, awkward and slow, stumbled into our presence. With him he brought a cloud of stench, the odor of rot so pure that I choked, unable to sing further, and almost gagged.

The man, his face a ruin of decay, his eyes sunken and empty, was Lesto dar Ostaferion. He turned toward me and came on.

Shallia screamed. Hers was a wail of horror, and she curled into a tight ball on the bench where she sat, unable to run, unable to tear her gaze from the dead admiral, unable to stop shrieking.

And yet I knew he was the spirit who had heard me, and he meant us no harm.

"Halleyne?" Kin's voice, hoarse, shouting from outside. He charged into the King's tent and seized dar Ostaferion's cloak, pulling the admiral backwards and off balance. The admiral stumbled back and turned to face him.

I saw Kin pale. He raised a hand to strike the admiral, but dar Ostaferion turned away from him and again walked toward me.

Kin interposed himself between dar Ostaferion and me and held him at bay, his hand on the admiral's chest. The admiral three times tried to reach me, but could not push past Kin. Then the admiral's knees buckled and he fell, a stinking mass, at Kin's feet.

I knew then that he was lifeless again. The spirit eyes

were gone, fleeing instead of approaching, and I became aware that I could move and think again, but had no strength to speak. Shallia had not ceased to scream, and I could not rise to comfort her.

Chapter Ten

Kin

Men crowded in behind me, shouting distress and confusion, adding to the sheer noise and smell filling the King's hut.

I rounded on them and spoke with the stern voice of a judge. "You and you, get that carrion out of here. You, fetch the King from dar Bontine's hut. You, fetch the Terosai doctor Ha—no, I don't care if you don't like it, fetch him or you'll find yourself walking watches on the beach all winter. You, get something to burn in here to clear out the stench. And you, keep everyone else out of this hut. Everyone out."

Halleyne seemed dazed but unhurt, so I knelt before Shallia, who was curled like a knot on her bench and did not stop shrieking until I shook her. "It's gone," I told her again and again, until I saw some light of comprehension in her eyes; then she lay, unspeaking, in her fetal pose and would not answer when I spoke again.

I turned to Halleyne and tried to speak to her. Her gaze drifted as though she were drunk. She finally did

123

fix her attention on me and said, "He came to help. He was not going to hurt us." Then her eyes closed and she leaned forward against me. It took me a moment to realize that she had fallen into sleep.

I carried her from that place and to my own hut, a few steps away, past the curious guard and past the stinking mass of dar Ostaferion's body, which the lazy sailors had left just outside the King's hut.

The King and Maydellan Ha arrived at the King's hut mere moments after I returned. They crowded into the doorway at the same instant; they bumped, the dwarf's shoulders at the level of the King's hips, and the dwarf shoved himself through before the King, a breach of decorum. "What has happened here?" the King bellowed. "What is that stinking mass outside my door? What has happened to my Queen?"

So I explained. The King went white as I told him what little I knew. It was interesting to me that he never knelt beside his wife nor took her hand in his; he waited for the doctor to be through with his examination.

Finally Maydellan Ha did rise to face us. "She has experienced a tremendous shock," he said. "I am going to give her an herbal infusion to help her sleep. I hope whatever horror has its hold on her will loosen by the time she awakens."

"Will she recover?" the King asked.

"She should. Though she has always been a bit high-strung, which cannot help." The dwarf frowned at the two of us. "Has she been under much strain recently?"

"Yes," I said.

"No," the King said, and scowled at me.

"Which?"

The King opened his mouth to answer, but I spoke up more quickly. "She is going through a difficult adjustment, doctor. I would say she has grown more brittle of spirit since she has come to the Liedans."

The King glared openly. "Kin, do not make up stories to entertain the doctor. She has flourished here. If she is more quiet than before, it is because she has found great contentment as my wife."

The dwarf stared at the King and did not respond for several moments. Then he turned to me. "Hot water, please."

When I returned from the campfire, he'd ground herbs to powder and poured them into the King's leather mug. I poured in water heated over the campfire. He stirred the mixture until the herbs released some of their color into the water, then had me draw Shallia to a sitting position. Though she would not focus on what was before her, Shallia accepted sips of the brew until it was gone.

"Now," Doctor Ha said, "Halleyne."

"My hut."

I made to precede the doctor, but the King said, "Kin, a moment, please."

"But—"

"He can find your hut. It is adjacent to mine. No great trick. I need your ear."

The doctor left, and the King continued, "What think you, Kin? Is she broken?"

"Broken?" I must have gaped at him. The word from his lips was so wrong, so uncomprehending, that it confused me.

"Yes. She is obviously not dead—but not whole, either. Is she broken? Do I need another?"

"Another woman?"

He gave me a look of impatience. "Yes, Kin. Another woman, another queen. What think you?"

I thought of putting my fist through his face. The vision was so richly rewarding that it took me a moment to get my breathing under control. But, no, if he was back, so was his bodyguard Garris, who must be just outside. "No, Majesty. She is not broken. I think her mind is just bruised. Give it some time to heal. I will ask the doctor about what sort of care she needs. She will be well." I did not know whether or not I spoke the truth—but I feared for Shallia should the King believe her to be truly "broken."

The King beamed at me like a child told that his favorite toy could be repaired. "Good. Go, then. Make sure that Terosai doctor leaves our camp without stealing anything."

I found Doctor Ha still in my hut. Halleyne was awake again, if drowsy, seated on my cot and wrapped up in the patchwork of melthue hide I used as an overblanket.

"Get some sleep, then," the dwarf told her. "Perhaps it will come back to you by morning." He nodded to me on his way out.

"Are you hurt?" I asked Halleyne.

She shook her head. That eerie calm still seemed to be with her.

"But you can't remember what happened to you?"

"I remember," she said, barely over a whisper. "But I did not want to tell the doctor. I wanted to tell you."

I sat beside her. "So tell me."

She did, without embellishment.

"Gods, Halleyne, I thought you were going to wait until you knew more about dealing with—"

"Wind spirits, yes. But that is not what I called tonight. I was looking for a friendly spirit."

"And you found a corpse. A walking dead man. I've heard of such things, monsters walking abroad at night . . . Stories to frighten children."

"He wanted to help. Perhaps my song made him want to. He responded to my call. I thought of the admiral while I was singing; perhaps that is why he came and not some other spirit."

"Well, whatever you did to call him was very

effective. He should have been hard-frozen in his grave. Halleyne, if anything had happened to you—"

"If anything had happened to me, what?"

"I would have been damned lonely, that's what. On the whole island, you're the only one I can talk to."

She smiled. "That was very sweet of you. I mean protecting me from the admiral. You couldn't have known he meant no harm."

"Only a woman would use a word like 'sweet' to describe such a thing."

"Well, brave, too." She heaved a sigh. "I need to return to the Terosai camp. Herself will be waiting."

"I think you should stay."

She looked startled; her glance eloquently asked what I meant.

"It's cold and you're tired. You'll have to walk across the river ice, face Herself . . ." My voice trailed off as I realized all my words were lies. No, I just wanted her to stay with me tonight, in my cot, where I could warm and protect and love her through the night.

The thought caught me by surprise, and suddenly words just would not do. I kissed her instead.

She pressed herself against me, wrapped her arms around my neck, and returned my kiss with a sweetness and strength that caught me off guard.

Then a heavy hand rapped against my door; startled, we sprang apart. "Kin?" It was Teuper's voice. "Is Halleyne well enough to move? I've come to walk her home."

Halleyne

I told my story to the Queen. She laughed as she heard of Shallia's distress.

Laughed. My friend lay in pain and she laughed. My friend was suffering a gruesome mockery of a wedding and she was laughing. Cold, hungry winter stayed on us and we thinned like melting wax and she laughed. I thought of dragging her outside and putting her head through the ice of the river and holding her there until it froze again.

But, no, it would never happen.

I did not admit to my part in dar Ostaferion's return, so she speculated. "One of us, a Terosai I mean, must have some necromantic abilities. He brought the admiral to a semblance of life to go kill their king or terrify that treacherous girl. Halleyne, find me some way I can discover which of us has this skill. I must make further use of it." Her eyes glittered as she plotted, and I did not lie when I said that I felt ill and would much like to go lie down.

In the crude hut I shared with the Queen's other court-ladies, I lay shivering in the cold and turned my thoughts away from the Queen. Instead, I plotted some grim fate for the oh-so-helpful Teuper, whose rescue of me this evening would have put me in a foul mood even without the interview with the Queen. It warmed me to think of tying him to a melthue and sending them out into the chilly water together, or dropping a rock on him from some high place, or just not telling anybody if I spotted him standing naked atop another hill.

And on that chilly, vengeful, satisfying thought, I finally did drop off to sleep.

Kin

I awoke the next morning, the day everything changed, to the sound of hammering upon my door. "Kin! Wake up!" It was the voice of Garris Bricker, the King's bodyguard, sounding more distressed than I had heard him.

I rose groggily, threw on my cloak, and opened the door to peer at him. "What?"

"There is trouble. Someone threw a rock at the King."

It occurred to me, uncharitably, that such an event might knock some sense into the man. "And?"

"They are talking. The sailors, the commoners. Terosai too. On the beach. They are becoming a mob. I was walking with the King not long past when someone from a hilltop hurled a stone the size of my head down upon him. It nearly struck him."

"Damn. What does His Majesty want of me?"

"He wants you to go to the beach and quell this trouble."

"Me? You'll find me buried under stones the size of your head." But, still, I might have some sway with the sailors and common men; perhaps some of them remembered how I labored among them. Perhaps. I shooed Garris back to the King's door and finished dressing—making sure my knife was well concealed but easily at hand—and emerged into the chilly, windy morning.

Rather than take the common trail, which passed through the south end of the Terosai camp, I walked across the river farther south, managing with fair skill not to slip on the ice, and moved through hardy, stunted evergreens to the southern portion of the beach. I heard the gathering as I reached the edge of the trees, but could not make out the words; I moved north along the treeline toward the cluster of men and women I saw huddling in the distance.

As I neared, I could see it was a mix of the two camps, perhaps twenty Liedans and ten Terosai, nearly half the people on the island. Finally, I could hear that it was Jenina Morlin speaking, her strident tones rising above the gusting wind, her words more eloquent than I might have expected: "—madness moving among us like sickness. The Terosai Queen laughs over misery;

you have all heard her." Most of the Terosai present looked among themselves and nodded. "Now, madness has struck down the Liedan Queen. The gods are angry. The gods have listened to our prayers. The prayers we speak as we toil while *they* eat the food we smoke and *they* wear the furs we stitched together with cold-numbed fingers." The crowd made a grumbling noise of assent. "Prayers we speak as Herself beats us." Another growl.

"And now," she continued, "Daneeth Po has heard the King murmuring of casting his Queen aside and choosing another. Against her will, as Shallia was taken. Who among you," she pointed one by one at the women present, "wishes to be his next bride?" No voice answered her, and she drew herself up to her full height. "If he were to choose me, I would plunge a knife into his heart, even if it meant my own death, before I would let him lie with me. Put his children into me." More noise of assent. "And there's another sign the gods hate him: Which of his children has survived? When the gods hate a man, do they not make him watch his children die?"

Several of her listeners cried yes, looking between themselves—seeking, I thought, mutual assent as they crept toward a conclusion they already had arrived at.

This was bad. The only conclusion could be an assault on the King. The thought of such a thing did not much disturb me any more, but such a mob up-rising would inevitably spread and make victims of the other nobles. I would be among the first. Garris Bricker would die in defense of his king. If the violence raged among the Terosai, and it appeared it might, Halleyne could perish. Teuper, too, guilty of nothing but loyal service.

But it had not progressed to the point that they were maddened. Jenina the huntress had not yet whipped up these dogs or unleashed them, so I might be able to dampen their anger. A weight as hard and cold as the rock hurled at the King settled in my gut, but I prepared to step out and confront them.

And, farther ahead, Sheroit dar Bontine, swathed in his heavy woolen cloak, moved out of the forest verge to stand before them. Like me, he must have been concealed among the trees, listening to the growing rebellion. I sighed in relief; dar Bontine would soon have them calmed and dispersed, though he would doubtless be bringing demands to the royals.

The crowd faced him, Jenina Morlin openly glaring at this intruder. "You'd best leave, dar Bontine," she said, her tone mocking. "This is no place for the willing tools of kings."

"That makes it a place for traitors and murderers," dar Bontine said smoothly. "Which are you, Jenina?" Before she could respond, he continued, "We must remember that man lives by laws. Without laws, which are nothing but agreements between men that are written down and made customary, we become bandits and robbers. Traitors and murderers. And King Jerno has done nothing that is against any law."

"Laws made by kings." Jenina's face was twisted into a mask of anger.

"Laws we know. Laws which we can turn to when men have disagreements they cannot settle peaceably between themselves. Who among you wants to forego peace forever?"

"Who among us wants to die of cold while the King sleeps in the warm hut we made for him? Who wants to see another woman torn from her preferred companion to grace the King's bed? Who wants to hear another lady-in-waiting kicked to death by Herself?" The crowd rumbled approval of her words.

For once dar Bontine seemed nonplussed. "The King is the king by virtue of the gods' will. Defy the King and you defy the gods."

"Is it not clear the gods hate him? They sent a messenger to his home to kill him! They brought a Terosai hero back to life to punish that fat slug!" Her words, somehow transforming a stinking corpse into a resurrected champion, brought a cheer from the men and women around her. "And then the King's judge killed him again!" The crowd began to move out and around dar Bontine, enfolding him, not yet threatening him.

"You do not know the gods did this."

"I know no man or woman here did it! We know the measure of Teuper and Shallia; they have often enough admitted their failings in magecraft. They could not have done it. That leaves the gods."

And Halleyne. But I could not just stand out and tell the story she told me. I did not want that mob's attention directed at her. Nor could I be sure that I would even survive if I confronted them, not after Jenina roused them against me for the "murder" of the admiral.

Dar Bontine stood silent. Jenina gave him a bare moment to reply, and then, seeing that he had nothing to say, smiled in victory. "Take him and tie him," she told the others. "But do not hurt him. We only want to prevent him from warning the others."

Dar Bontine lunged for the edge of the crowd, but the men around him seized him and bore him roughly to the ground. Jenina turned to the others and began issuing orders in a tone too low for me to hear.

I cursed dar Bontine and the gift of persuasion that had obviously abandoned him. Then I turned away and raced back the way I'd come.

After all the work we'd done to survive the winter storms, we might just all perish before a storm of a different kind.

Chapter Eleven

Kin

I ran as fast as rough ground and slippery footing would allow me.

The thirty people on the beach had to be most of the ones Jenina thought she could count upon. That was less than half of us. That gave the rest of us an edge in numbers—if I could assemble and prepare us in time.

At the King's hut, I pushed past Garris and dragged him in with me. "The situation is bad," I told the King. "They will be coming soon to kill you. Take Shallia to the newest smokehouse and hide there with her."

"I cannot hide there with men working," he protested.

"No one is working. It's a rebel's holiday." I turned to Garris. "Make sure they are safely hidden. Then go through the camp and to all the work stations. Tell anyone you think to be loyal to the King, or me, or you, to meet in the little glade west of dar Bontine's hut and *stay silent* while they are there. I will join you shortly.

But send Ardith Netter and the Axer brothers to me here."

"They're scarcely loyal," Garris said.

"Ardith knows he can't become wealthy siding with rebels. And I can bring the Axers back into the fold. Go, now."

The King, no longer inclined to protest, enfolded the silent Shallia in a cloak. Garris ushered the two of them out.

I waited, desperately aware that precious time was streaming by. If Jenina's force finished its weapon-gathering too soon, they would catch me here and kill me.

Nerrin and Viriat Axer arrived first, and together. In a few words, I told them what was coming. "I need the two of you to fight for the King," I said.

Nerrin scowled. "It wasn't enough that you asked me not to kill him, now—"

"There's no time for argument. I think I can convince the King to restore Shallia to you . . . if we win. If we lose, Shallia might end up dying with the King—most of the rebels like her, I think, but we can't count on all of them. Or you might end up dying under a loyalist's knife and she'll be sad forever. What's it to be?"

He fumed, then nodded assent. I glanced at Viriat, who nodded without showing emotion. I told them to join the others in the glade near dar Bontine's hut. Before I was done the messenger Ardith Netter joined us.

I explained again. "My plan depends on you, Ardith. What you must do, and it is some risk, is stay here in the King's hut and convince Jenina and her men that the King has taken refuge in dar Bontine's hut. Doing this means you save the King's life. All by yourself." That was a lie, but one designed to appeal to Ardith's self-centered way of thinking.

"I can do that." His eyes glittered as he realized that, at last, he was to be a hero before the eyes of the King. "But why would I stay here when I could pursue the King?"

I looked between him and the others. "I hadn't considered that."

Viriat shrugged. "Because Garris beat him so severely that he could not follow."

"Good idea." I turned to Ardith. "Can you stand a few blows, Ardith? Just enough to make them think you've been in a fight. Say, one to bruise your face, a deep one on your thigh."

He sobered and considered, but nodded. "I can. But I want you to strike them, Kin."

"Why me?"

"I just want it to be you."

"Very well." I sent the brothers on their way. Then it was time to beat Ardith, a task I might have enjoyed under other circumstances. Now, though, I had to be deliberate, precise.

With my fist, I struck him hard on his left cheek, just below his eye. The blow knocked him to the floor, and when he rose his cheek was already reddening. The blow also did my fist little good.

Then I kicked Shallia's chair to pieces and, with its leg, twice hammered upon Ardith's thigh. He could show them that bruise if they wanted further proof of his injury. He groaned under the blows, but took them well, and barely glared when I was done.

I heard distant voices, an excited babble gradually closing. I wished Ardith luck, then fled.

Halleyne

The Terosai camp was deathly silent, and when Herself sent me out to discover why, I could find no one within its borders other than the Queen's ladies and Doctor Ha. The workers who'd been assembling the Queen's "summer hut" had taken their crude tools with them, not returning them to the pouch in the hut where they were kept.

I returned to the Queen's presence and told her what I had found.

"I asked for answers, Halleyne. You have brought me none."

"I am sorry, Majesty. Shall I go out again? Venture farther afield?"

"Why bother? You've proven yourself to be completely inadequate. I wish I had a cat instead of you. It would be similarly useless, but it would be self-sufficient and easier to look at."

"Perhaps Your Majesty would like to see the last of me." I was by then fuming, and failing to completely conceal it. The Queen's handmaidens unobtrusively drew away from her, in case she went off on one her rages.

"Perhaps I would. You could build yourself a lean-to in the depths of the forest and we'd find you hard-frozen come spring." She laughed at what she took for her own wit.

"Perhaps I'll find out if King Jerno needs a scribe."

She stopped laughing. "Oh, you'd like that, wouldn't you? Go off to live with your old friend Shallia. I'm certain she could use you after last night. Perhaps the King would assign you to wipe the drool from her chin and undress her for his bed each night." She smirked at me.

A veil of pure rage descended over me. Someone reached out and struck the Queen across the face. I saw her expression go to shock and anger—anger she turned toward me—and I belatedly realized that it was I who had struck her.

She slapped me in return, a blow I barely felt.

"Down on your knees, Halleyne, it is time for you to learn—"

I struck her again, harder, rocking her head. "Lie down so you can kick me to death like Jiarna? I'd sooner die standing—"

She threw herself upon me, and suddenly we were on the floor, biting and tearing and striking, while the Queen's handmaids shrieked and called for help.

Someone wrapped me about the waist and lifted me—lifted *us,* for I had the Queen in a clinch and was loath to release her. But I did and she fell to the rough planks that served her as floor. I bit the arm that held me and heard a yelp, but whoever it was did not release me; he pulled me further away from the Queen, toward the door.

Queen Lia rose to her full height and shrieked, "Halleyne, you condemn yourself to death and your family to ruin! Teuper, by my command, you will take her forth from this place and put her to death. Get her out of my sight."

Teuper, for it was he, dragged me out her door. "Stop struggling," he whispered. "You're in no danger."

I took a few deep breaths of cold air and complied; he set me down on my feet. "Let's get out of her sight and hearing," he said.

He led me to the hut he shared with the Queen's oddly-absent bodyguards and sat me on his cot. I was shaking, either from anger or cold or both, and he wrapped a tattered patchwork blanket around me. "You're going to have to leave the Terosai camp," he said.

"I know. She'll never forgive me, or back away from a sentence of death." I felt neither ashamed nor regretful, but I was suddenly very tired. "It looks as though I'm a Liedan now, like Shallia."

"Perhaps not." He pressed a crude wooden bowl full of water into my hands. Green speckles floated at the water's surface. "This will calm you. Drink up."

"I don't wish to be calm. What do you mean, perhaps not? There's the Terosai camp and the Liedan camp. Oh, and dar Bontine, I suppose. Or I could do as she said and go live in the forest."

"Or go home."

"Someday, I hope." If I could have more luck when next I tried to summon a spirit . . .

He shook his head. "No, soon. Within a day or two. I have a way."

I shook my head. "I don't understand."

"Do you remember the day you and Kin found me on the hilltop?"

I couldn't restrain a smile at his expense. "It was very memorable."

"I was making a summoning, Halleyne. A wind-summoning. I've been more careful since, never doing it alone. And I've found a wind that will carry a small boat back to the mainland."

"I thought such a casting was beyond you!"

He shrugged. "I lied. I wasn't ready before. I didn't wish anyone to count on me."

"So you'll go home and send a rescue ship back for us?"

"No." He looked very serious. "Think on it, Halleyne. Think of the survivors on the island. Two decrepit, half-mad rulers and their courtiers. Terosalle and Lieda are better off without them. The boatload I lead home will be the 'sole survivors' of the wreck, and the rest can freeze on this rock. Are you with me?"

"Why me?"

"Because you're beautiful, Halleyne. So many times I have spied upon you as you've cleansed your public face away, or alone with Shallia, have revealed your true self." He lowered his tone. "Before the storm, when I invited you, it was half in jest. Now I am serious. I want you."

His words, knowledge that he had been peering at

me during my few moments of privacy, sent a chill through me. I struggled to conceal it. "Can I bring Shallia?"

He grimaced. "I suppose so. There's room."

"And Kin?"

His expression darkened. "Why Kin?"

"He doesn't deserve to be stranded here."

"Yes, he does. He married Shallia to that pig, didn't he?"

"I suppose you're right. We won't worry about Kin, then." Once back on the mainland, I could break away from Teuper and tell the court of Terosalle or Lieda; a rescue expedition would surely follow. Though it broke my heart to think Kin would believe I'd abandoned him.

"Are you lovers?"

"No."

But something must have crossed my face, for his scowl deepened. "You are, aren't you? All that time you spent among the Liedan's wasn't just with Shallia, was it?"

"Teuper—"

His expression became an unfamiliar mask of anger, the face of a baby denied a toy, ready to explode into rage and tears. He stood and, from beneath the cot, grabbed a knotted club cut from a tree branch. "You bitch."

I hurled the bowl of speckled water into his face and ran for the door. But I was slowed by Teuper's blanket.

I remember feeling a mighty blow to the side of my head, the dirt floor rising to meet me, and nothing more.

Kin

No guard stood outside Queen Lia's hut—the better for me, as I had no time for proper decorum. I gave her crude door the barest knock, then shoved my way in.

The Queen sat in her throne-chair, which, owing to the scarcity of furnishings, she had carried with her from place to place. One of her ladies was making up her face with cosmetics. I idly wondered if she'd managed to salvage many such decorations from the shipwreck, or whether, like Halleyne, she'd made more for herself while here. She was surrounded by nervous-looking handmaidens whose composure was not improved by my sudden entrance.

"What do you want?" That was the Queen, her tone unconcerned.

"If you wish to live, hide in the forest until all the trouble is done," I told her. "Men, rebels, seek to kill King Jerno. When they're through, they'll probably come after you."

That got her attention. She brushed her lady's hand away and sat up. "This had best not be a joke."

"Hide or die, Majesty." I made my lack of concern clear to her with my tone. I looked among her women. "Where is Halleyne?"

She smiled. It wasn't pleasant. "Off with Teuper, I expect."

I left her and ran through the small Terosai camp, poking my head in Teuper's hut, then others, and calling for Halleyne and Teuper. But neither answered, and I could hear shouting and crashing from the Liedan camp.

Too much time was passing. I moved north out of the Terosai camp and headed for the glade where I'd told the others to assemble. En route, I found a likely-looking fallen branch and began breaking twigs from it to make a crude club.

A score or more of Liedan men and women awaited me. They knew trouble was coming and had brought the clubs, tools, and other weapons available to them.

I told the Axer brothers, "Creep to the edge of the trees where you can watch dar Bontine's hut. One of you come back to warn us when Jenina's force comes." They nodded and left.

I looked among the rest. Most were high-born courtiers and had done light duty, such as protecting or entertaining the King, while the lower-born had labored to make sure we were sheltered and stocked with food. But a few of them were low-born sailors, loyalists. "You know some of what is happening," I told them. "Jenina Morlin and others have whipped up a mob, mostly of commoners. They're out to kill the King and the rest of us."

Garris Bricker spoke. "So we kill them."

"No. We beat them, scatter them. Take Jenina prisoner if we can. Give everyone time to calm."

"They won't." That was Casseyl Vinner, a common sailor; I'd been surprised to see him among us. "King'll do something else, make 'em mad, they'll rouse again."

"Why are you here?"

"Better the King than Jenina. He's sane some of the time. She eats ice and spits fire." He put his arm around Eleyn Kitter, one of the women sailors, known for her skill in climbing shroudlines. "But if King tries to take Eleyn, I'm on the other side." There was a murmur of assent from the other commoners present, and, I was surprised to note, from some of the nobles as well. This assembly was on the verge of siding with Jenina.

"The King won't take another woman against her wishes, and he'll let Shallia go."

"You're guessing." That was Garris again.

"No, I've decided. You, all of you, have my word. If the King doesn't put his thoughts in order, I'll—" I hesitated over the words; they were big ones and it took me a moment to be sure of what I was saying. "I'll cast him down myself."

Garris stared at me. As the King's bodyguard, he was obliged to react to the sort of treason he'd just heard. I returned his gaze as evenly as I could.

Finally, he nodded. "You won't hurt him."

"You won't let me."

He almost smiled. "I'm with you, then."

There was a hiss from the edge of the glade. Viriat crouched there. "Men coming," he whispered.

We crept as silently as we could with him to the beach edge of the trees, a few yards from dar Bontine's hut. By the time I reached the verge of the sand, most of Jenina's force was already fanning out to surround the hut. We didn't need to be as quiet as we were; they were making plenty of noise, calling out to the hut, demanding that the King emerge to face his fate. I saw Jenina directing them; Daneeth Po and Gulbuk were among those most noisily haranguing the absent king. Handsome Raldan was there, and at least one of the Queen's ladies-in-waiting. Ardith Netter was among them, limping, supported by a female Liedan sailor. I did not see Sheroit dar Bontine and hoped the negotiator had not been harmed.

I sent word down the line: "Spread out behind their entire line. When they move in on the hut, or when I cry 'Byriver,' attack with all speed." They began to move down along the treeline.

It did not take long. The rebels circled the hut, shouting, whipping one another up to the dread task of murdering a king, but not entering. Finally Jenina shouted, "Just go in and get him, will you?" And the majority of them charged the hut's door, all of them crowding in where only one or two could pass.

I leaped out from the treeline, Garris Bricker to my left, Casseyl Vinner to my right, and charged. I did not need to cry out: Other loyalists were emerging from the trees all down the line. A couple of the rebels saw and shouted, but their cries of alarm were drowned out by the shouts of anger coming from within dar Bontine's hut.

And then we were upon them. I swung my club at the back of a burly sailor; the impact jarred my arms to the shoulders and the man staggered forward. I lost track of Garris and Casseyle, so fixed was I on the enemies before me. I spun in a wide arc and cracked my club against the head of a woman, Jenina I think, knocking her down, then reversed my spin and hit my first target a second time.

There was shouting, screaming. Someone hit me from behind and bore me to the sand. I twisted around to face him and the sky and struck the man a blow in the throat. His counter-blow to my gut hurt only a little through my bulky jacket. I managed to sweep his arm aside with my free hand and swung the club again, cracking it against his temple; dazed, he toppled from atop me. I rose.

It was already almost over. A few fights raged on, personal battles between club-wielding men and women. Several victims lay on the sands, some of them moving a little, one of them throwing up. More were running—them fleeing, us chasing. I shouted, "Don't follow! Regroup!" I stepped up and struck the club-arm of one of the still-active rebels; the blow did not break bone, but the man dropped his club. He backed away, his free hand up in a gesture of surrender.

Among the fallen, unconscious, was Jenina Morlin. I turned to Garris, who'd come through the fight unscathed. "Take her to King Jerno's hut, to the 'throne room.' We're going to settle matters there."

Chapter Twelve

Kin

We assembled in the drafty, unfinished throne room. I kept our best fighters on hand and armed in case the rebels returned for another assault, and sent others off to fetch King Jerno and Shallia, Queen Lia and her women, and Doctor Ha.

I waited in the King's hut and thought over all the details I had to manage. I knew that in one stroke I might resolve many of the problems that beset us. I was distracted, though, by worries about Halleyne, whom no one appeared to have recently seen, and about the actions of the other rebels. Viriat Axer had followed them for a time and came back to say that they were congregating on the northern tip of the island.

I heard Queen Lia arrive; not even the great expanse of the adjacent throne room could contain her petulant complaints. Then Garris Bricker brought King Jerno and Shallia in through his door.

The King looked troubled, vague. I motioned for him to take his seat and I helped Shallia sit upon the cot.

"Is it over, Kin?"

"For the moment."

"Then all is as it should be."

I stood before him, deliberately looming over him, and shook my head. "All is not well. If we do not act soon, there will be another riot. You might die in that one."

"Then have all the rebels executed." There was no strength behind his words, and he could not seem to look me in the eye. I thought perhaps he was still having trouble coming to grips with what was happening.

"As the one judge on the island, I have come to the decision that some of their complaints are justified. The office to which you appointed me compels me to rule in their favor."

"Oh." I knew then that he was far gone. He could not even question the logic of a judge ruling against the ruler who'd appointed him. He finally did look at me. "What must be done?"

I moved beside him to speak quietly in his ear. "You know that your queen is . . . broken. You have said so yourself."

He nodded, saddened.

"Majesty, you must give her up. Divorce her. Perhaps, elsewhere, she can become herself again."

The King looked at his wife for a long moment. I saw a tear creep down his cheek. "So be it."

"And there will be rebellion again if the nobles, courtiers and officers have an easy life of it while the common men and women toil. I will assign everyone to the same amount of work."

"Even me?"

"Not you. You are the king."

"Will I have no bodyservant? No bodyguard?"

I hesitated. "One. One man to be both. Until our lot eases, we cannot spare more."

He sighed, then nodded again. "Must I make these proclamations before my subjects?"

"I will do it. You rest. You have had a trying day." I felt like an uncle telling his fractious nephew to take a nap.

The King nodded. His gaze slid from me and he closed his eyes.

I shrugged at Garris, then took Shallia by the hands. She rose as I drew her up, but did not look at me or anyone else in the room. It pained me to see her so far gone, but perhaps her trials were almost done.

I led her through the door into the throne room. Those gathered there fell silent. I saw that Jenina was awake; she stood scowling at those around her, then at me, and her hands were bound before her. There was still blood on her brow where she had been struck; Doctor Ha, making his rounds among those injured in this chamber, had not yet reached her. Nerrin Axer moved toward the two of us, but I waved him back; he hovered at the edge of the crowd, anxious.

I moved to stand between the throne and the upside-down ship's boat, and leaned on the latter rather than sit upon the King's throne. "Attend me. I have announcements to make.

"First, as I with my judicial powers wed King Jerno to this lady, Shallia dar Kantrin, I today declare that marriage ended. This day, King Jerno publicly divorces Lady Shallia for reasons—" I hesitated over the cause, but would have to come up with one for the document to be written later "—of irregularities in the original proceedings."

Someone in the crowd had the temerity to laugh. It was Sepeter dar Tacha, a sailor I'd not seen among either the rebels or loyalists. Perhaps he'd been hiding. I shot him a glare, then turned my attention elsewhere. "Nerrin Axer, I'm appointing you to care for Lady Shallia during her recovery."

He moved forward to take her hands. He spoke her name and she turned a bit, as if hearing it called from a long distance, but did not look at him. The pain on his face was wrenching to see, but he concealed it and led her from my side, speaking quietly to her.

"Second," I continued, "there will be changes in the way work is conducted. Except for King Jerno and Queen Lia, the ranks we enjoyed on the mainland will have no bearing. Everyone works, nobles and officers just as hard as commoners. The King and Queen may have one bodyservant each. This is my judgment."

Queen Lia made a noise of outrage, then shaped it into words. "You have no jurisdiction over the Terosai, you stinking mass of entrails. I decide how many bodyservants I have. And that is *my* judgment."

I gave her a cold smile. "Oh, absolutely, Majesty. You rule your subjects. But understand this. Except for your principal servant, all those who act as your servants must do so after their day's duties are concluded. If one of your subjects decides to abandon his duties to tend to your every little need, *I will personally kill him. Or her.*"

She gaped at me as though I'd struck her. I realized then that she *had* recently been struck; her makeup did not conceal that her cheek was bruising. She sputtered for a moment, then looked around and said, "Sepeter, kill him."

The sailor looked between us and gulped, but dutifully moved toward me. But Nerrin Axer momentarily abandoned Shallia's side to stand before me, against Sepeter. The sailor looked grateful for the two-to-one odds against him: He shrugged and backed away.

The Queen spat at him. "Coward. As you wish, Judge Underbridge." She made an insult of the title. "Doctor Ha, I order you to cease attending the Liedans. Henceforth you will only care for Terosai. Let them sicken and die."

The dwarf heaved a sigh and continued with his duties, tending to an injured Liedan.

I saw the Queen flush scarlet. Then she turned and flounced toward the main entrance, her handmaidens clustered nervously around her.

"Third," I said. "Jenina Morlin. You've led a force of men against your ruler. That is treason, punishable by execution. But I have told the King that there were mitigating circumstances, and you will not be killed."

"I drip with gratitude," she said.

"Will you live by the tenets I've set forward here?"

"No."

"Why?"

"Because Jerno is not fit to rule, nor is Lia, nor you, nor anyone we marched against. You are all pigs and deserve only death." Her tone was as matter-of-fact as though we were discussing sailing matters.

"Then I exile you from this island. Anyone who cannot abide by the laws I've set down can accompany you."

She laughed. "That's a death sentence, then. The sea is too choppy for that little boat. Shall I swim to my place of exile?"

"You'll walk. The strait between here and Hopeless Island is frozen fast."

"And then we'll starve."

"We'll provision you from the supplies we have. Whatever proportion of our numbers your followers represent will be the proportion of the island's stores you receive. Viriat, get her out of here. Take as many men as you feel you need to make sure that she and anyone loyal to her make it across the strait to Hopeless Island." The former bodyguard nodded, then led her forth.

"That's all," I said. "Return to your works and duties. Those who know how to set a bone or wrap a bandage, I imagine Doctor Ha can make use of you—"

"I can."

"So please stay. And has anyone seen Lady Halleyne? Or Teuper?"

No one would admit to having seen Halleyne since this morning, but Doctor Ha said he'd heard Teuper say he was off to find and free Sheroit dar Bontine. I realized belatedly that the lean negotiator had not been present for this gathering.

A captured rebel, one who chose to accept the laws I set down and stay with the Fishtail colony, said that dar Bontine had been tied to a tree not far from where he'd been captured. Increasingly worried about Halleyne, I went off in search of her or Teuper, whom Queen Lia said had seen her last.

And for some considerable time I had no luck. I searched the trees near where dar Bontine had been grabbed, and finally found cut leather thongs marking where the negotiator had been tied; it appeared Teuper had already freed him. I scoured the Liedan camp, annoying Queen Lia, who was barricaded within her hut with her serving-ladies. I looked in at dar Bontine's hut, but it was empty. I walked all the paths and trails we'd made across Fishtail Island. And still there was no sign of Halleyne, Teuper, or even dar Bontine.

I eventually returned to camp. Not much later, shortly after nightfall, Teuper arrived in the company of dar Bontine; I admitted them to my hut and, without preamble, asked, "Have you seen Halleyne?"

Teuper looked grim. "Perhaps you had best sit."

"I don't want to sit. I want an answer." His solemnity sparked a fear in me.

"Today was insanity," Teuper said. "Many things were done that cannot be undone. Halleyne assaulted Queen Lia this morning."

"And?"

"Herself ordered Halleyne's death. Told me to drag her forth and kill her."

"You didn't—"

"Of course not! What do you take me for?" His indignation immediately gave way to sorrow and sympathy. "But it scarcely mattered. Not long after, a band of rebels found us. Attacked us, because we were nobles. Halleyne—" His voice rasped and he swallowed several times. "Halleyne was struck by one of them. A knife. Her heart . . . She died almost immediately."

I found that I could not stand. I made it to my cot just before my knees gave way.

"And then they went after her with their clubs. Her face . . . I couldn't get to her. I had enough skill to elude the others as I shouted at them to stop, as I told them what she'd done this morning, but not to save her." Tears rolled down his cheeks as he relived his failure. "Then they understood what I was saying. That she'd assaulted the Queen. That she was one of them. And they, too, knew sorrow."

"When . . . Where?"

"Not far from the Terosai camp. We were talking about her coming to live among you Liedans. I sensed she fancied you, Kin. The prospect of leaving Herself did not displease her in the least. And then the rebels were on us. They were hurt, bleeding, angry. They'd just been in some sort of fight. Perhaps if they'd not been so savagely battered, I could have made myself understood. But they'd been blooded and had to have blood of their own."

And there it was. My own assault on the rebels, the battle to save my life and the lives of the nobles and loyalists, had led to Halleyne's death. I stared dumbly at the wall of my hut.

It couldn't be true. I rose. "I must see her. Her . . . body."

Sheroit dar Bontine, his expression full of sympathy and pain, shook his head. "You can't, Kin. Teuper and I are just back from walking with the rebels, and with the guards escorting them, to Hopeless Island. We hoped to convince some to return. They bore Halleyne's body with them. They honor her as one of their own, for the blows she struck against Queen Lia. They will bury her with all due ceremony where they make camp."

"I'll go to them. I have to see." I made to push by them, but dar Bontine restrained me.

"Kin, the strait is still frozen over, just barely, but it's thawed a bit. It's treacherous. Three people fell through the ice. One we were unable to recover in time, and he died. This was in broad daylight. If you try to cross now, in the dark, you'll die . . . and there will be no one here to check King Jerno. Everyone is looking to you, Kin."

"To hell with them." I felt myself waver. All strength had left me and I sat again. "There's not one man or woman on this island I care to help. Let them freeze. Let them starve. Let them kill each other." They'd allowed Halleyne to die.

Teuper asked, "Even Shallia and Nerrin?"

"Even them." Then I grimaced. I didn't sound convincing even to myself. "Leave me alone."

Teuper nodded and left. Dar Bontine hung back a moment. "Kin, if you need to speak of these things, come to me."

I nodded glumly and waved him away. I closed my eyes and heard him leave.

Halleyne dead. I had not known whether anything might have become of us. And now I would never know. She was gone, leaving behind only a hard knot in my chest.

And that was the first of the two revolts. It had taken most of the day, so it was the longer of the two.

Chapter Thirteen

Kin

I awoke shortly before dawn to someone rapping at my door. "Who is it?"

"Garris. The King needs you." The bodyguard sounded troubled.

"I'll be along."

I lay there several minutes debating whether or not it were worth my time to rise and face this new day. More out of habit than for any other reason, I decided to do so. I dressed and crossed the few yards to the King's hut; Garris admitted me, avoiding my gaze.

The King, too, was dressed. He sat on his throne and stared glumly at me as I entered. "Kin, I need a Queen."

"Again? Majesty, you're barely rid of the last one."

"And what a choice she was. Melancholy, half-mad . . . now all mad." He shrugged. "I have a way to ensure that my next choice will be the correct one."

"Yes?"

"To start, I want you to make a decree that all women remaining on Fishtail Island—except Shallia,

153

of course, and that bitch Lia—are henceforth off-limits to the other men."

"Majesty—"

"Then assign workers to complete the throne room. Make it a true shelter. It will become a long hall where all the women shall live."

"Your Majesty, this plan—"

"I know what you are going to say. There will be trouble if I take another woman against her will. So I will not do that. I will just keep them all here until some of them decide to choose me of their own free will. Then I will choose the best of them. Is that not fair?" He didn't wait for my answer. "So, see to it."

"No."

"What did you say?"

"I said no. I will not do this. If I do, the men and women will rise up against you, and I doubt you can be saved a second time. They will kill you."

I expected him to rise, full of bluster and fury, and insist that his orders be carried out. Instead, he looked at me sadly, silently, for a long moment. "This is rebellion, Kin."

"Yes."

"Are you casting me down as King?"

"No. You still rule Lieda. But I think I must govern on Fishtail for a while."

"Kin, am I mad?"

I drew a deep breath. "I think so, Majesty. A little."

"I must have caught it from Shallia."

"I think not. I think it started when Jernin died."

"You'll take care of me, won't you?"

"Yes, Majesty."

He bowed his head and I left.

Outside, I asked Garris, "Did you hear all that?"

"I did, Judge Underbridge."

"And what do you have to say about it?"

He shook his head. "My task is to guard him, not to impose his rule."

And so I became ruler of Fishtail Island.

Queen Lia protested, of course, and tried to countermand my orders whenever she heard about them. But in truth, only a handful of people, mostly ladies-in-waiting, remained loyal to her. After the admiral's death, she had ruled thirty-two Terosai; but sixteen of them, nine men and seven women, had turned rebel and departed. Shallia had joined the Leidans. Halleyne was dead. The rest had stayed out of sight during the aborted rebellion and most seemed content to follow my guidance. Eighteen Liedans had also left with the rebels.

This left me in charge of thirty-two Liedans—twenty-one men and eleven women—and fourteen Terosai—seven men and seven women. Plus King Jerno, Queen Lia, and Sheroit Dar Bontine. I made no effort to persuade the two rulers to make good use of their time, and doubted whether either one had any skills relevant to our survival. Dar Bontine remained as neutral as he always had been, accepting guidance from no leader, trading his skill as a leatherworker for food.

The rest of the population I put to work, dividing them regardless of birth-rank or social standing among the many tasks we needed to accomplish. I joined them at that work, returning to my position among the smokehouse crew. There was grumbling from the upper classes, of course, but no one could complain that I was treating him unfairly—just that I was not according him all the benefits of his station in life.

The task of organizing the work assignments, which I thought essential to preventing another rebellion, occupied me for two days. I wanted nothing more than to make the crossing to Hopeless Island and see Halleyne; I needed to look upon her and truly know, truly understand that she was dead. To say goodbye.

But for those two days I could not leave my work, and when things were settled enough that I thought I could leave, Teuper pointed out kindly that they had to have buried or cremated her by now.

So when I was not working I thought about her, and wondered what might have become of us.

Halleyne

For a long time I knew only cold and dizziness, pain in my head, and brief moments of consciousness. I would awake with a sensation of motion, and see that Gulbuk or Daneeth Po was carrying me along cold, bleak shorelines. Then I would lose consciousness again.

One time I woke up in the midst of men and women huddled around a pathetically small fire. The sky overhead was clear and the air was icy. I was propped up in the lap of Jenina Morlin, and she was trying to feed me a bowlful of melthue stock. I managed to take a few swallows of it before dizziness and darkness claimed me again.

This morning, when I awoke—I think another day or two must have passed—I awoke on another shore, beside a different campfire. Two people were with me: Jenina, tending the fire, and a Liedan sailor whose name was, I believe, Seiner, lying wrapped in a blanket on the other side of the fire.

I managed to say, "Thirsty."

Jenina spun and smiled. "Awake again, are you?" She reached under her cloak and brought up a crude waterskin; she knelt beside me and helped me drink from it. "Are you better today?"

"My head hurts."

"Small wonder, with that madman trying to bash your brains in."

That brought back the memory of what had

happened—Queen Lia, the sentence of death, Teuper's attack on me. I looked around in confusion, but nothing of this campfire looked familiar; I could not even determine where on the island we were. "Where are we?"

In a few words, spoken proudly, Jenina told me of the rebellion, of the attempt on the life of King Jerno, of the attack on the rebels—the "treacherous ambush," as Jenina put it—outside dar Bontine's hut, of the sentence laid down upon her and the other rebels by Kin.

"We have walked for two days," she said. "Across the hard ice to Hopeless Island—we lost Shean dar Petris through the ice. Then we decided that there was nothing but rocks and melthues on Hopeless; we had to have timber for fires, after all. So we walked across Treacherous Strait to Turtlehead Island. That's where we are now, far away from those maggots back on Fishtail." She nodded at the blanket-wrapped figure on the other side of the fire. "That's Seiner. A Liedan. We just lost him. Walking around for two days with injuries inside because some loyalist bashed his guts in with a club." She didn't seem too saddened by the loss. "They're raising a cairn for him now. Ground's too hard to bury him."

"Why did you bring me along?"

"Teuper said you walloped the Queen and she wanted you killed. We can't allow that to happen. Not to a fine young girl with enough sense to slap old Lia silly." She laughed.

"Where *is* Teuper?" I'm sure my tone became cold; Jenina noticed.

She laughed at me. "Still mad at him because he couldn't save you from a clubbing at the hands of the loyalists?"

"*He* was the one who hit me!"

"Ah, you're confused. Remembering it wrong. He

and Sheroit walked with us for a while. Teuper was trying to keep you safe, but you insisted on bolting and ran right into that damned Viriat Axer. He came near to killing you before Teuper drove them off."

"That's a lie! Think about it. Teuper couldn't drive Viriat off if he had a cavalry unit helping him."

"Teuper said you'd be addled when you woke up." Jenina shrugged. "He went back with the loyalists. I think he's going to make another attempt on King Jerno. I wish him luck."

Then men came for the body of Seiner and Jenina helped them bear him forth.

I found that my big pouch, with my journal and inks, had survived the voyage, so I have spent the last few minutes transcribing these events.

In the midst of thirty people, I'm alone here. My only friends in the world are back on Fishtail. But if nothing else good has come of these events, I'm free of Queen Lia and the need to appease her.

Kin

The weather warmed rapidly over the next few days. The ice sheets encrusting the straits, lake and river thinned, becoming too frail to sustain a man's weight.

We were all low on stores and hungry, but Doctor Ha said no one was in immediate danger of starvation. "No," he told me privately, "I think our greatest danger comes when things warm up a little more . . . and the snakes begin to emerge. The Gloriana vipers."

"Are they as deadly as they seem?" I asked. "As with Admiral dar Ostaferion, a single bite and you're dead?"

"Possibly. But perhaps the one that killed him was unusually large. Perhaps his age or a natural reaction made it deadlier for him than it would be for you or me. Or maybe he was merely paralyzed by the toxin and chilled to death." He shrugged. "Or, perhaps they *are* that deadly. It would be good to know before they begin to emerge."

"And how do we do that?"

"Capture one."

"While they're in their burrows? That stick-and-rope I made you isn't much good there. What do we do, stick our arms down a tunnel and drag one out?"

"Just so." My grimace must have amused him, for he laughed. "Give it some thought. Find someone who is willing to help me with this. We must know, Kin."

I put Eleyn Kitter on the task. The Liedan sailor was known for her daring on ship's yards, had long, slender arms, and evidenced no undue fear of snakes. I asked dar Bontine to make her a hide glove that would reduce the likelihood of her being bitten when reaching into snake burrows.

A week later, I had report from Eleyn that she and Doctor Ha had had their first day of searching; they'd found two burrows, both empty, and had not captured a snake. By then, the weather had warmed to the point that ice only clung to the river and lake along the banks, but the nights were so cold and windy that everyone stayed huddled in his hut, shivering and shaking.

That's why it was such a surprise that night to hear a knock upon my door. "Who is it?"

"It's Sheroit, Kin."

"Dar Bontine?" I rose, my blanket still tight around me, and hobbled to the door to open it. A blast of icy wind entered, then the negotiator, then young Teuper. "What are the two of you doing out on a night like this?"

Dar Bontine looked serious. "Matters are very bad, Kin, and Teuper has something to confess."

"What is it, Teuper?"

The younger man shook his head. "I have to show you. It's not pleasant."

"Something outside?"

"Yes."

"Damn."

I dressed as warmly as I could, then accompanied the two of them out into that chilling, blustery night. No one else was about, and although not one fire or torch guttered in our cluster of dwellings, the full moon was bright; it made the camp an eerie image, as if this were a long-abandoned village perfectly preserved by the cold and recently occupied by howling wind-spirits.

They led me to the river and then downstream. Once we were past the outer ring of huts and approaching the lake, Teuper began talking.

"Really," he said, "you have to understand, very little of it has been an accident."

"Very little of what?"

He waved his hand around us. "This. The entire spectacle of our shipwreck. The real accident was that they came too early."

"Who did?"

"The winds. The winds I called."

"You can call winds."

"Oh, yes. I'm not very good at it. It requires bribes and promises and long preparation, all of which I must use in place of strength of will and great magical knowledge." He laughed, apparently to himself. "I'm not much of a wizard, Kin. I've told you that before. I'm just a little better than I let you know."

"So you called the winds that wrecked the *Wave-Breaker* and *Thunderer*?" I stopped, stunned, but he kept walking, maintaining his pace along the lake's rocky shore. Dar Bontine kindly waited for me to regain my composure and the two of us struggled to catch up to the younger man.

"I did," he answered, as though there had been no break in our conversation.

"Why?"

"That's a long story. The first and most basic reason was so that the rulers of two kingdoms would die. Drown, drown, glub glub glub."

"Give me the long story, Teuper." What he was saying had finally sunk in, and his casual attitude made it clear to me that this boy was an uncaring murderer—or a madman confessing to things he had not done. Either way, he was probably dangerous. I fingered my left sleeve to make sure my dagger was still sheathed there, and was reassured by its presence.

"It's simple enough. My name is Teuper, which is not Terosai, and the dar Hiaro name is false. My family name is Hiaran, and my father's name is Jehan, which is also foreign.

"A few years ago, my father was gravely injured, his head half bashed in, while he was executing a plan to become ruler of a nation called Suinomen. Ever heard of it?"

"Yes. Arachnean traders bring us goods from there. Across the western seas, isn't it?"

"Yes, very far away. A very cold place. One reason I haven't minded the winter here so much. Magic is highly regulated there, but my father was convinced enough of its importance that he had me brought up in its traditions.

"Anyway, though I was very young at the time, my arts were adequate to save my father's life and get us clear of Rozinki, the capital. Together we fled here. Rather, to Feyndala, where you Terosai and Liedans squabble pretty much like nations everywhere else in the world."

We were by now nearing the far side of the small lake. Teuper continued to press forward along the trail, heading toward the western shore of the island, obviously with a destination in mind—something that also increased my unease. I glanced at dar Bontine; his attention was on Teuper, his expression sad, as if trying to withhold judgment.

"So," Teuper continued, "we saw this land full of opportunity. You know when opportunity is at its greatest? When vast fortunes and thrones are changing hands. So the idea is to put yourself where you'll profit most from such a change and then set it in motion."

"You planned to take the thrones of Lieda and Terosalle?"

"Oh, yes. And the plan was itself simple. Find heirs to the respective thrones. Persuade them that they should participate in a plan to bring them those thrones. Concentrate the current rulers in a single area. And—"

"And eliminate those rulers."

"Yes."

"Who do you have standing by to take the thrones?"

"Standing by? Kin, they've done so already. It's been a season. But the answer is Buyan and Thaliara."

"They're dead!"

"Far from it. They're lovers. Have been for years."

I had difficulty keeping up with him while I digested this. "So Buyan's kidnapping was false?"

"Oh, very. The gold Jerno paid was real, though, and financed our operations for some time. The gold Lia paid for her daughter likewise."

"And Thaliara was part of this from the start."

"Oh, yes. She's quite a work of art, that one." He licked his lips. "Beautiful, smart, ambitious, the ethics of a bird of prey. Hates her mother—and who doesn't hate the Queen?"

"I thought she loved Prince Jernin."

Teuper made a gagging noise. "She was already in my father's camp when Captain Buyan conducted Prince Jerno to Terosalle for his state visit. My father saw an attraction between her and Buyan, learned about his none-too-secret paternity, and jumped on the opportunity, bringing Buyan into our fold. Thaliara was happy to keep up a pretense that she loved the oh-so-noble Jernin, and it did make things easier, didn't it?"

We reached the last verge of trees shielding the west beach. Where the river broadened as it ran into the sea, the *Wave-Breaker*'s ship's boat was beached and tied off to the last of the trees.

It would have taken at least two men to shove the unwieldy thing across the short stretch of land from the King's "throne room" to the river.

Teuper was watching my face, perhaps to judge my reaction when I sighted the boat. I gave him no satisfaction. I just asked, "So why are you here?"

He shrugged. "That was the mistake. I'd done everything I needed to—killed that nuisance, my 'master,' Kiaran dar Delerio so he couldn't feel the winds coming, arranged for the deaths of the Liedan wizards likewise—and left on a little raft. I was just heading off for shore when the winds hit. They were supposed to wait a few hours—do you know when the best time is to summon a wind?"

"When?"

"When it's not doing anything else."

"That would seem to be obvious."

"It's not. People try to summon cold winds in winter and warm winds in summer. But that's just backwards! In winter, all the cold winds are already hard at work making life miserable. At and after the change of seasons, when their tasks are done, *that's* when to get them. But I digress. I was caught out on open water and had to paddle frantically back to the *Thunderer*. Barely made it back. And then, on that whole long storm ride, I had to communicate with the wind, telling it to fetch us up on a shore somewhere so I wouldn't die. It's taken me all this time to find another wind, a southern wind this time, and convince it to come visit me now, when its winter duties are all done."

"That's what you were doing on the hilltop."

He nodded.

I turned to dar Bontine. "What's your role in all this?"

He looked startled and made a face as if to begin a denial. Then he shrugged and left off pretense. "I was responsible for getting the two rulers out on the water, and I was on the raft with Teuper." He looked apologetic. "You would have done what I did, Kin. It's in our nature to wish to better ourselves. The messenger from Teuper's father came to me before Jerno's messenger did. He made an interesting offer. I'll rule my own nation, made up of disputed parts of Terosalle and Lieda . . . and mountains in between, which is where my own people are from. I'll make a most effective king."

"You are a most effective negotiator."

"I am."

"Which is why it was so odd to see you fail the other day, when you whipped the crowd up into a fury of rebellion rather than calming them down."

"Noticed that, did you?"

"I noticed, but I didn't realize. Not until tonight."

We reached the ship's boat. It was almost ready to sail; it merely had to be cast off and the little mast stepped. I saw bundles of provisions, blankets, leather bags full of unknown contents. "Why didn't the King and Garris hear you moving this?"

"Asleep," Teuper said. "I made up a warm drink for them and Sheroit had them drink it. A powerful drug, a bit slow-acting; they'll be dead by morning."

"Ah. And that's the fate you have awaiting me. Were you supposed to stab me, Sheroit, while I stood enrapt by Teuper's story?"

The negotiator shook his head. "Absolutely not. I want to offer you a place with us."

"Of course you do."

"It's true. We've gone to considerable lengths to ensure that this motley collection of royalty and their hangers-on die here. You've impressed us by spoiling some of our efforts. You've demonstrated good abilities to manage. Come with us, and Emperor Jehan, King Buyan and Queen Thaliara, and I will doubtless all compete for your services."

My shadow, lying across the hull of the boat before me, grew slightly broader. The flesh on the nape of my neck crawled. Here was the third conspirator, standing behind me. Sheroit worked to keep my attention with his smooth words, but a glance at Teuper showed that the younger man was staring over my shoulder, ready to give the command that would end my life.

"You have a deal," I said.

Teuper lost his concentration and glanced at me. Even Sheroit looked startled. "We do?"

"No." I stepped to my right and drew my knife. I turned as I moved and struck with my fist at the man behind me, at Teuper before me with my knife.

Both blows connected. Teuper gasped as my blade punched economically between his ribs to the crossguard. And I smashed the nose of the man now to my left, sending him staggering back—Ardith Netter.

"Get him!" That was Sheroit, giving unnecessary orders in the manner of someone who talks for his living.

I was shouting, too, words I do not remember, cries for the guards of the encampment to come aid me. I did not follow up immediately on Ardith or Teuper; instead, I circled around to get Ardith between me and the other two, that I might have all three in sight at the same time.

This may have saved my life, but it also gave Ardith time to recover. With blood streaming down his face, he switched his own knife from a stabbing grip to a fighting grip and advanced on me. "Bastard!"

"You killed the Solunes, didn't you?" I asked, retreating, keeping well away from his blade. "Dar Bontine and Teuper didn't have the run of the *Wave-Breaker*. They couldn't have killed our wizards. You could. You were also on that raft paddling for shore when the wind hit."

"I'm going to cut your throat."

"You're an incompetent messenger, not a—" I was going to say "barber," but in my retreat I stumbled over a root of the nearest tree and fell over on my rear. Ardith, screaming, leaped at me, crashing down upon me and bearing me flat.

I got my free hand up under his descending arm and caught his wrist, then stabbed at his side. The blow struck, but did little harm through the layers of his cloak and hide tunic. Before I could strike again he'd gripped my wrist as well. There we strained at one another, a battle to the death between two minor court functionaries.

But terror was my strength. I leaned up and clamped my teeth squarely on his already-damaged nose. The crunch of cartilage giving way was drowned out by his sudden scream of pain. He tried to draw his knife-hand back and I went with him, rolling him over on his back as blood gushed out and flesh tore under my teeth.

He let go my knife-hand and his fingers sought my throat. I stabbed him in the side, a direct blow this time, then twice in his gut and chest.

His scream strangled off. His hand gripped my throat tighter for a moment, then fell away. I drew back from him, stumbling again as I stood away, but automatically brought my knife back in line against a charge by the other two.

No such luck. They'd already cast off the ship's boat. I could not see Teuper; he had to be at the bottom of the boat. But dar Bontine was rowing with more strength than I'd have given him credit for. As I rose he looked at me, fright in his expression, and increased his efforts.

But he was already a dozen paces out in icy water; I'd be up to my chest and half-frozen before I reached the boat, easy victim to a blow from an oar.

Instead, uselessly, I screamed oaths at him and ran up and down the shoreline looking for rocks. These I heaved at him as I found them. My third rock, a sharp-edged stone the size of my fist, caught him in the temple and he went down.

But he was up again a moment later, raising the little mast and lowering the sail. Despite my best efforts, I only hit the boat with one more rock, and that one merely bounced off the hull.

As soon as he lowered the sail, a wind filled it. Though I felt little breeze where I stood, the ship's boat raced northeast as if caught on the leading edge of a storm. Within moments I could no longer make out its occupants' features, and within minutes it was lost to sight. I shook from cold and anger, and both were still with me when the boat was gone.

I returned to Ardith and stood on his wrist. His knife-hand opened. So did his eyes.

I carefully stooped to recover his knife.

"I'm going to die," he said. I didn't know whether that were statement or question.

"It appears so."

He coughed and blood stained his chin. He looked angry. "It's your fault."

"I don't think so. If you hadn't spent your life trading information for favors and whoring your honor—"

"Your fault." He stiffened, arching up, and then relaxed. His eyes closed.

I left him and set about my errands.

Chapter Fourteen

Kin

Under Doctor Ha's care—and after his application of an emetic to both of them—King Jerno and Garris swiftly recovered. The next day, they were both listless and weary, but suffered no further problems from Teuper's drug.

Workers found Ardith the next morning, on the river trail. He'd apparently not died when I thought he had, and had crawled about a hundred paces from where I'd stabbed him, then frozen to death.

I felt some qualms about that. Had I known he was not dead from the wound I struck him, I would not have left him there.

Oh, I would not have brought him in. He was a self-confessed murderer. Had he survived, he would have had to be cared for. After recovery, he would have had to be imprisoned, which would require that vital resources be lavished upon him, or exiled, which would leave him a danger to the rest of us. In my capacity as Judge, then, I'd have passed down a sentence of death and finished him there.

But the thought of him dragging his way desperately toward light and warmth, only to perish of cold and exhaustion, bothered me through the day and long afterwards.

At noon, I gathered the island's remaining population into the throne room to tell them what had happened. I told them everything that had occurred.

"You're a liar," said Lia. "My Thaliara would never do such a thing."

"I'm not a liar, Majesty. Teuper and Sheroit dar Bontine demonstrably have been. Perhaps they lied to me about your daughter."

"Well, they did."

"But considering that they planned to kill me immediately after, it makes little sense to lie to me."

"Then you're a liar."

King Jerno said, "I have a son still living."

"Yes, Majesty. Though he has conspired against you."

He waved the objection away. "A shrewd diplomatic move. A bold plan. I will forgive him after a due period of penance."

"Of course, Majesty." I turned back to the assembly. "None of this affects us now, of course, except that it removes the danger that Teuper, dar Bontine and Ardith presented in our midst. I would appreciate it if you all would spend some time recalling to mind what you know of their activities since we were stranded here; if you remember anything of interest, tell me. Just in case they set other events into motion that we need to stop."

I dismissed them and they left slowly, falling into small groups to talk about what they'd just learned. But Nerrin and Shallia lingered and approached.

I hadn't had much time to follow Shallia's progress. She seemed wan and somber, but the light of intelligence had returned to her eyes, and it was she who spoke first. "Kin, if Teuper and dar Bontine lied about so much, might they have lied about Halleyne?"

"That's what I spent the rest of the night thinking about. Yes, they might have. She may still be alive." I tried not to let myself feel the hope those words represented. I didn't want to suffer the blow when hope was dashed again. But I couldn't help myself.

Nerrin asked, "What do you intend to do about it?"

"Build a raft." I shrugged. "My personal interests aside, with the ship's boat gone, we need something so we can reach the other islands. So I'm going to start on a raft."

"Have you ever built one?"

"I've never joined two pieces of wood together for any reason."

He smiled. "I'll help, then."

"So will I," Shallia said.

"It will have to be after our normal work hours are done."

"We know," she said.

"I'll meet you after evening meal and we'll begin planning." I made to return to my duties, but Shallia surprised me by stepping up to kiss my cheek before they left.

Halleyne

Life on Turtlehead Island is meaner than it was on Fishtail, if only because we were used to the huts and now have to make do with lean-tos and natural windbreaks again. And, already, trouble is starting.

It began with Jenina insisting that we encamp near Treacherous Strait, the better to "defend our new home from invaders"—and, I think, the better to launch raiders across the strait to Hopeless and then Fishtail, for Jenina has made it well known that she intends to punish Kin and the rest who exiled her.

But I pointed out that, according to the maps Kin

made—maps I remember with fair clarity, as I helped him copy them—fresh water was available on the east side of the island, a body of water they'd named Marille Lake. The lake was sheltered by hills that would protect us from punishing winds. Despite Jenina's objections, most everybody wanted to have a better situation than Jenina's preferred camp, despite the fact that her site would have been better for melthue hunting.

We walked down Turtlehead's jagged east coast and soon found ourselves on the beaches of the lake, a much larger and prettier body of water than the pathetic little King Lake, but fed by a waterfall that lacked some of Gloriana Falls' beauty. Even Jenina had to admit that it was a more comfortable-looking site than the one she'd chosen. So there it was, but she was still cross with me for a few days.

As everyone looked to Jenina for leadership, but her mind was always set on long-range plans, it fell to me to make out daily work assignments. I did that at dawn, was cook during the three meals, and worked on carving myself a new woodwind whenever I had time and could borrow Gulbuk's knife.

We lived off the supplies we'd brought while we built our new camp and explored the island. There were some gulbuks left here, and I said we ought to impose punishment on anyone who killed a female— else there would be no gulbuks at all by next year. But Jenina overrode my objections, saying, "We need to eat now, so we'll hunt whatever we need now," and was able to persuade most of the others to that way of thinking. Hungry men and women just do not consider next year.

Daneeth Po has turned out to be a surprisingly good scout. He has made us maps of his travels, cruder than Kin's and Teuper's but adequate. We knew already that Turtlehead Island narrows to a thin strip of land, from which you can see both east and west beaches, and then widens toward the south, and he reports that there is little of interest south of the narrowing.

Jenina has put some of the men to making a crude boat; they chopped down a tree, a horribly demanding task when the trees are as cold and hard as rock and all we have are stone hatchets, and will eventually burn out the middle to make a hollow. Even suspecting that she plans to use this to make raids onto Fishtail, I've expressed enthusiasm for the dangerous-looking craft . . . because if it can be made seaworthy and I am counted a loyal member of Jenina's circle, I might be able to secure passage back to Fishtail on it.

Kin

My manner, subdued and surly after Halleyne's death, did not improve in the days to come, but some things did.

Shallia, for one. I could hear her singing in the hut she shared with Nerrin, Viriat Axer, and a few others. She sang more at work, for with her craftsman's skills she replaced dar Bontine as our incidental leatherworker. Sometimes her songs were melancholy, but they were strong and beautiful.

She told me one day, "Spring is on us and spirits are awakening all over these islands."

"That's good."

"I'm not so sure. There are so many . . . with my songs I can reach out and feel them, and they cluster in their masses more numerous than any other place I've been."

"Here on Fishtail?"

She shook her head. "Some. But more off to the east, probably Turtlehead. And still more in the middle."

"In open water."

"No, below, on the seafloor or even below that."

"Ah." I looked at her, helpless. "Shallia, I don't know what to make of that."

She gave me a wan little smile. "You mean, are these the ravings of a madwoman?"

"Not precisely."

"Sometimes my feelings come crashing down on me like a wave, Kin. They overwhelm me and bear me down. But this is only sometimes . . . The rest of the time I'm me again, and this is when I sense what I'm telling you."

"I'll think on what you've told me, then."

"And Kin—I know I'd be dead if not for you."

"Now you're raving again."

She smiled and left me.

On my departure from the smokehouse one day, I was joined by Doctor Ha. He was as brown and stubby as ever, but wore a brilliantly colored new belt—made from the hide of a Gloriana viper.

I looked at the doctor. "Eleyn was not bitten obtaining that for you?"

"She was bitten, yes, but her glove protected her. The last good thing dar Bontine did."

"Let's walk along the river." This discussion was one I wanted to have away from others' ears; I did not know what answers the doctor had for me. When we were clear of the encampment, I continued: "So, what sort of danger do these snakes pose to us?"

"Not much, I think."

"You surprise me. I thought their poison was deadly."

"Deadly to dar Ostaferion, certainly. Deadly to you, maybe. Deadly to me and to many of the others, probably not."

"I don't understand."

He paused a moment to fish out his flint and tinder. He packed his pipe with what looked like shaved bark and lit it, then took a couple of puffs before we began walking again. "Their poison is strange," he said. "A paralytic of sorts. When it is introduced into your blood, you lose volition, but your mind remains mostly clear. You experience visions, hallucinations."

"How do you know this?"

"I've allowed myself to be bitten."

"*What?*"

He waved my objection away. "Only after testing. I arranged for Eleyn and Casseyl to bring me animals. I allowed them to be bitten and observed their reactions. The birds died. The melthues and one gulbuk survived; I am reasonably sure that the difference lies in body weight, the proportion of viper toxin to the weight of the victim. The animals acted oddly while the poison worked its course through them; they watched things that weren't there, as cats do."

"And then you allowed yourself to be bitten."

"No. I told my helpers that I was going to do so, because I wanted to know what the venom was about. But Eleyn said that the doctor should not be the one poisoned and she volunteered. Then Casseyl, not wishing to see his lover hurt, volunteered. He pointed out that he had twice her weight and so the poison would affect him half as much, which is nearly true. We had two serpents, the larger of which was nowhere near the size of the one that bit dar Ostaferion, and I had the smaller bite Casseyl."

"You should have consulted me first."

"I think not. You're not qualified to advise me on matters of medicine."

"I *am* qualified to evaluate the danger you think this experiment poses to someone in my command, and then decide whether we can afford to risk losing someone like Casseyl."

"Humpf. Are you interested in the rest of this story?"

"Just keep it in mind, doctor."

"So, Casseyl became very complacent and began

talking to things he saw that Eleyn and I did not. Speaking his name, telling the story of our shipwreck. He talked of lovemaking with Eleyn in such terms that she became very embarrassed; she was angry with him afterwards. Later, when I allowed myself to be bitten, I experienced much the same thing."

"Lovemaking with Eleyn?"

"I knew you would ask that; you're far too crass to be a judge."

"True."

"No, I saw snakes that I did not fear, men made of burning rock, vistas of steam and smoke and black stone—nowhere near so menacing as it sounds; they were all very comforting images at the time."

"Were you asked questions?"

"Not really; I just felt the need to explain. Casseyl said it was like that for him as well. A need to explain, a certain peacefulness."

I sighed irritably. "If it's so comfortable an experience, why did dar Ostaferion die?"

"Two possibilities. One is that he might have been bitten several times. He could have been bitten and lain down atop the viper's hole, making the snake afraid and angry. But I don't think that is the case; I found only one set of bite marks on him.

"The other possibility . . . well, I experimented while under the venom's influence. I tried to move. I decided not to explain myself, despite the urge to do so."

"And?"

"I fell sick with headaches, the worst I'd ever felt. They only began to diminish when I stopped fighting the effects of the venom, and did not completely leave me until hours after the venom's other effects were past."

"So he might have died of headaches?"

"Well, of the condition that induced the headaches. Some very deadly things can give you headaches, Kin.

Brain fevers. Abnormal growths in the brain. Things that only magic can detect, such as ruptures in the brain. I think that the struggle to overcome the venom's effects caused one of these results, such as a rupture, and it is from this that dar Ostaferion died."

"So your advice is, if you're bitten, don't fight it."

"Yes. I don't think the venom is nearly as deadly if you don't fight its effects."

"That is a relief."

He shook his head.

"Not a relief?"

"Not to me, no. It bothers me that I've never heard of any serpent venom with properties like these. I know a fair amount about poisons and their effects; this is a strange one. Some plants can cause listlessness and hallucinations, but they tend to make the victims lose clarity in their thinking, and the visions are not so uniform from victim to victim."

"Well, let me know if you have any further thoughts on it. For now, I'll pass on your instructions about not fighting the venom's effects." I rose, but paused before leaving. "Could any of this have something to do with dar Ostaferion's . . . moonlight walk?" I knew of Halleyne's involvement in that incident, but it now occurred to me that her calling might not have been the only element involved.

He shrugged. "I hope not. Shall I duplicate the circumstances of the admiral's death to find out?"

"Ah, no."

"I meant, perhaps with an animal."

"I'm sure you did. But that sort of experimentation just does not seem wholesome." *Nor might you have any success without Halleyne's participation,* I thought. "Thank you, doctor."

But from that curious errand I was able to turn to a much more congenial one.

As winter had loosened its hold on the islands and

on us, the men and women of the island had begun to have a little more time available to them—the load of work needed to keep us alive had lessened, and we needed to spend less time and energy making sure we were warm enough to survive. Not surprisingly, many of the castaways began to act on plans they'd made during the long weeks of hard winter. Two women I knew of were showing that they'd caught children during the winter months.

At dusk of this day, most of the people of Fishtail Island, the King included (but Queen Lia not), gathered in the throne room. Everyone made an effort to dress up—a difficult task on an island where every garment had been worn almost daily to stave off cold. But the people of Fishtail wore jewelry made of stones and shells, or pre-shipwreck decorations carefully unearthed from where they'd been hidden, and looked as festive as they could.

This event I did not shorten. There were long words of encouragement and advice—recommendations that were more than a little hypocritical, since I had never faced the fate the two before me were about to share. Then, exhortations of the gods to favor them on their journey into mystery.

Then: "Casseyl Vinner, sailor, do you consent to be wed to this woman?"

"Damned right."

The audience tittered, and I fixed the seaman with a stern look.

He wiped away his grin, but I saw it lurking just beneath his more serious expression. "Yes, yer honor."

"Eleyn Kitter, sailor, do you consent to be wed to this man?"

"Yes, your honor."

I don't know how she'd gotten it, the ankle-length spring-green dress she wore. It was cut in the Terosai style, so it had to have been a gown worn by one of

Lia's ladies-in-waiting during the shipwreck, carefully patched up. It had probably been dyed green with local plant extracts. I imagined I would be seeing it again on other brides. Whatever its origin, Eleyn had decorated it with strands of small seashells. Barefoot, her hair unbound, she looked like one of the legendary sea-girls who sometimes come on shore to tryst with handsome men.

"Present your hands."

They did, extending his left and her right.

With a cord of melthue hide, I bound their wrists together. I knew the secret, from the wedding of one of my older brothers: By tradition, the judge shows his personal feelings on the wedding by the way he binds the couple. Too tight, and he expects them to cause one another pain (or he simply does not care for them). Too loose, and he expects them to slip away from one another. I bound Casseyl and Eleyn comfortably but snugly and tied the cord with a sailor's knot of excessive complexity that I had learned just for this occasion—a mark both of their mutual profession and of the regard in which I held them.

"Gods grant that the children of this union be numerous and strong," I said, and added to myself, *and reared in Lieda*. "By my right as Judge of Byriver, under the eyes of the gods, I declare the union of marriage between Casseyl and Eleyn. Let happiness find them."

This time there was applause from the audience, and the couple was swarmed by well-wishers.

I spared a glance for the King. He wore a little smile, but his eyes were sad, and I saw him glance at Shallia and Nerrin. He had to be wondering when they, too, would choose to be wed, but I knew the answer to that: They would wed tomorrow if Halleyne were here to witness, or if they knew she were no longer alive. They waited only for the raft to be finished so we might find out her fate.

Halleyne

The people of Turtlehead gather every evening beside the communal fire. It is there I announce who will be working where tomorrow—usually the same assignments as today's—and Jenina makes other announcements, including exhortations to work hard and threats against the Fishtail islanders.

Jenina interrupted me when I had barely begun. "You will have to plan around Daneeth, Gulbuk, Leiala and I tomorrow. We will be practicing with the canoe."

"As you wish," I said. "Please, make the rest of your announcements while I make changes to my list." I did not need any time to do any such thing; an adjustments like that took only a moment. But if she went first, I could eat before my bowl of food went cold, and fish stew that is barely appetizing when warm is much less so when chilly.

Daneeth Po spoke up. "No canoe for me," he said.

We all looked at him, then at Jenina, who usually was not very congenial when her orders were counter-manded. But her expression was civil enough. "Are you sick? Hurt?"

"No."

"Then you'll be on the canoe tomorrow."

"No."

Jenina lowered her head just a little, but still managed to look bigger than before. I imagined her as a cat with all the fur just starting to stand up. "Hunting is so appealing to you?"

"Yes."

"Well, we all must do some things we don't want to if we're to survive. Me, for example. Do you imagine I enjoy all this muck-a-muck with canoes and weapons?"

"Yes."

"What did you say?"

Daneeth drained his bowl, shook free the last droplets of fish broth, and instead of setting it aside tucked it into his tunic. "There's going to be a big fight with the Fishtailers. You're going to start it because you're angry. We're going to get killed because you're angry. But not me."

"You'll do as you're told or you'll be exiled. You'll die out there alone, cold and hungry."

"I'll take exile. I've already found a better place to live."

"You're an idiot, Daneeth."

He shrugged and rose, picking up his bed-blanket— which, we saw, was already rolled and tied around his other goods—and the crude spear he used for hunting.

"Leave the spear, Daneeth. You didn't make it, you don't get to keep it."

He merely gave her a scornful look and turned to leave. "Take it from me," he said.

But no one did, and he passed from our company while we watched in silence.

Jenina looked between us. "Anyone else?"

Again, no one answered. She continued, "Well, then, tomorrow it will be Gulbuk and *Raldan* and Leiala and I. And if anyone out hunting sees Daneeth tomorrow or any other day—he's fair game, too. Anyone who brings in his ears gets double rations for the day."

We looked at one another, but did not speak. I hoped no one would take her up on her offer.

Chapter Fifteen

Kin

The raft was made up of eight-foot planks, their rough-cut surfaces unplaned, lashed together with hide cords and crudely-spliced bits and pieces of salvaged ship's rope.

Two poles protruded from it. On one side was a mast that might carry a small sail without tipping the thing over. On the other was a tall oarlock, a forked thigh-high pole in which we could set the long oar we'd use to move the raft.

In the calm waters of the eastern bay, it—we could not bring ourselves to dignify it with the term "she"—looked about as safe as a shepherd's cottage moving downslope in a mudslide. It rippled with every wave; cords became wet, stretched, and came loose. But after a few practice attempts and inevitable repairs afterwards, we decided that it was approximately seaworthy.

I said, "It's not too bad."

Nerrin said, "It's good for a first attempt."

Shallia said, "We're all going to die."

On the first day the sun was warm enough for me to work without my jacket and cloak, we three made a few last repairs and adjustments to the raft and then embarked on our first voyage, rowing it out from the bay and north along Fishtail's coast until we came to the northern tip of the island. It was hard, tiring work and took us hours. When it was done, we sat with our raft on the beach and watched the sun settle into the sea.

"Tomorrow?" Shallia asked.

"Yes . . . and no."

"What does that mean?" asked Nerrin.

"It means," I told him, "that tomorrow I sail for Hopeless to look for the others . . . and you and Shallia stay here."

"Don't be ridiculous," she said. "We all worked on the raft. We all deserve to drown together."

I looked at her intended. "Have you noticed, over the last few days, that I have been making you learn most of my tasks and duties?"

"Yes," he said.

"Why do you think I was doing this?"

"I reasoned that you hated me and wanted to see me suffer."

I snorted. "So if we go and we all die, who runs things?"

He fell silent. Shallia answered for him. "No one. Until King Jerno and Queen Lia and anyone who can force others to listen to them have it out."

"Ah. And if only I go, and only I drown, who runs things?"

They both fell silent.

"You two do. Because everyone I deal with has learned to work with you. Between you, you can keep our little village full of rulers from shaking itself to pieces."

Nerrin glared at me. "You've changed the rules when I wasn't looking."

"You were looking. You just weren't seeing. And now you're caught up in the same fisherman's net of responsibility that snared me, and I have no sympathy for you."

Shallia pitched a handful of sand at me, but her expression told me I'd won. It pays to set up the battlefield before you enter it—it truly does.

The next morning, they came out to see me off, and made sure that the bag I'd tied off to the mast held enough dried meat and skins of water to see me through the several days this trip might take. They helped me shove the rickety craft out into the cold water, and helped shove me aboard; and then I was on my own, pushing back and forth on the oar to propel me toward Hopeless Island.

The oar blade was the size of a large fish's fin, and the back-and-forth sweep of the thing was somewhat greater than that of a fish. So I calculated that the oar displaced water much as a large pike would. The prospect of the time it would take a harnessed pike to tow this ungainly craft across Duckhead Strait, along the beaches of Hopeless Island, and possibly as far as Turtlehead was daunting.

Then it was tiring. To my surprise, the raft held together during the strait crossing and showed no sign of separation or collapse, but my arms were tired by the time I reached the near shore of Hopeless. I hopped off, refreezing my lower half, to push the thing up onto the rocky shore, one too stony and dismal even for the melthues, and when I turned I could still see the distant Nerrin and Shallia. They waved, I waved back, and then finally they left.

After a period of rest I pushed off again and maneuvered the raft east along the shoreline. This was a much longer stretch, but I would not be out over deep water.

As the sun climbed in the east, I worked through the unaccustomed ache in my arms and fell into a more efficient rhythm of motion; my rate of travel increased a trifle, but most importantly, the effort was less a strain on my arms and back. Still, as hours passed I longed for a steady eastward breeze to pick up so that I might raise my cloak as a crude sail; but none ever did.

Just past midday I was at the eastern tip of the western headland of Melthue Bay. I'd passed no sign of exile settlement, nor seen a fire; and from this vantage I could look over the entire shore of the bay, and there was still no sign of Jenina's followers.

Ahead of me was a choice, and so I put the raft in to shore to think about it. I was very mindful of snake burrows, but more mindful of my afternoon meal; even the familiar, monotonous smoked fish and melthue meat were a welcome treat.

My choices were three. I could raft around the beach of Melthue Bay, staying safely close to the beach during my travel; I would be partway around by nightfall and might have to make my bedding among the melthues. I could cut straight across from headland to headland, a trip about a third as long as my travels so far, but over deeper, choppier, open waters; this would put me not far from Treacherous Strait before nightfall, and away from the greatest concentration of melthues. Or I could camp here tonight and make the same decision in the morning.

After eating, I examined the raft. It had continued to hold together well. I repaired a couple of places where the bindings had rubbed themselves frayed, but overall I was pleased with the way the craft had held up.

In the end, I decided on the straight-across trip, due to the condition of the raft and my own impatience. Though my slightly-rested arms screamed pain at me to convince me to continue my rest, I set out again.

I had to stop a few times to drink water and rest. Still, it was well before nightfall that I reached the stony coast south of where the admiral had died. I continued rowing until I reached a beach that was sheer rock. I grounded there.

I built no fire—there was no wood to be found within short walking distance—and so ate another cold meal. But in the distance, from somewhere in the center of Turtlehead, I thought I saw a faint plume of smoke arise, sign that the exiles had indeed made their way there. I watched it during the last minutes of daylight and then made my bed atop the raft. Tied off, it should not float away at high tide . . . but if it did, I wanted to be on it.

It was not many hours later that I awoke to answer nature's call. Even that simple task was not simple; the muscles in my arms and thighs burned like a blood pudding fresh from the fire. Then, when I turned away from the sea, I saw the Gloriana viper.

It was no more than three steps from the raft, clearly visible in the moonlight, laid out over a flat stretch of the stone shore. I thought perhaps it was dead, but it reacted to my movement, curling around itself protectively. Then I saw another beyond it, several paces away, and another, and realized with a shock of fear that the shore was littered with them.

Unmoving, I looked over the raft and saw no sign of the things. That didn't mean there weren't others beneath the raft, where gaps might allow them access; but there were none atop. Only when I was sure that I was alone did I finish adjusting my trousers.

Were they here to menace me, attack me, or just warn me? And then I knew the answer and I almost laughed. This was a flat stone shore; it had to have been warmed by the sun. Like ordinary snakes back home, they'd stretched out on warm rocks for the heat. I had nothing to do with it.

With what I knew of the serpents from Doctor Ha, I reasoned that I would be no less in danger shoving off again now than I would be staying here. Carefully, I sat leaning against the mast and watched the snakes to make sure none came near me.

And then I opened my eyes again and it was dawn. The snakes were gone.

Halleyne

Yesterday was my first day to try the canoe.

I'm certain the others thought I would be of little worth on the inelegant craft, but I surprised them. Despite my slight stature, I have been made fit by the last several months of living on Fishtail; I was able to row as long, though not as powerfully, as any of the others practicing with me. I was quicker to pick up tricks of timing, so my strokes would complement rather than compete with the other rower's. I did not have to be shown that when my partner leaned one way, it might be a good idea to lean the other, to keep the awkward log from tipping over so easily. At the end of the day's practice, Gulbuk, who taught me, praised my efforts.

Jenina did not. She just frowned and asked, "But what will happen when you are faced with a big Fishtailer fighter with a club in his hand?"

"I won't be," I told her. "I am small and quiet. I'll serve best as a scout. I'm much more nimble among the trees than giant Gulbuk here. While you're pounding the skull of some big Fishtailer fighter with a club in his hand, I'll creep into Queen Lia's quarters and pop her in the face again."

The others laughed, except Jenina. It was a ploy on my part; I was best known now for hitting Herself, and could often turn peoples' thoughts to other things by mentioning the event. No one who really knew me would believe I wanted a rematch with the Queen, but—and a little touch of sadness always accompanied the thought—no one here really knew me.

That was yesterday, though, and we have had trouble since. Yesterday evening, Leiala failed to return to the campfire by dusk and missed evening meal, nor had she shown up by dawn today.

"What was her assignment?" Jenina asked, her tone cross.

"She said she'd seen good-sized crabs on the beach south of Bucketfish Bay, so I said she could harvest some."

"Well, go find her."

So that was my morning's task. Ever mindful of the Gloriana vipers, which the hunters and foragers had reported in growing numbers—and had killed in growing numbers near our encampment—I set out to the lonely stretch of beach where Leiala was supposed to have been.

Bucketfish Bay is about the size of Salvation Bay back on Fishtail, perhaps a little larger, and stares out into empty ocean. It's pretty enough, being shallower than Salvation, with a nice white beach and clear blue water. It also teemed with fish, and the more knowledgeable fishermen among us plied it every day. I greeted them as I passed—some hunted with spears, some with crude nets—and listened to each one grumble.

Raldan's comments were typical. "Give me that canoe and this net and I'll get more fish in a day than I usually get in a week."

"Well . . . true. But nothing stops you from making a canoe when your day's work is done."

"Why should I? We already have one made!"

"That was Jenina's project—"

"With our labor!"

"Yes. But without her driving us like a herd of oxen"—a deliberate choice of words, designed to be unarguable but offensive—"it would never have been done, nor would most of what we all do together, like the new huts. Raldan, if you want to take over her prerogatives where the canoes are concerned, you want to take over all her other duties, too. Assigning work details—"

"*You* do that."

"But she's responsible. Making plans. Settling disputes. Allotting measures of food. Do you want to have to do all that?"

"I never said anything about taking over."

"Yes, you did. When you talk about taking away one part of her leadership, you talk about taking it all, and you know that. Everybody seems to be willing to rebel, but no one wants to do all the work when the rebellion's done. Think about that before you start in again with loose talk." And I moved on.

I liked doing that. I'd taken a simple brag and turned it into something Raldan would have to think about. For there had been increasing noise, as Jenina talked more and more about raids against Fishtail, that perhaps she shouldn't be in charge. Privately, I agreed. Publicly, I supported her . . . but tried to leave the complainers with something to think about.

Maybe this time they'd have a plan in place when they decided to remove her from the captain's role. Maybe they'd realize that the whole exile was a mistake: That King Jerno and Queen Lia, too, had been cast down, and been replaced *by someone willing to do their work*. To be responsible for everything.

I missed Kin.

And I moved on, passing the other fishermen and having the same conversation with them, then moving out past the tip of the headland and turning south along the shore.

I walked the length of this eastward-facing shore, searching in vain for any sign that Leiala had been there. When the shoreline curved toward the east and became stonier and less friendly, I turned back and moved off the beach a few paces; perhaps she'd left some sign off the sand.

And, again, there was no sign of her, though I did see a couple of viper burrows; I walked well clear of them.

As I neared the headland, I saw someone ahead of me on the beach, a man—and then realized it was Daneeth, the exile of the exiles. He had his spear in one hand and the other hand tucked under his cloak; as he came close I could tell that his expression was more solemn and thoughtful than I had yet seen it. There was some sort of gray chalk or dust sprinkled everywhere on his cloak.

"Fair morning," he said.

"And to you."

"Are you here to collect Jenina's bounty?" He turned his head this way and that to display his prize ears.

I laughed. "Of course. With my mighty arms, I will pluck your head forth and then worry the ears off. No, Daneeth, I have another errand. By chance, have you seen Leiala?"

He glanced down and was slow in answering. "No."

With another Terosai, I would have then asked, "I apologize—I meant in the last day or so." That would have given him time and opportunity to offer another answer without loss of dignity. But I could not remember how to politely tell a Liedan that his answer was a lie and another answer would be better. So I said, "There is something odd about your 'no,' Daneeth."

He heaved a long sigh, then looked up at me again. "She is dead."

It was a moment before I could answer him; it seemed that the air was very thin in my lungs just then. "How did—where is she?"

"Snakebite. Found her on the beach yesterday, just

where it faces that big rock that pretends to be an island." He shrugged. "Buried her. She's gone, Halleyne."

"Oh, gods." Leiala had been the quietest of the ladies-in-waiting, thus the one who received the least punishment, and was tall and gawky enough that the Queen had no need to persecute her for excessive beauty. Her size had served her well in exile; she'd become strong and fit. "Show me."

"What?"

"Her grave. I'll need to show it to Jenina and others. They will want to go there. Conduct the appropriate rituals."

"I did that."

"But they'll want to see it. I do. To say goodbye."

He was again slow in answering. "Halleyne, when I was done digging and planting and refilling, that's when I saw the snakes. They'd been drawn out by the sound of my effort. Lot of snakes there. I barely got away alive. You go to the grave, take others there, and you'll be planting another body. No." I saw his hand moving under his cloak and tunic, back and forth, as though he were stroking something hung around his neck. It was an irrelevant motion and for that reason disturbed me.

"If I have to tell that to Jenina, it may make her more determined to do you harm. You know she doesn't care to have people tell her no."

"Since coming to Turtlehead, you have become much prettier, Halleyne."

Others had said that. I let them think it was mere joy at being away from Herself. No one here knew that I had simply abandoned the cosmetics I used to make myself plainer under the Queen's eyes. I shrugged. "Thank you, But that is not an appropriate topic for conversation under these circumstances."

"I think everything is better here. Improved by

Turtlehead." He slowly brought out his hand from under his cloak and reached to take mine . . . and yet I saw the movement of his hand under the cloak, still stroking something beneath his neck.

I flinched away from him, heard a hiss from behind me, and jumped to the side just in time to see a snake strike the ground where my heel had been. I backed away from both snake and Daneeth, half-stumbling toward the water in my haste. The snake coiled where it was and watched my movements, ignoring Daneeth.

"Don't go," Daneeth said. "We must talk." He looked down, noticing the viper for the first time. "Oh. A snake. Turn away, Halleyne. I don't want you to see me kill it."

"I'd have to be as mad as you to turn my back on you." I ran past him toward the bay, and did turn my back as soon as I was past, the better to run full-out.

"Don't go!" This time it was a command, but it only made me run faster. Finally I heard his running steps, but on a sandy beach his clumsy, patched boots, a blessing throughout the hard cold of winter, were for once a great hindrance. I quickly outdistanced him.

On the beach of Bucketfish Bay, I told this to each fisherman I passed: "Don't trust Daneeth. I don't know what's wrong with him, but he seems half-mad. Don't let him near you." And then it was back to the main camp on Marille Lake to tell Jenina.

Chapter Sixteen

Kin

Treacherous Strait is so called because an ocean stream moves from south to north through this narrow gap between Hopeless and Turtlehead. The strait constricts it and increases its speed. Several times on the ship's boat Teuper and I found ourselves in danger of being swept through and out into open sea before reaching the opposite side. This was no great danger to us—it would probably merely have made us work harder to get clear of the current and make a landing elsewhere on the island.

But on the raft, the current could be dangerous or fatal. I did not think it would take much effort on the part of the water to break up or capsize the poor thing.

So instead of moving up to the closest promontory of land to Turtlehead, I departed the shoreline some distance away from that point and cut due southeast, aiming to cross a stretch of water as broad as the mouth of Melthue Bay. Doubtless the current would move me toward or into the strait, but by then I hoped I'd be most of the way across.

The trip started off well. But when I was a few minutes into it, I saw an object detach itself from the Turtlehead coast and begin moving in my direction. It took a few moments for that tiny dot to resolve itself into a crude boat, a canoe, manned by two rowers . . . and on a course to intercept me.

As we closed, I made them out to be Jenina in front and Gulbuk behind. She seemed to be shouting; I faintly heard snatches of her harangue, and finally they resolved themselves into words: "You are intruding into Turtlehead waters. *Our territory.* You are our prisoner. Heave to and prepare to be boarded." I listened to this, repeated with only minor variations, three times until I was sure of what she was saying—and sure that she'd be able to hear me in turn.

"Boarded? Jenina, the last thing we need is more border wars!"

"You started it! You exiled us! We are now a sovereign nation. You are our prisoner. Prepare to be boarded."

They'd come another few paces closer during this exchange. "Thirty people do not make a nation. I come to talk, Jenina."

"I'll kill you before I'll talk to you!"

"And what will you do if you take me as prisoner?"

"Kill you!"

"Then I have little incentive to surrender, do I?"

They were within easy javelin-cast by this time, and I saw Jenina pull up a crude javelin. But Gulbuk was talking to her, shaking his head, apparently arguing some point.

She won. He picked up a javelin too. Jenina shouted, "Those are the fortunes of war, *Judge* Underbridge. I advise you to surrender. A knife will be quicker and cleaner than our spears."

"You don't have spears, you have sticks with crude points on them. Care you don't stab each other."

Now they were no more than ten paces away, and Jenina half-rose and let fly with her weapon. It was a good throw and arced in straight for me; but the weapon was so crude, her throwing position so precarious, that I found it simple to just step a little to one side and catch the thing as it descended. I couldn't restrain a smile; a pity only two enemies had been present to see the skill of my maneuver. Then I saw my oar sliding out of its lock. I hopped back to grab it before it left me.

"Throw!" Jenina said.

Gulbuk appeared to have reservations. I heard her command him again before he was willing to heave his weapon at me. He rose partway and let fly.

I didn't even have to move aside. The spear hit the water in front of my raft and disappeared, then bobbed to the surface a little left of my raft. It began drifting north; the current had it and us.

"Well, that's that," I said.

"Board him!"

Gulbuk's wince displayed his feelings.

I shouted, "If he doesn't sink you leaving your canoe, and doesn't sink me trying to board, I'll just hit him with this stick you gave me. By the gods, I don't want to fight you, but if you keep after me I'll have to give you a drubbing."

"Board him!"

Gulbuk visibly sighed. He stripped off his tunic and boots. I took the opportunity to maneuver the raft around the canoe and a little farther toward the island; if we waited much longer, we might get caught up in the speedy, dangerous part of the strait.

Gulbuk slid into the water. He did so very skillfully, barely tipping the log canoe, and in a moment he was swimming strongly toward me.

I wrapped a thong around the oar and oarlock where they met to keep the oar from slipping easily away.

Then I brandished the spear. "Gulbuk, this is not necessary. I am not your enemy."

He dog-paddled a mere pace beyond the edge of my raft. "No choice," he said. Then he swam the final pace in and put his hand on the raft edge.

I swung the spear and slammed the butt into his hand. He cried out and snatched his hand away.

"The next time it's your left hand, and after that your head. You'll find swimming hard with no hands and even harder when you're asleep."

He upended with some skill and disappeared under the water. I saw a suggestion of him moving beneath my raft.

Which side would he come up? That was an easy choice. I faced Turtlehead; Gulbuk, no master of tactics, he would try to come up behind me. I turned.

When his left hand came up to grip the raft, I smacked it. He snatched it back and emerged from the water, wringing his injured fingers.

"I told you."

"You shouldn't make me mad." Instead of trying again, he reached up, grabbed my oar above his head, then raised a foot and pushed off from the raft . . . taking my oar with him, despite the restraining thong and my grip on it.

"You miserable thief!" I ran to the very lip of the raft, threatening to tip the thing over myself, and swung again.

My spear butt caught him against the temple. The blow was heavy enough to jar my hands. He looked surprised and let go of the oar. Then he sunk beneath the water and hung there, suspended, a foot or two beneath its surface.

I looked at him in alarm for a long moment. "Jenina, I hope you like Gulbuk."

"Why?"

"Because he'll drown if you don't save him." I sat down pulled off my own tunic, boots, and belt.

"Well, you're obviously going in to save him."

"I'm going to save my oar. I need it. Don't need him."

Yes, it was a bluff. I had no wish to see Gulbuk die. But if I had to rescue him, I'd lose the oar and Jenina would have me.

"Liar."

I jumped off the raft and swam toward the oar—

No. I jumped off the raft, hit the water, felt cold blast through my body as though every drop of my blood had turned into mountain runoff, and curled into a tight ball while I tried to keep from sucking in a lungful of air. I felt parts of my body shrivelling and contracting.

Then I bobbed to the surface and realized I could breathe again. How had that madman Gulbuk swum ten paces in this cold? He had to have become used to it through practice. It was all I could do to kick myself up a little higher—and then I spotted my oar, and then, finally, I swam feebly toward it.

Jenina swore like a good sailor. When I dared look back, I saw her following my example, taking off garments that would weigh her down in the water or warm her up if left dry on the boat. A moment later I heard her splash into the water, too.

A day or two later—or so it felt—I reached my oar, seized it, turned back with it. Actually, I did not need to swim so much as stay in place; my raft, caught up in the current, was headed toward me. Soon after it reached me I could place my precious cargo aboard and climb up after it.

I wrapped myself up in my cloak and sat shivering at the base of the mast. As the shudders took me, I knew I could not help Jenina; to go into that water again would kill me.

Fortunately for Gulbuk, she did not need my help. I saw her already dragging him through the water back toward her craft; so ungainly was her canoe that even in the current she could gain on it, and did, towing a full-grown man.

It took her a long minute to get up into the canoe and drag Gulbuk up as well. I marvelled at her skill and strength; I knew I'd never have been able to do it without capsizing the thing. Then I saw her turning him over, manipulating his arms, persuading him to cough up the chestful of water he'd taken in.

He coughed on his own a moment later. Then I heard him throwing up. In these circumstances, they were welcome noises.

My raft and I were now some fifteen paces north of them and we were both headed into the strait. I was nearly halfway across and could definitely make the crossing before the fastest waters caught me.

I finished blotting as much water as I could off myself, dressed myself again, and began rowing back toward Hopeless. A minute later, I heard Jenina's jeers following me: "Coward! Come back and fight!"

"You win, Jenina."

"I'll kill you next time!"

"Probably so."

For if I made the crossing today, it would be under Jenina's eye. She would turn out her followers and I might be found. Worse, the raft might be found and seized, or destroyed. It was best to let her think I'd been beaten back.

"Coward!"

Halleyne

Jenina was not in camp when I returned. That was no surprise; she'd spent most of her time the last few days in the canoe. I told those who had remained in camp to cook and repair what I'd seen of Daneeth Po.

After midday, Jenina and Gulbuk returned to camp. He was subdued, quieter even than usual. She was ebullient.

"Our first naval battle!" she cried. "And Turtlehead Island was victorious!"

In a few words, she told us of Kin attempting a raid in a large, preposterous raft and how she and Gulbuk had chased him away.

I did not let my feelings reach my face, but the news made me nearly dizzy. Kin alive, and trying to reach us!

"The Fishtailers now know they can't just come here with impunity," Jenina said. "We are sovereign. Next, we need to establish control of Hopeless and its resources. The melthue herds are ours. Let the Fishtailers starve next winter."

Silence greeted her statement. She glanced around angrily, doubtless looking for support for her plan.

I firmly set my feelings to the side. "I've been told that Leiala is dead," I said. And then in a few words I told her all the details of my encounter with Daneeth.

She thought about it. "Pity about Leiala," she said. "She was a good worker."

"If she's dead."

"You think Daneeth lied?"

"I think he's changed. Maybe he is mad. Maybe he lied. I think we need to know."

"We do. But we cannot afford to spare anyone to find out. We've lost both Daneeth and Leiala, and now we know that we have to defend our northwest shore from invasion."

"*Invasion?* We can't compare this threat we don't understand, whatever has become of Daneeth and Leiala, to the possibility of a mere visit from Judge Underbridge."

"True. We can't. Underbridge threatens everything we stand for. He'll trick people into going back with him and accepting King Jerno's rule. *We will never be ruled by Jerno again*, Halleyne. Do you understand?"

"Daneeth—"

"*Do you understand?*" She had her head down like a bull and glared at me as though she wanted to charge.

"Yes."

"If you want to find Leiala's body, you can look for it yourself. So long as all your other duties are done, that is." She turned her back on me.

The others were looking at me. I gave them a little shrug, a you-see-how-unreasonable-she-is gesture. If none of them yet felt there was enough reason to disagree with her, it was not yet time to cause a scene with her.

Kin

I timed it carefully. Just at dusk I set out again. Any sooner and spotters on the Turtlehead coast might see me. Any later and the air might get so cold that my movement would be impaired. It was dark enough as it was to kill me if I ran over any submerged rocks.

I rowed across the stretch of water just south of Treacherous Strait—a shorter distance than the one I'd tried to cross earlier, but still far enough from the strait opening that I thought I could beat the current.

A night crossing. It was an idiotic idea, but I had every reason to believe that any attempt to cross during the day would end up as today's effort had. Or worse.

So I rowed, fast and hard, hoping to have some of the last light available to me by the time I reached the Turtlehead shore.

I thought about the coldness of the water, the way it had leeched away all my strength. The way another minute or two might have leeched away even my will to live.

I thought of hungry fish and sharks, not that we had yet seen a shark in these waters, and of turbulence and reefs.

I thought of Jenina Morlin and what she would probably do to me if ever I came under her hand.

And I thought of Halleyne and kept at the oar.

Eventually I heard a noise over my clumsy thrashing about. I stopped rowing and could hear water lapping against stone, not far ahead.

But it was full dark. The moon gave me some light, little glints of edges of stone outcroppings ahead. There could have been fair beaches beneath the stone, but I couldn't see any sign of sand. So I turned due south, fighting the current, and tried to move along the shoreline.

The sound of something scraping along the underside of the raft froze me for a moment; I redoubled my efforts until the sound was done. I'd never be able to see in time if crucial cords and ropes had been frayed by the contact; perhaps the raft would split in half and I'd find myself suspended between the halves, unsuccessfully trying to control both.

The stony shore became trees, perhaps just as treacherous; then, before the ache in my arms became quite unbearable, I saw the jutting silhouettes of evergreens give way to glimmering sand.

Within moments I'd beached. I sprawled on the sand and rested.

But there would be no sleep here. If I left the raft exposed on the beach, it might be found by Jenina or her followers, and I'd never leave this island. After the ache in my muscles settled to a tolerable level, I rose again and moved to the trees I'd passed to reach the beach.

Moving slowly, ever mindful of snakes, slippery

stones, and sudden falls into the water, I traced the path of the shoreline along the trees. I did this mostly by stepping into water and discovering that that was how far up the waves came. Once I stepped into nothingness and would have fallen but for the tree bole I caught; that was how I found the tiny niche in the shore, overhung by branches, that became my raft's hiding place.

I shoved the raft back out and, wading waist-high in the chilling water, pushed it into that little niche and tied it off. Then, after a long time of sitting wrapped in my cloak and blanket while waiting for my legs to unfreeze, I spent quite a while tripping over roots and finding small branches I could break off and drape over the raft.

I could not see how effective my camouflage was, so I went by touch. As the moon climbed higher in the sky, I kept at this task, ranging farther afield, until I had assembled nearly enough branches to cover the craft. Once I lost track of where I'd hidden it and had to walk up and down the shore until I found it again.

By the time all was done, the night was half over. I was as tired as a farmhand and had worked a longer day. I walked and stumbled twenty paces inland from my raft and set up my bed.

It was a hedge against the snakes—a net hammock I'd made from cast-off strings, cords, pieces of rope, and scraps of melthue hide. It was awkward and ugly. But we had never seen sign that the burrowing vipers would climb trees, so I tied it off high and clambered into it. As I twisted and writhed in its grip to make sure my cloak and blanket were wrapped fully around me, I felt some of the strings snap; it sagged here and there as portions gave way under my weight. But when I was done, I still swung feet over the forest floor and felt that I was in no danger of breaking through.

That was my last conscious thought.

Halleyne

Raldan did not return from his fishing yesterday, nor did we find him among us when we awoke this morning.

"The snakes got another one," said Jenina. She heaved a sigh that looked like genuine regret. I supposed that she, like most of the women on Turtlehead and Fishtail, had liked the dark-haired, dark-eyed Raldan; he was both decorative and helpful.

This put me in a quandary. I knew what I wanted to do today: Get myself set up as the lookout on the northwest coast, so that I might "protect us from further invasion"—and give Kin clear passage in if he tried to reach the island again today. But I also knew what I *ought* to do: Find Daneeth, or Leiala, or Raldan, or all three if they were together.

Just this once, I opted to please myself. "I'll stand watch against the invaders."

Jenina shook her head. "The crew practicing in the canoe will do that."

"Then I'll join them."

"No . . . while there is immediate danger of Judge Underbridge returning, I want only real fighters on the canoe."

There are times I want to strangle her. But for me to try would do her little harm and me no good, so I smiled as though she'd granted me some useful wisdom. "Well, then, I'll hunt for crabs south of Bucketfish Bay."

"Was Leiala's bucket ever found?"

"Well, no." I looked around and spotted an object that might do. "I'll use Raldan's hood."

"Mind you don't get bitten like Leiala and Raldan."

"I won't.

"And if you run into Daneeth—"

"I won't run into him, I'll run from him."

"Good."

So I set out fully intending to be a complete failure at crab-catching. I would first try to head inland from where Leiala had disappeared to see if I could find trace of her. I took up one of the rough javelins Jenina had kept us working on last night to replace those *she* had lost, then headed off southward from our camp.

The day was bright, the sun almost enough to warm me as I walked. My path to Bucketfish Bay was well marked; in our weeks of occupancy of the island we had made quite a trail to the sites we commonly visited. So I was as comfortable as I could be in circumstances where I might find a deadly viper or dangerous madman around every bend.

And yet I felt edgy, as though I were under someone's scrutiny, and once I was out of sight of the encampment it occurred to me that Daneeth Po might not be waiting for me to find him.

I turned back. No one, except perhaps Jenina, would fault me for asking for company on the walk down to the bay.

Then I turned again toward my original destination. Ask someone to walk me to the shore? My companion would then need to leave to be about his business, leaving me alone anyway. There was no point in asking for protection that ultimately meant nothing. But I walked more slowly, as alertly as I could, on the long walk down to the bay, and I kept my hands firmly gripped on the clumsy javelin I'd taken.

At the northeastern edge of Bucketfish Bay, the trees come up beside the trail we'd made. I was especially careful there; those trees could have hidden a company of skulkers.

And yet as I came up on the last of the trees I felt a hand fall upon my shoulder.

I shrieked. Mind you, I hate women who shriek almost as much as I hate those who swoon; but a great wail of surprise and, yes, fear was out of me before I could contain it. I shrieked and swung around, wielding the little spear like a club, and I smacked my assailant across the jaw.

He fell down.

It was Kin.

Chapter Seventeen

Kin

It gave Halleyne pleasure to tell people that she knocked me out that day. It was funnier in the telling, but it wasn't true. Her blow caught me completely off-guard and I stumbled as I stepped back, so I fell. The blow was hard enough to daze me.

And she fell upon me, calling my name until I took hold of her and shook my head (an act more painful than helpful) and swore, "I'b noh dead, ih doesn'h hurh."

"Oh, gods, Kin, is it truly you?"

When first I'd seen her this morning, as I hid among the trees beyond the verge of their encampment, I'd felt my heart race. She was alive and well, in a position of some authority among the exiles, stronger and more beautiful than I'd ever seen her—even taking into account her trick with cosmetics. It was within my power to walk right up to her. And, of course, be attacked by Jenina and her followers. I decided against that tactic.

Now, with her in my arms, I swear I felt my heart

stop. I could not answer her, not with words. I looked at her a long moment while, she told me later, she tried to determine whether she'd knocked my brains loose.

Then, in spite of the pain in my jaw, I kissed her.

She made a little noise of surprise and kissed me back.

It was more than a kiss. In it were sweetness and desperation and longing and thankfulness.

And love, recognition of it no longer kept at bay by the fear that she was dead, that we would never meet again.

And a promise. When at long last we broke, and looked at one another in some measure of surprise, we both knew that the kiss had been barely a hint of what would come . . . later. "We have to get off the trail," she said.

"That would seem to be a good plan," I said. "It's hard and lumpy here."

She looked exasperated, more like her old self. "Others will be coming this way on their work assignments. We'll be seen." She stood and dragged me up, then led me into the trees.

When we were deep enough within them that we could no longer see the trail, we sat upon a fallen log not swarming with insects and wrapped our arms around one another.

She told me of her time on the island and of the events of the last few days. In turn, I told her of the changes on Fishtail, of the upturn in Shallia's spirits, of the snakes and what Doctor Ha had learned.

After a few moments of reflection, she said, "I think the snake that tried to bite me was doing Daneeth's bidding."

"He's no Bard, no sorcerer."

"Nevertheless, they were cooperating. It paid him no mind while it watched me. He had no fear of it. Perhaps Daneeth was doing *its* bidding." I felt her shudder. "I wish Shallia were here. There are Bardic ways to find people. She always swore she had little skill with them . . . but we are only a few people on Turtlehead. Maybe she could find Leiala."

"I want you to come back to Fishtail with me."

"I will! But not yet." She looked distressed. "Kin, all this confusion with the snakes, and Daneeth and Leiala and Raldan, and maybe even the admiral's walk that night are wrapped up together as tight as, as—"

"Snakes coupling," I suggested.

She grimaced. "I need to know, before I leave, what is happening. If I don't, it might get worse."

"For Jenina and the other rebels."

"And then us. And Kin, what if Leiala and Raldan are dead? Does Jenina deserve to die for what she's done? Does Gulbuk? How about the others? What if leaving now leads to their deaths?"

I sighed, defeated. "What do you want to do?"

"Look for Leiala and Raldan."

"Perhaps in an hour?"

She gave me a sweet, sympathetic smile but shook her head.

So we spent the morning walking. Tricky business that was: To stay away from the areas where the other rebels might be working, we had to avoid the trails they'd worn and paths they'd found in their weeks of exile.

Fortunately, I knew this island from my explorations with Teuper. "If Leiala disappeared from the south and you encountered Daneeth there, we may assume, for now, that he's hiding south of the narrow neck of the island," I told her. "The neck has Bucketfish Bay to the east, then the hilly rise your trail passes along; then on the west is more hillside, and the inlet to the sea. But between the two hills is a defile, like a little valley, and it does not sound from what you've said as though your islanders spend much time there."

"I've never heard it spoken of," she said.

So that was our path to the south: A little more distance inland through the trees, then southward to where the ground stayed level before us but rose to the east and west. This defile was very rocky and hard going, but it was not within sight of the Turtlehead pathways.

Ahead the ground rose into the central hills of this southern portion of the island. Teuper and I had spotted caves among those hills; I suggested that Daneeth might have made his shelter in one of them.

So we climbed up into the highest reaches southern Turtlehead had to offer. And when we were not negotiating dangerous rises, we held hands like the young lovers on the beaches of my home city, Bekalli.

From one of the highest and most southern hilltops we had an unimpeded view of most of the island, not to mention the more distant Hopeless and Fishtail. From this altitude it was such a pretty chain of islands, growing green as we approached the spring, hilly enough to be varied, the three islands ideally arranged to protect the blue water between them from the worst of summertime winds. The sea between the island would be a good place to sail for entertainment and practice.

I could even see little plumes of smoke rising from Fishtail, and imagined that they had the cookfires going for the midday meal. Halleyne and I shared my smoked melthue strips and wineskin water while we rested.

"What's that?" she asked, and pointed.

I followed her gaze. Farther north, toward the center of this southern portion of the island, there was a white scar on a hill slope.

No, several white scars, like angry gouges from the paw of the god of lions. "I don't know, but they were not there when Teuper and I were exploring."

"Some sort of plant growth, then?"

"White growth? Maybe. It looks more like incisions into the hillside, though. We'll go look when we've rested."

An hour later put us at the bottom of the hill slope where most of the scars were situated.

Up close, these hills were covered in grasses and shrubs, with few stone outcroppings, and the white scar material seemed to be unearthed dust. "Much like what they were finding deep in the soil on Fishtail," I said. "Closer to the surface here."

"So someone has been digging."

"Yes indeed."

I took a step up the slope, then thought better of it when I saw the first of the snake burrows. It was perhaps ten feet above us, just a little spot of inky blackness in the soil. It might have been a shadow from the rock above it, or a natural cleft, but then I saw another not three paces away, and another, and as I took the hillside into perspective I realized that there were countless holes on the slope before us.

Halleyne's grip tightened on my hand as she saw the same thing. She quickly looked behind us and around. "No snakes, though."

"I wonder why. We've seen no sign that they're night feeders, so they can't all be in their holes. Do they range so far afield for their food?"

"Perhaps they do. I've never seen such a concentration of burrows."

"Nor I."

"Do you want to leave?" she asked.

"Yes."

"I, too." But she took a tentative step up the slope. I followed, keeping my attention on the ground behind us.

We climbed the slope, carefully tracing a path that would not require us to put our hands to the ground or come within striking distance of any of the holes we saw.

We came to the first of the scars. It was a trail of ash and dust flung out from a hole in the slope—a hole made by a man using some sort of crude spade. The hole went five feet into the ground . . . and ended against a flat surface made up of cut stones.

"That's a wall," I said. And felt stupid for announcing the obvious. To cover my discomfiture, I began to squeeze into the hole.

"Kin, don't!"

"There are no burrows here," I said. In the dimness, I could only be *almost* sure that what I said was the truth.

It was definitely a wall shaped by man. The stones were cut and dressed, smooth as any made for the walls of Bekalli. They were of different sizes, but assembled with a great deal of skill . . . and no mortar. I tried to slide the tip of my knife between them and could drive it no farther than a fingertip's length.

I emerged with gray chalky dust all over me.

Halleyne gave me an odd look. "What?" I asked.

"That's how Daneeth looked the other day."

"Now we know how he got that way."

Farther up the slope, we came across several more small digs. Most ended against stone walls. But with two, the stone wall had a window or niche in it, easily large enough to accommodate a grown man; I saw only blackness beyond. In another case, the hole did not end; it just kept descending until distance and a bend hid its farther reaches.

But the biggest gash of all was still above us, and when we reached it we saw that he—for we had little doubt that this was Daneeth's work—had dug a sloping tunnel tall enough for me to stand upright in. This hole was driven a dozen feet into the ground and ended in a doorway, made up of stone like the wall and complete with a lintel. A more modern addition, a barrier of melthue hide, was tacked across it.

I looked back at Halleyne. From the tunnel opening, she shrugged. I could tell she wanted to be here no more than I, but had to know what lay beyond that curtain.

I reached out and swept it aside. It was dark beyond, with still air, and a faint odor of smoke.

"Have you a candle?" I asked. "Or anything I can burn for light?"

"No," she said. "Wait, yes. I can tear a page from my journal."

I heard her fumbling with the pouch that hung from her belt. I stepped in through the doorway; there was enough light from behind me that I should be able to see some of the chamber I was entering, and I could already see enough floor to know that no snakes were within striking distance of me.

No snakes. A pity I wasn't as alert for other dangers.

I woke up much, much later with my head throbbing, so sick to my stomach that I imagined for a moment that it was again the first few days aboard *Wave-Breaker*. But as my vision settled I found I was in no ship's cabin.

The walls seemed to be of ancient plaster, crumbling away from the sort of stones I was used to from our recent explorations. I could make them out with fair clarity by the light of the candle set before the hide-curtained entrance to the room.

I turned and saw Halleyne lying uncomfortably against the far wall. Her feet were bound, her arms were drawn up behind her and, I assumed, bound as well. Her eyes were closed.

Fear for her jerked me into motion. I sat upright, only to find that my own arms and legs were bound as well, by leather strips. My hands and feet were numb, and the limbs they were connected to were

cramped and awkward. I could also feel the source of
my headache, a greater throbbing near my left temple.

But my motion awoke Halleyne; her eyes opened.
"Kin! Are you—"

"Unhurt," I lied. I was groggy enough to be grateful for the wall beside me; I maneuvered around as best
I could with my legs bound and sat with my back to
the wall. "What hit me?"

"Daneeth," she said. She was keeping the pitch of
her voice low. "He was standing beside the entrance,
hit you with the butt of his javelin. He said he'd kill
you if I didn't come in . . ." Her voice broke on the
last word, and the fear behind her calm exterior showed
through.

"Oh, Halleyne." *Why couldn't you have run?* But,
to be fair, in her position I wouldn't have been able
to flee. I silently cursed Daneeth and whatever game
he was playing.

Perhaps my curse was a signal to him. He swept the
heavy curtain aside and entered the room: Thinner than
I remembered him, his cloak more ratty. He kept one
arm underneath it, moving it up and down across his
chest.

He smiled at me. On someone else it would have
been a friendly, hopeful smile. On him it seemed alien.
"Judge Kin. I hope you are well."

"Untie me and we'll see."

"I will. Soon." He entered. "I'm sorry I had to hit
you so hard. I did not know what you wanted."

"What do *you* want, Daneeth? And what is this
place?"

"A home," he said, in the tone of a man who'd never
had one before. "It was a home, long ago, for the men
of this island. And it will be again, now. Thanks to me.
And you."

"I don't understand."

He brought his arm from beneath his cloak. Wrapped

around it was one of the Gloriana vipers, as peaceful and content as a pampered cat. It looked indifferently at us as he stroked it with his free hand.

"I don't understand the whole thing myself," Daneeth said. There was still wonder in his tone. "What I have learned comes in little pictures. Images. Like dreams. Slowly I have assembled them, like a mosaic, into what I understand now.

"A long time ago there were the people, and the serpents, and their mutual goddess. On the island."

"On Turtlehead."

"No, *the* island." He was cross with me for a moment. "Turtlehead and Hopeless and Fishtail and all the rest. They were *one island.* And everything on it belonged to her. The serpent in the earth. The crawling fire. I don't know how to speak her name. The snakes can't tell me. I can't read the writing yet."

Halleyne spoke. "There's writing?"

"Oh, yes. Carved into many stones, painted onto many walls. Not this one. Since I don't know her name, I just do what the snakes do. I call her Mother."

"Of course." I felt a shudder ripple through me.

"A few men and women fought Mother. They were born the wrong way. They didn't care for the life of sacrifice. Some of them fled. Others profaned her rituals. She arose in anger and spit fire, then sank to cool and sleep. The last men killed one another. All dead, all dead." He rocked back and forth as if trying to encourage the snake to sleep.

"And you know this from the snakes."

"Yes. You will, too, soon enough. They aren't just snakes, you know. They're carriers of Mother's spirits. When they bite you, the spirits enter you. Talk to you. Return to Mother and speak into her dreams." He smiled. "She's waking up, slowly, slowly. The more she learns, the more she awakens. We have to be ready for her."

"Ready what way?" Halleyne asked.

"Willing to serve. Understanding the ways."

She paused a moment to phrase her next question. "Did you bring Leiala here to serve, to understand the ways?"

His smile grew broader and even more childlike. He nodded. "Yes! And to be my mate." His expression fell. "But she did not want to. She was willing to endure the pain and even die rather than be mine. So I asked whom she would prefer."

"Raldan," she said.

"Yes." He looked vaguely disappointed. "Always Raldan. I'll find another who will be my mate. Are you willing?"

"No," she said.

"I thought not." He shot me a disappointed look.

"Are they here?" I asked.

"Oh, yes. But I've told them not to talk. They're fresh from the fangs, so they dare not disobey, or the headaches will claim them. We don't want that."

"What does that mean?" I asked. "Fresh from the fangs?"

He didn't answer.

Halleyne again paused to consider a question. "Daneeth . . . you know about the night Admiral dar Ostaferion went for a walk."

"When he was dead, you mean."

"Yes."

"I know about it."

"Did the serpents have anything to do with that?"

"Oh, yes. Sadly so." He did look mournful. Whatever had happened to Daneeth, he seemed unable to keep his true emotions from his face. "Spirits, I told you. In with the venom. Connecting serpents to those they bite. Shared spirits, do you understand?"

"No."

"When the serpent lives and the man lives, they

share a spirit. There is talking between them, though others cannot hear it. But when one or the other is dead, there is no sharing."

"That makes sense," I admitted, as though I understood.

"But when both are dead, they are tied together again. The original spirits of both have fled, leaving only Mother's little spirit. They can act again as she wishes." He looked confused. "Mother is not awake, so she could not have called the admiral. But something did, so he walked. Had the serpent been intact, it would have come too." His expression became one of satisfaction. "That is how I know Mother will have her due. Some men will do her bidding. Some will refuse, and die, and when they have died we will sacrifice the life of the serpent, too. Then these stubborn men will serve anyway."

A shudder ripped through me. "Daneeth . . . you're the son of a man and a woman. Back in Lieda."

He nodded. "I remember."

"They wouldn't like this."

"They'll like it when I take Mother's servants back to Feyndala. Everyone in Lieda and Terosai will like it."

"Oh, gods. Daneeth, you're one of *us*."

"No. *You're* going to become one of *us*." Without another word, he turned and left us.

Halleyne and I looked at one another helplessly.

"Do you think you can get your hands free?" she whispered.

"Maybe if I'd started working on the bonds just after I was tied. But now my hands are numb. Maybe if I can scrape the bonds against something sharp . . ."

Daneeth reentered. This time the serpent was wound around his neck. In both hands he carried a bundle of items: I saw cooked or smoked fish, my water-skin, Halleyne's pouch, my cloak. This bundle he sat on the stone floor.

He unwound the serpent from around his neck. "This is my companion," he said. "She has no name that I could understand. I call her Hardaport because she curls to the left when frightened."

"How nice," I said.

"She *is* nice. We share thoughts and spirits, and she talks to Mother for me."

He brought the snake near Halleyne. She tried to draw away, but before she or I realized what was happening the snake struck, sinking its fangs into her ankle and then recoiling. Halleyne hissed from the pain and then glared at Daneeth. I'd told her that the bites were not necessarily fatal; I prayed to the gods that she remembered and was not enduring mortal fear.

Daneeth brought the snake to me. I kicked at him, but he swayed back from my clumsy effort and lunged at me while I was recovering my balance. I felt white, burning pain against my right cheek; then Daneeth and his pet were drawing back from me as well.

Dizziness swept over me. I slid over until I lay on my side, and my stomach lurched. But except for my cheek there was no pain.

And suddenly it didn't matter what I knew about the serpent venom. Fear swept through me that in spite of Doctor Ha's experiments, the stuff was deadly poison and we were both shortly to die. "Daneeth, you *bastard*."

"You'll repent saying that when you realize how much I like the two of you," he said. He wrapped his snake around his neck, then drew a knife.

My knife, I saw, and anger intruded on the alarm I felt. "What are you going to do with that, Daneeth?"

"Free you, of course." He addressed Halleyne. "Roll over. On your stomach."

Reluctantly, clumsily, she obeyed. He carefully leaned down and cut the bonds on her wrists. She put her hands on the floor and tried to roll over again, but her pale, bloodless hands couldn't take the pressure; she stayed where she was.

"Now you," he told me, and we repeated the actions. I then rolled onto on my back through sheer stubbornness, sat up in spite of the dizziness, and began rubbing my tingling hands together.

"I'm not letting you go," he said. "This is just to make you more comfortable. Let me show you." A step brought him to the doorway, and he swept aside the curtain there to reveal—

For a moment I imagined that the floor outside was made of a different variety of stone, one made up of geometric shapes that swayed as I watched. Then I realized that the stone was literally covered with a carpet of Gloriana vipers. They were a thick mass, keeping its shape, none of them spilling through into our little room. "Gods save us," I said.

"Mother will save you." Daneeth smiled. "I must leave now. I have things to do before dawn. I will be gone several hours, until dawn at least. If you do not try to leave, you will be safe, warm, and comfortable here. If you do try to leave . . . well, their venom *is* deadly when you've been struck enough times. Stay and live." He left again.

Chapter Eighteen

Kin

It took me several minutes to restore my hands to something like working order, and then only a matter of seconds to free my feet . . . for while Daneeth had relieved me of my knife, he had not taken Ardith Netter's. I retrieved it from my boot and sliced the bonds on my ankles and Halleyne's.

I couldn't blame him for the mistake. Weapons, other than crudely-made spears and clubs, were so rare among us that to have two steel knives was an unimaginable luxury, and one I would not have enjoyed had I not beaten Ardith.

I tucked the knife away. Two steps brought me to the doorway. I swept the curtain aside.

The carpet of serpents was still there. There had to be hundreds of the vipers, stretching up and down this corridor, which was lined with the dressed stone. The corridor dead-ended immediately to the left, and was some fifteen paces long to the right, before it turned away and out of my sight.

Scores of the serpents hissed at me as I looked at

them . . . and I felt my head begin to pound. This was different from the headache caused by Daneeth's blow; it was deeper, harsher.

I let the curtain swing back into place and stepped back. The headache subsided. I sat beside Halleyne and held her.

"You were right," she said at last. "I'm dizzy. But I do not feel too bad. I don't feel myself . . . slipping away."

My own dizziness was neither growing nor fading. And with it was a distant noise like surf breaking on a faraway shore, rising and ebbing. In it I thought I could hear faint words, whispers, queries I couldn't make out. It would be so easy just to sink into the sensation and listen to it all . . .

Halleyne closed her eyes and began humming. I recognized the tune, some lilting Terosai melody I'd first heard during the negotiations off Hanuman's Point. "You sound happy," I said.

She broke off for a moment. "I'm not," she said. Then she resumed her tune.

"It could be worse," I told her. "We're unbound. I'm armed. Daneeth is crazy. We have these advantages."

She nodded and kept humming.

I fell asleep then, without meaning to.

In my dream, I stood on the streets of Bekalli, except the capital city was somehow transplanted to Hopeless Island so the docks swarmed with melthues instead of seamen. A dirty street urchin was talking to me, asking what my role was. I was still valet then, so I talked of serving the King: Keeping distractions away, choosing attire appropriate to every occasion, teaching the ruler's children.

As I talked, the boy grew more and more excited, and offered me praise every time I described a new task. But eventually I grew tired of accumulating praises from the dirty boy and my answers became curt. He shot me a hurt look and wandered off to play with the melthues.

I saw one of the melthues finish loading crates onto a small merchantman. It came flopping down the ramp, onto the pier, and then up the road toward me. It waved as though it recognized me; then as it reached me, it reared up taller and higher than a real melthue could and planted a moist kiss upon my lips.

Surprise woke me. And again I was sitting against the wall of this subterranean prison.

Halleyne was leaning up against me, smiling, her face a fingerspan from mine, and her kiss still lingered on my lips.

The candle had burned down a fingerspan. I'd been asleep for a while, but not the whole night. At some point, she'd risen and laid my cloak out upon the floor.

"Through with your songs?" I asked.

She nodded.

I drew her to me and kissed her. Again she relaxed into my embrace; again, she held and kissed me with a strength and passion I never would have imagined in her. When at last we broke, and we did so only for air, desire lay heavy on both of us.

"This is scarcely the place and time," I said.

She shook her head a little sadly. "I know. But we may never have another. We may be dead tomorrow. Or . . . changed."

"You have convinced me."

We drew one another down onto the cloak and pulled at one another's clothes. In moments we were flesh to flesh, impatient with our need for one another, as dizzy with passion as we were with the venom in our veins.

And that was our lovemaking, on a cloak that offered too little protection from a stone floor, with only a leather curtain separating us from an audience of vipers, with poison in our blood. Halleyne was a virgin, but kept me from knowing of any pain she might have endured. And though I, through calculation and practice, could keep up with barracks boasts of wenches and conquests, I was a virgin too . . . a late bloomer in my military family.

And yet we transcended our inexperience and awkwardness, even the menace of our situation. The world became only the two of us, my cloak a magic carpet carrying us away from this serpents' tomb.

Afterwards, we held one another, inseparable and inextricable, while the candle burned its way toward dawn and Daneeth's return.

"I love you," I told her.

"I know," she said, and smiled.

"I have for a long time."

"I know."

"Stop smirking. If we live," I asked her, "will you be my wife?"

"No," she said.

"Why not?" Her words burned me more than the snake's bite ever had.

She laughed. "You're the only judge. There's no one else to marry us."

"Wretch. If we live and return to Feyndala, will you be my wife and come to live in Lieda with me?"

She was slow in answering. "Yes. But if we live and return to Feyndala, will you be my husband and come to live in Terosai with *me*?"

"I—" Give up my family and position, everything I'd ever known? Had she any idea of what she was asking me to do?

Well, yes. Just what I'd asked her to do.

I weighed two halves of my life on scales no one could see. "Yes, I will."

Her smile grew. "Come. I want to try something."

"So soon?"

"Put your clothes on."

"*On?*"

She suited action to words, rising from my clinging embrace to slip back into her garments. Grudgingly, I followed suit while she explained.

"What Daneeth said made sense to me," she said. "That night, I sang for spirits. My song found one. The spirit that had entered Admiral dar Ostaferion's body with the venom the day he died. It still occupied him. My song gave it reason to move his limbs."

"So he walked, and he came."

"So my song can affect the very spirits he spoke of. A little while ago, I tried to do just that. That's when I was humming."

"And?" I had my trousers and tunic on and was struggling into my boots.

"And . . . my song can keep them at bay. Hold their desires, their orders back. At least for a while. *Even the ones within us*, Kin."

I shot her a sharp glance. "You're certain?"

"I'm certain. I felt them. I spoke to them. I gently pushed them back. While I sing, while I push, they can do nothing to us. While you slept, I stepped out into the hall . . . and though it made me tired, the serpents there made way for me."

"No headaches?"

"None . . . unless I slip. Lose concentration."

I winced. "I won't have you killing yourself because of a slip in concentration."

"If we stay, we won't have to kill ourselves. Besides, the grip of the spirit within me has weakened. Perhaps it is because the venom is weakening. My hope is that I can keep the spirits at bay until their hold is too weak for us to worry about."

"Damn it. You're right." I finished up and rose to bundle our few possessions. "What about Leiala and Raldan?"

She shrugged. "If I were a Bard, maybe I could look

for them with a spell. As it is, we'll just have to look for them as we leave."

"All right. Are you ready?"

A stupid question. She was ready long before I was.

I picked up the candle and positioned myself beside the doorway. Halleyne began singing.

Her choice of music surprised me: "Drover of the Little Birds," a Liedan song. It tells of a real event, of some two centuries ago, when a plague descended on the swamp city of Naisley. The magicians determined that it was brought by mosquitoes from the swamp, but could do little for it but heal a small number of the afflicted and burn off the worst-infested areas of the swamp.

That is, until the somber Bard named Isbian came, saying he knew a way to lead the stinging insects away. He arranged for the city to pay his family; then he walked into the swamp and became infected. Through his magicks, he convinced the insects that he was one of them, their king, and let them forth, promising them a new land . . . but led them into fires set by farmers in their fields. The mosquitoes perished, and those that hatched subsequently followed the trail of magic to die in the fires as well.

Isbian did not enter the fire, but was left with a mind little more developed than that of the creatures he had commanded—the price he had to pay for leading them. The mages of Naisley could have cured his body of the plague but chose not to, letting him die a hero rather than live as less than a man.

A sober, haunting song. I prayed that Halleyne would not become too close to the minds of the creatures she commanded.

She sang the first verses, making sure of herself and the music, then nodded to me.

I pulled the curtain aside. The carpet of vipers still writhed there, and they hissed at me.

And—the vaguest pressure in my head, then none.

Halleyne stepped forward . . . and the leading edge of serpents retreated, curling away, hissing. I'd always doubted that snakes could express emotion with their features, but these seemed to demonstrate outrage as they were forced back by her magic and her song.

I walked as close to Halleyne as I could, timing my steps with hers. And slow steps they were, for the snakes could only be compelled to retreat at a sluggish rate.

We walked down the hall outside our prison room, the living carpet coiling around us, but never striking, never approaching within a pace of Halleyne as she kept up her song.

To the bend in the hall; it turned left, and we saw more doorways, all open. There were not so many serpents in this hall, but more were crawling toward us, alerted by whatever means to our jailbreak. Farther ahead, small patches of white ash discolored the stone floor.

Another ten paces through the ever-thickening carpet of reptiles . . . and the next doorway to the left was curtained, while the opening opposite it was a side hallway. I gestured to the curtain and she nodded; when we reached it, I swept the cloth aside.

Beyond, darkness. I waved my candle in.

It was a chamber much like Halleyne's and mine, but there was a cot. On it, curled together, were Leiala and Raldan. They looked sluggish, blinking sleepily at us.

"Get up," I said. "We're escaping."

They shook their heads.

"Damn it." We entered their chamber and I forcibly dragged them from their cot, insisted that they put on their boots and shoes *fast* while Halleyne stayed at the door. Still they shook their heads and would not speak, in spite of my protests that Halleyne was holding the spirits at bay.

I cursed, shoved Raldan down onto the cot, and picked Leiala up over my shoulder. She struggled, but feebly; I wondered how much venom was in her blood.

Raldan caught up to me as I reached the doorway; he grabbed Leiala and tried to pull her from my shoulder. But passive as he was—and smaller than I—he did no more than slow me. I got an arm around him, too, and dragged him forcibly out into the hall.

"You see?" I said. "You're not dead. There is no headache. Do you understand?"

Raldan looked dazed, still, but was considering what I said.

I looked around. The hallway we'd been following headed into deep blackness, but there was some light in the turnoff hallway, which was stained along its length with the white ash. I nodded for Halleyne to go that way and I dragged Raldan in that direction.

It was only a few more steps before he caught on and came willingly. I heard him clear his throat. "No headache," he said. "I can talk. Leiala. Try it."

The hallway bent a little before us. Past the bend, it was only a few more steps before it became filthy with the white ash and opened up into a larger room. Beyond, an opening led out onto a ramp of ash and dirt—the very one I'd just descended when Daneeth clobbered me. Beyond was a line of hills and the first signs of dawn.

"Put me down," Leiala said. I did, careful to set her well within the area Halleyne was keeping clear for us. The snakes still clustered around, a deepening mass of them, hissing in vexation as though their anger could keep us at bay. More were slithering in through the tunnel mouth as we watched.

I asked Halleyne, "Are you holding up?"

She nodded, concentrating. She was almost through the song's last chorus, and a moment later started over with the first stanza.

"Time to leave," I told the others.

With four walking in the same constricted space that had previously accommodated only two, we had to coordinate our steps especially well. A single slip could drop one of us onto the serpents . . . and Raldan, apparently suffering worse than the rest of us from the venom's effects, was prone to slipping. Leiala kept him upright as we marched out of the last chamber and up the treacherous ash slope to the hillside beyond.

Fresh air, the moon high overhead, the sun peeking up beyond the distant hills . . . and a slope full of serpents working their way up to us. Even so, we were less hampered than before, because the tunnel exit had acted as a bottleneck for the vipers, most of whom were behind us. We descended the hill slope, me with an arm on the distracted Halleyne to keep her from stumbling, Leiala doing the same for Raldan.

A score of paces down the hill, the ground was open enough that we didn't have to plant each step with the same excruciating care. Our pace increased.

"Stop!"

Daneeth Po emerged from another of the holes cut into the hillside. He and the snake he carried—and the spear in his hand—were covered with ash, but it didn't obscure his shocked, dismayed expression. I stooped to pick up a fist-sized rock.

"You can't go!" he cried. "We're not done. Why won't you do what you're told?" He came toward us, his spear up in one hand as if to throw.

I hurled the rock, a straight flight for his head.

Well . . . not so straight. It hit his arm and his serpent. He let out a shocked cry and fell back, rolling several paces down the hill slope. I grabbed up another rock and we continued.

He was up in a moment, backing away from us, stroking his precious viper. "I know what you're doing," he said. "They tell me. Your song protects you. It doesn't matter. You can protect three or four, but not everyone. We'll come for you."

We continued to pick up speed as we descended.

"Raldan and Leiala already belong to us!" Daneeth shouted after. "Do you know what they did?"

We ignored him.

"They did as they were told. They loved one another with the venom and the spirits in their veins, in the heart of Mother's temple of fertility. The child they have will be born the right way, will belong to Mother."

That stopped us cold. Leiala and Raldan bumped into my back as Halleyne and I looked at one another, dismayed, her song choking off.

The hiss snapped me out of it. I saw the viper curl for a stroke at Halleyne. I kicked at it; its fangs hit my boot leather, ejecting twin dribbles of poison, but my kick send the thing downslope. Halleyne stumbled on her lyrics a couple of times but quickly regained the tune, starting over at the song's beginning.

A few steps more and the slope was clear and level enough that we could run, even the barefooted Leiala and Raldan. We did, putting the hill and its madman behind us. We could still hear him shouting, "We'll come for you!"

We walked in silence for several minutes as daylight continued to spill out over us. There were snakes out, seemingly called even from a great distance to help prevent our escape, but we were cautious enough and they were rare enough that we avoided them with fair ease. We circled around mad Daneeth's hill and headed down into the defile by which we'd entered this part of Turtlehead.

"Is he telling the truth?" Leiala finally asked.

I looked at Halleyne. Her gaze was haunted. "I hope not," I said. "Perhaps no child will issue. Perhaps he was wrong. If he was right, perhaps we can find a remedy for the situation."

"We need to get you to your raft," Halleyne said.

"No, no. First, we get you to your encampment."

"Not with you among us! Jenina might have you put to death before we can convince her of what has happened."

"I doubt it."

"We can't chance it." We were at the far end of the defile now, rising into the trees that marked the northern portion of the island, and Halleyne began walking west with determination. I sighed and followed.

"Besides," she said, "you *have* to get back to Fishtail, and as fast as possible."

"Why?"

"Because our only real Bard is there. Because we may be spending the next days fighting off snakes—we won't have time to build the rafts we need to get off this godsforsaken island. You have to do that for us."

"*We?* Halleyne, you're coming with me."

Pain crossed her features, but she shook her head. "Raldan and Leiala won't be able to influence Jenina. I will. Without me, Daneeth may poison all the exiles before Jenina understands what is happening. I have to stay."

I looked at Raldan and Leiala—exhausted and obviously far more badly poisoned than we had been, and never the most assertive people under the best of circumstances. Then at Halleyne.

I was filled with anger at the exiles of this island: That they, just by being here, put Halleyne in danger. I weighed the value of their lives and found them to be worth little. But if I just carried Halleyne off . . . I knew she would never forgive me. I slumped, defeated.

She wrapped herself around me and kissed me. "I'm sorry, Kin."

"I, too."

It was midmorning by the time the four of us—stinking, exhausted, and far from through being scared—reached the stand of trees on whose coast I'd hidden my raft. I found it, unmolested, after a few more minutes of searching.

I drew Halleyne aside while the others rested. "I don't want you to take any risks."

She gave me a weary smile. "I won't."

"Don't even cook. You might poke yourself with a stirring-stick."

"Now you're being ridiculous."

"Because if when I come back *anything* has happened to you . . . I'll make them pay in the god-courts and the halls of hell."

She silenced me with an embrace and a kiss that seemed to last until dusk . . . though the sun had not moved when next I glanced at it.

Then I did what I least wanted to do in all the world. I kicked the concealing branches off my raft, cast off, pushed off from the shore with my oar . . . and watched my love wave goodbye as she grew smaller and smaller.

When I could no longer make her out among the trees, I turned and rowed as hard as I could with weary limbs toward Hopeless Island.

And for the first time since I was a child, I wept bitter tears.

Chapter Nineteen

Halleyne

"Kin Underbridge was on Turtlehead," Jenina said. She was already puffed up and head-down.

"Yes."

"And you let him go."

"Yes."

She slapped me. I wasn't entirely unprepared for it, so the blow did not stagger me. But it hurt. That, and the knowledge that I did not deserve it, and the certainty that I was sick of her and her bullying, made the world before me swim red.

I slapped her in return, as hard a blow as I could manage. It hurt my hand probably as much as it did her face, but the look of shock she gave me was a rich reward.

She came at me with her hands extended and I shouted, "Go ahead! Strangle me. When you die, you won't even know why."

Gulbuk stepped between us, facing her. Jenina made to shove past him but he did not let her. "Jenina," he said. "Let her talk."

"She's a traitor!"

"Maybe. Let her tell us why."

Jenina glared at him, then stepped back reluctantly.

So I rubbed the sting out of my cheek and told them all that had happened since Kin found me.

Well, not everything. Nothing of our lovemaking; it was none of their business, and it would give Jenina more reason to suspect me. Nor of that between Raldan and Leiala; that was none of their business . . . *yet*.

When I was done, Jenina gave me a harsh smile. "You've kept a secret all this time that you have some Bardic training."

"It wasn't worth much. Until today."

"So you admit you're a liar. And yet you really expect us to believe that Daneeth Po can command an army of snakes to come kill us."

"He's not in command," I told her. "He's just a soldier, like they are. Their . . . mother . . . is in command."

Mother. The word finally took me back to the way Shallia used to awaken from sleep. With her greater Bardic sensitivity, perhaps she'd had a sense early on of the original inhabitant of this island.

I hastily continued, "And, yes, I believe it. I've seen it." I gestured to Raldan and Leiala, who sat huddled beside the fire used to cook the midday meal. "They've seen it."

"They're hysterical. And you're a fool."

I opened my mouth to speak, but did not have to. With more energy than I would have guessed she still had, Leiala pushed herself to her feet and stalked up to Jenina. "*You're* the fool, Jenina. You don't have to kill us all to prove you're in charge. Halleyne's telling the truth. *They're coming for us.*"

More words than she'd ever spoken at a time since the shipwreck. Jenina just looked at her, her gaze meant to intimidate, but Leiala returned it.

"Very well," Jenina said. "Greffia, Bient, you know the part of the island she spoke of."

Bient nodded. "I've seen it from afar."

"Go there and tell me if what she says is true."

I moved up beside Leiala. "You're sending them to die. Or become what Daneeth wants them to be."

She looked at me. Her gaze was still intent, but it was different. Intimidating in a different way. I'd seen Kin stare at people that way when trying to burn a layer of lies and fabrications from the truth underneath. "You really think so," she said.

"Yes."

"Greffin, Bient, belay that." She moved past me and took up her spear. "I'll go myself."

"Then *you'll* die."

"That's what you want, isn't it?" She turned her back on me and left.

We all watched her go . . . then the eyes of the others turned on me. "What now?" asked Gulbuk.

"Half of us will set up all the lean-tos we can manage on the beach," I said. "We'll sleep there tonight. It will be easier to see snakes crawling across those light sands by moonlight and torchlight. The rest of you, go out and bring in everybody working across the island. From now until we can leave, we'll live off stores and what we can fish from Marille Lake."

Gulbuk looked dubious. "Why don't we go to the north shore and use the canoe to cross to Hopeless?"

"It barely seats two, and is so heavy it takes two to paddle. Not all of us are as strong as you are, Gulbuk. In fact, only you are. You're the only one of us who could act as ferryman. How many trips across Treacherous Strait do you think you could make?"

He shrugged. "A few every day."

"And in the meantime, we set up camp on that shore with all its rocks and crags and places for snakes to hide . . ."

"Never mind. You're right." He sighed. "I'll bring in the fishermen from Bucketfish Bay."

In minutes, I had those who'd come in for midday meal to go out and gather those who hadn't. The rest of us began dragging sleeping goods, food stores, clothes and weapons out from the new long huts . . . and were painstakingly cautious against the possibility of snakes as we did so.

But all these plans, all this watchfulness I accomplished by habit. Mostly, I thought about Kin. About him rowing for safety on that laughable excuse for a raft. About our time together in that dismal prison.

I prayed for him, and bargained with the gods to keep him safe on his voyage. And I found a little time to write these words . . . for all that I will ever be able to read them, with tears staining the pages.

Halleyne

The words above were written two days ago; it has been that long since I put quill to paper. Much has happened since then.

By dusk, Jenina still had not returned, nor had Baltrion, a Terosai sailor who had become Gulbuk's good friend; he was supposed to be hunting, and it would be nearly impossible to find all the places he'd been today.

We had moved our gear, the fires, and all the sleeping rolls and lean-tos to the beach and had set up a perimeter of poles for torches. It might be a cold night, but I doubted crawling serpents could reach us unseen . . . and they would have to burrow some considerable distance in order to dig their way up from underneath.

"Baltrion!" called Gulbuk. And there the sailor came, emerging from twilight's gloom, the bag holding his day's catch slung over his shoulder.

I sighed in relief. Now only one was missing. And in spite of her words, I did not want Jenina to be out there dead or in Daneeth's hands.

Gulbuk walked toward his friend, to take his burden—

"Get back!" I shrieked.

I'm not certain what warned me. Some oddness in the sailor's walk, some stiffness in his pose. But suddenly I was sprinting toward Gulbuk, telling him to stand back, shouting at the others to arm themselves.

Baltrion flung his bag at me. It was not tied shut and living serpents spilled out of it as it flew. I turned away, wrenching my side, and one of the serpents landed across my leg. Before it could strike I leaped away. It came crawling after me across the sand.

A dozen serpents were among us. There was shouting and confusion; I backed away from the snake pursuing me until I was almost in the fire, then snatched up a brand and beat the viper with it. I only swung when its neck was at extension, and after three good blows it lay still. I was through with it twenty blows later.

Only then could I look up. Men and women were running around the camp, striking at serpents and at shadows on the ground. Gulbuk rolled across the sand, locked in his struggle with Baltrion, and I saw with horror that there was a serpent among them, too, and it struck Gulbuk time after time.

More than thirty people, less than twenty snakes. A whisper like one of Kin's analytical thoughts brushed the back of my mind. I turned away from Gulbuk's fight and looked out across the beach.

There they came, another swarm of snakes, emerging from the grasses at beach's edge, crawling toward the line of torches we had set up. Unseen by all but me.

I took my torch toward the line. Before me, Raldan beat another serpent into a bloody mess. It was long dead. I seized his ear and shouted, "Look!"

He did. He blanched. He joined me at the torch line, a brand in his hand, and his shouts alerted others.

So we were a dozen at our line before the snakes reached us. We hammered at them with clubs, spears, and torches as they came within range. And though whoever directed them knew enough of tactics to arrange a distraction, he had not imparted any tactical skills to the serpents; instead of some of them racing through our lines and falling upon us from the rear, they all stopped at the line to hiss and strike . . . and die. I battered a second snake dead, my torch burning its beautiful hide, and hammered at a third while sheer terror within me was replaced by simple, reasonable, desperation.

In moments, we were joined by another dozen men and women. Some were reduced to throwing rocks and handfuls of sand at our attackers. But even that helped.

The serpents never retreated. More spilled out from the underbrush. We destroyed them. And only one of us, Bient, was bitten.

I saw the bite land, saw him back away from the line, his face stricken. I also backed away and let Greffia step over to fill the hole I'd left. "Don't fight it!" I told him. "Don't be afraid. It won't kill you if you don't resist."

He looked at me with fear and stumbled, sitting down. "Don't let it kill me."

"I won't. Don't fight it. Tell me everything that comes into your mind. You'll be well." I pushed him prone and took the club from his hand.

"Nothing. Nothing in my mind."

Under other circumstances, I would have laughed. But he was in mortal fear, and shook with it as he lay there.

I spared a glance for Gulbuk. Raldan was with him, and had pinned Baltrion to the ground with a spear. I saw him lean into it, driving the spear deep into

Baltrion's chest, but the man kept thrashing and fighting. Gulbuk held him down, and even in the torchlight I could see tears glittering on Gulbuk's cheeks.

In minutes it was over. Leiala directed the others to throw the bodies of the serpents into the fires, and soon the beach stank with burning meat and flesh.

And still Baltrion fought. Any man would have tired by now, but not him. Other men gathered around the fight, and there was a discussion I could not hear. Raldan had someone take his spear. He ran to his pile of possessions, then returned . . . with one of the stone axes they'd used to make the canoe.

I turned away as they took Baltrion to pieces.

I had Greffia relieve me and care for Bient. I instructed her quickly in what she needed to do, what she needed to say to him. Then I joined Gulbuk where he sat, yards from the bloody rubbish that had been his friend, his back to the carnage. Tears rolled unheeded down his face.

"He wouldn't stop," he said.

"He couldn't. He was no longer your friend, Gulbuk. His spirit had already fled to its new home."

He bowed his head. "I will join him soon. The snake bit me again and again."

Reluctantly, I looked again at Baltrion's body parts. The torso still moved a little. So did another piece, pinned to the ground by a javelin; I recognized it as the snake.

"The viper was dead, too," I told him. "I'll try to find out what that means for you."

So I sang to him. Not the depressing tale of Isbian, for all its resonance with this situation. I sang a lullaby of a bird watching over a baby, and use its rhythm and meter to compose my thoughts.

I felt for serpent spirits. I could detect none within Gulbuk.

"I don't know what the dead venom will to do you,"

I told him. "Or even if it injected any. Go to your bedroll and rest. Whatever you feel, whatever thoughts you have, tell me. I must know, for your sake and ours."

"I'm going to kill him."

"Daneeth?"

"Daneeth. That's my only thought. Kill Daneeth. I'll do to him . . . what we did to Baltrion. While he still lives." He wiped tears from his face and went to do as I told him.

Chapter Twenty

Kin

I beached on the northern point of Fishtail Island and walked to the village.

Walked? Staggered, really. How much sleep had I had in the day it took me to make the crossing? How much rest? I couldn't remember. All I could recall was desperation and Halleyne.

The first person I met was a Terosai man whose name I couldn't even remember; he tried to show me the string of fish he'd caught this morning, but saw my face and fell back from me, not speaking.

"Bring everyone to the throne room," I told him. My voice was dull with exhaustion, but he understood.

I told the next person I saw, and the next. And I walked so slowly that as I reached the village proper, I could see the word spread ahead of me like a ripple in a pond.

Shallia caught up to me before I'd quite reached the stream separating Terosai from Liedan. "Kin! Is she alive?"

"I hope so," I said. I think my expression discouraged further questions; she merely helped me to the King's hut.

People were already gathering. It would be some little time before everyone assembled from their disparate work assignments. I leaned on Jerno's throne and thought about what I would say.

And then he was there, the King, looking me over. "Kin, you seem . . . weary."

"I am."

"Oh." He thought about it. "Sit, then. Take my chair."

I would have snorted had I had the energy. *My chair.* No one sat on the King's throne. But I did, grateful for the respite.

They filed in, the citizens of Fishtail, in their twos and threes. They were curious about the summons, and more curious when they saw my condition.

When I counted nearly fifty of them, I told them the story. I was short with words and, I think, long with emotion. I don't remember exactly what I said about Daneeth Po and the snakes. I do remember the looks of worry, of fright that crossed their faces. Of recognition on Shallia's.

"What do you propose we do?" asked Queen Lia.

"Build rafts; we can lose a few days and eat the last of the stored meats. Then we go and fetch them from Turtlehead. And, if we can . . . do something about Daneeth. And his Mother."

That caused a burst of murmuring. Men did not set out to do things about the gods, after all. Or even dark spirits deep in the earth.

Queen Lia put on her reasonable face. "Judge Underbridge, they chose to leave. Let them manage their own affairs."

"No," I said. "Anything else?"

She was startled by my brevity and just stood, staring. There were no more complaints.

Shallia came up to take my hands. "You're half-dead," she said. "You're going to your hut."

"I haven't made the assignments."

"I'll do that."

That was the last I remember of that day.

But I awoke, come dawn, on my own cot, so sore of muscle that I could barely move, yet more clear-headed than I had any right to be.

No sounds of industry; had they disregarded my wishes?

I dressed and took up the crude spear I'd never had occasion to use; now it served me as a walking-stick. I leaned heavily on it as I walked through the village.

The deserted village.

Priests sometimes talk about the hells, a variety of dark places for your spirit to end up when you die. They suggest that some are shaped to your life, the better to agonize you through eternity. Could I have died there on the throne and found myself in an island hell, full of places familiar to me but no human being to talk to? No Halleyne?

I poked into hut after hut, on both sides of the river, and found no one. Until I peered into Queen Lia's.

She was there with her sole serving-maid, weaving bits of cord into rope; they started as I entered. "Have you no manners?" the Queen shrieked.

"Are you sharing hell with me?"

"What?"

"Where are the others?"

She waved a dismissive hand. "Up at Duckhead, of course. About your fool errand. Get out."

"What's the rope for?"

"Your rafts, of course. *Get out.*"

I did, shaking my head. I was not sure what convinced her to share in the work . . . though it was no surprise that she'd do so among the comforts of her own hut.

It was a long walk back to where I'd left the raft, and long before I reached it I heard sounds of carpentry: Hammering, men and women singing work songs. Missing were the sounds of saws, but then, we had none.

The northern beach where I'd left my raft was littered with workers. I saw at least thirty at work, and more dragging in logs and headed back to the forest verge for more. The workers waved as I approached; some cursed and made as if to hurl their hammers, but it was in good humor.

Four complete rafts, in addition to my old one, stood assembled on the shore. They were larger and far better than the crude thing Nerrin, Shallia, and I had made, being fitted and lashed together with something like competence.

And—it brought me to a halt as I understood what I was seeing—the King and Garris Bricker stood working together, driving stone wedges into logs and splitting them with blows of their hammers. I saw it was a competition between them, each trying to split his log with the fewest strokes . . . and the King was winning.

Nerrin Axer trotted up to join me. "Not a bad day's work, eh?"

"One day? I was about to ask how long I'd slept."

"One day. It helped that we had sailors working with us this time. People who know something about watercraft. You're lucky you weren't here for the howls of laughter our raft produced in them."

"How did you put the King to work?"

"I suggested that if he worked, Herself might feel obliged to do so, in order that Terosalle not be unrepresented."

I snorted. "You're getting too good at this."

"No." His tone was thoughtful. "It didn't fool him, Kin. Something is at work in him. Really, he decided to help for his own reasons . . . and yet used my reasoning as an excuse."

I walked among the work-crews. Four more rafts were under construction. "Eight," Nerrin said, "will be enough for us to bring everyone off Turtlehead. And to have two or three rowers per raft going across."

"Nine, you mean."

"Eight. No one will put to sea on our first one." He shrugged. "It's served its purpose, Kin. Let it die in peace."

Halleyne

Bient suffered few ill effects from his bite. He raved a bit, about his work assignments, but fell into a good sleep by midnight.

Gulbuk became very sick that night and threw up until he had nothing left to expel. He stayed sick. But he complained of no headaches. The next morning, though weak, he seemed to be past the worst of it.

Not me. Perhaps it was a reaction to Gulbuk's illness, but I slept from past midnight until dawn, and then woke up sick myself. After my stomach emptied, it refused to be refilled; even the smell of the morning meal, another day of fish stew, made me queasy.

Some long-term effect of the venom was affecting me, too. I wondered if Kin was as sick as I. But he was bigger, and Maydellan Ha said the venom did more to those of us who were small. I hoped the single bite would not be so bad for him.

Midmorning, Jenina came back to camp. Long-sighted Raldan spotted her coming up the beach and called a warning. Half the camp turned out to present the points of their spears to her.

"Stand off," Raldan called, "and be identified." A traditional sailor's challenge.

Jenina should have been infuriated. Her garments, more tattered than they'd been yesterday, and scrapes on her arms and legs suggested that she hadn't had a good night, which should have made it worse. But she just dropped her spear, with a bit of her usual irritability, and extended her hands to us, palms up. "I haven't been bitten," she said.

Raldan and I walked out to check her. He looked her over for bites. I sang my lullaby. There was no sign of serpent-spirits in her.

Once inside our safe perimeter, a mug of nause-ating-smelling stew in her hands, she explained. "I made my way to the next hill over from the scarred one. Watched it from my vantage point. Had to kill a couple of snakes." She grimaced. "Saw Daneeth Po hauling Baltrion's body up to his hole. Saw them both come walking out of there near dusk . . . followed by all the snakes in the world." She shuddered, then looked at me. "What have you decided in my absence?"

"To hope Kin and the others will come to take us back to Fishtail."

She looked away, surly. "I won't live under that man's rule."

"Then don't. Are you going to stop the rest of us from doing so?"

She took long swallows of her stew. Finally: "No."

"We have a task cut out for us. It will be days before they can reach us. We gathered up all the firewood we could yesterday, but we'll have to marshal our reserves if we're to have fires and torches every night. Prowling through the trees makes us too vulnerable to snakes."

She shook her head. "Green will do. Your Kin will have to come by sea, so we'll have to make our way down the river from the lake. True?"

"True."

"So we assign a work-crew to choose which bank to take. It's only a few minutes' walk to the sea, but there are too many places where snakes could spring out at us. The work-crew clears it as much as they can. Knocks down branches for our fires. Burns off underbrush when it comes too close to the bank. Makes it less bloody dangerous when we have to leave."

"A good point. I hadn't thought that far."

She drained her bowl. "I'm tired. I'll stay in camp unless you know of something only I can do."

"Go sleep."

An odd mania fell over the camp that day.

The fishermen, limited to Marille Lake, worked its banks with desperate energy. Most were spear-fishermen and, throughout the day, stabbed the lake as though it were a hated enemy.

Gulbuk appropriated two whole melthue hides and had begun cutting them before I knew what he was about. Then he explained his purpose to me.

"That is a good way to die," I told him.

"I don't care," he said.

So I helped him pattern and cut heavy leather pants from the hides. That, and stitching them together with our crude tools, took the two of us the better part of the day.

And all the while, we could feel, sometimes hear, the snakes massing out there in the underbrush. The work crew assigned to clearing one of the river banks reported many aborted attacks on them by snakes. The creatures recoiled from torches and fled from spear-thrusts, but there were no five minutes strung together without a snake attack. The work crew got away unscathed, by virtue of keen sight and desperate alertness . . . but they came back exhausted and only partly finished.

Kin

Not long after dawn, we pushed off. Eight rafts, twenty-four rowers . . . but I get ahead of myself.

At dawn, we had our final gathering in the throne room: the crew chosen for the rafts, the King and Queen, bodyguards, planners—over half our population. "Nerrin and Shallia, again, you're in charge while I'm away."

Shallia shook her head. "I'm going. As a Bard—well, partly—I can be of help. Do things no one else can."

"True. All right. Nerrin, you're in charge."

"If Shallia goes, I go."

"You're needed here."

"Then Shallia stays."

She shook her head. "I'm going."

In the silence that followed, King Jerno said, "I'll do it."

I looked at him. "Do what?"

"Organize things. While you're away. I have some practice at it, after all."

Queen Lia made a noise like a cat that had been stepped on. "Again with this. The Terosai will never accept Liedan rule. Not even your 'organization.'"

He regarded her levelly. "Then it won't be Liedan rule. I will govern . . . as Kin's subordinate. If he does not return, the populace can choose another Judge."

I can't describe the hush that fell over the assembly. I did not even hear breathing.

The Queen regarded him with suspicion. "You'd relinquish power?"

"In Lieda, no. Here, yes." He glanced at Shallia with something like embarrassment, then returned his gaze to the Queen. "It would work even better if you and I did this together. Perhaps only to prove we can."

She considered. "What terms do you offer?"

"Simplest is best. Two votes, yours and mine. When we can't agree, nothing gets done."

I opened my mouth to interrupt, then realized that this was the first real negotiation between the rulers since our shipwreck. I stayed silent.

"Done," she said.

They both looked at me. Suddenly I was allowed back into the royal presence.

I cleared my throat. "Very well, then. While I am gone, Lia and Jerno govern in my stead." I saw her eyes flash as I omitted her title, but she said nothing. "If I fail to return, the populace may choose its next . . . townsman." No greater title would have been appropriate.

There was a relieved nodding of heads and smattering of applause.

Then we walked to the beach and launched, an invasion force of twenty-four castaways.

Halleyne

The camp awoke in good spirits, surprised that no evil had befallen us during the night. The sun came up over the forest and the lake, a dim glimmer beneath the fog that clung to the ground in long tatters and rolled with oily undulations over lake and sea.

And then the snakes came out from south, west, and north, the entire land approach to our beach. They crawled at us in their hundreds, perhaps thousands, a living flood of green. We seized our weapons and sprang to defend ourselves.

The snakes reached our lines and began to die. Since the last encounter, we'd made more weapons suited to their disposal, especially short spears with forked ends that took a terrible toll on the serpents. In the first minute of that assault, not one of them passed our line.

It was our very success that made me suspicious. Daneeth had been capable last time of at least a crude distraction. Why this simple assault now?

I looked back over the line of approach the snakes could not take—the lake itself—and saw our canoe. It emerged from the glare of dawn and the mist over the lake. It moved slowly, apparently guided by no man, toward the beach behind us. It looked like a whole log again, with no cavity.

Then my vision cleared. Daneeth was in the water behind the canoe, pushing it, and it seemed whole because its cavity was filled nearly to overflowing with serpents.

My yell alerted the line. Jenina and Gulbuk, not hesitating, dropped out of the battle and splashed out into the water. I saw Daneeth's face contort with anger; he gave the canoe a final shove and then swam away.

Jenina reached the canoe. She grabbed its bow and heaved, slowly tipping the thing partway over. A serpent struck at her and she was forced back; but her motion had stopped the craft's forward progress. And Gulbuk, swimming hard and fast for Daneeth, stopped to give the canoe's side a final shove, capsizing the thing.

We found out then, for certain, that the Gloriana vipers could not swim. Gulbuk and Jenina backed away from the spill of serpents and watched them thrash in fury and terror as they sank and died.

Daneeth made good use of Gulbuk's distraction. He was lost in the morning lake mist before Gulbuk could return to the chase.

I returned my attention to the line. This time, the serpents fled not long after Daneeth did, leaving behind hundreds of their slain kin.

Chapter Twenty-One

Kin

Rowing three to a raft was faster and much easier than going it alone. By nightfall, we'd beached at the point we'd be jumping off across Treacherous Strait, all of us in fair shape. We could even post guards through the night to keep an eye open for serpents, and I was awakened twice by the sound of crunching and chopping as they found one.

Again, we set out at dawn and crossed over some distance from the strongest point of the strait. There was no sign or marker on the Turtlehead shore; Halleyne had promised to leave one, and a note with it, if they were to be found anywhere but the encampment on Marille Lake. Of course, Daneeth could have found and removed such a marker, and that worry gnawed at me.

Staying as close as we dared to the Turtlehead shore, we poled into the strait, letting the current take us north, and needed only use our oars to steer. Then came the long stretch, around the north tip of the island, then down the long shore southeast.

Late in the day, weary, we rounded the final promontory and in the distance could see where Marille's stream let out into the sea. We beached not far from there.

"What now?" asked Nerrin.

"Up to the lake."

"By foot or raft?"

"Foot, I think. I'm not sure the stream is navigable by raft, and foot is much faster."

He made a face. "It's almost dark."

"I know. But I want them to know *tonight* that relief is at hand."

I made ready to set off. Nerrin, Shallia and Viriat joined me. We all carried spears.

Within a couple of minutes of travel upstream, it became obvious that the people of Turtlehead had been working on one of the banks, clearing it. We splashed over to that side and our pace picked up; even in the growing gloom, we'd be able to see serpents crawling out at us.

And they did come, one every forty or fifty paces. They seemed to have no sense of self-preservation, and this dedication to our destruction, so unlike the behavior of a normal serpent, was chilling.

We'd racked up a count of thirty-two dead snakes by the time the bank opened up into a beach and the lake lay before us. On the opposite side I saw a main fire and a line of torches, people walking before them and being silhouetted—they had survived.

In a minute we were among them. I fell upon Halleyne, half-crushing her, while my companions and the people of Turtlehead laughed.

She beamed at me. "It's nice to be able to do that in public."

"Oh, be quiet."

They sat us down, gave us some of their dwindling supply of fish stew, and told us of the attacks—wave after wave of serpents over the last few days. Every one accompanied by some sort of trick or diversion. So far, Halleyne and Jenina had outthought Daneeth at every turn, but the fear was rising in them that he would grow more clever.

"He knows you're here," Jenina said. "The serpents are his eyes."

"He'll have a nasty surprise if he attacks our rafts," I told her. "We brought melthue oil, quite a lot, and they're digging a little trench in the sand around the rafts. If the serpents attack, they'll crawl into a literal wall of fire."

Her expression brightened. "I don't suppose you brought any—"

"Viriat, Nerrin?" The Axer brothers swung down their packs and produced several wineskins full of the stuff we'd been using for lamp oil. Jenina gratefully handed it out to the guards on duty.

I saw that the people of Turtlehead were weary, but they were not defeated; our arrival seemed to have given them hope on top of the combatative edge they already had.

I asked Jenina, "You've doubtless given this some thought. How, precisely, do you plan to get your people to the beach?"

"On foot on the north river bank when we can, for speed," she said. "If the serpents press, we take to the water. We've spent some time the last few days making those who can't swim or are afraid of the water splash along the shallows, getting used to it. The canoe will bring up the rear; if we have any injured, we can put them in it and push the canoe. Pray to the gods we have no more than two or three injured."

And when none but Halleyne was around to hear, I told Jenina, "Your anger at me seems to have . . . well, dwindled."

The look she gave me was frank, and there was still

some hostility in it. "You surprised me," she said. "You showed up." Then she rose and left us.

That night, Halleyne and I slept in one another's arms for the first time. In full view of the camp, we could do no more than that . . . yet it was the best and most restful sleep I'd had since leaving Lieda months ago.

I awoke some two hours before dawn, alerted by some distant cry. I could see the guards at the torch line; they looked to the east, discussing the noise among themselves. There was a little glow above the treeline. So the snakes had attacked our rafts. But this was nothing I could do anything about, so I fell asleep again.

Shortly after dawn, I awoke to singing. Halleyne's sweet voice and Shallia's better-trained one, a lullaby. I smiled and rolled over to look.

They sat on the sand with a Gloriana viper between them, in easy striking distance of both.

A chill like a runoff stream went through me. But the snake was still. Of the people gathered around the two singers, some wore expressions of fear and hate; others were merely intrigued.

I dared not jump up and run over to stomp the snake to death; I didn't want to interrupt the singers' concentration. But, thankfully, the song ended moments later. The two women nodded at Gulbuk, who, with greater nerve than I could have managed, reached to pick the snake up by the head . . . and twisted its neck, killing it instantly. I saw something like regret cross Shallia's features.

Halleyne saw I was awake and joined me. "What was all that about?" I asked.

"Shallia had an idea. She'd sung animals to sleep before. Including grass snakes."

"Where did you get the viper?"

"Gulbuk. He walked out into the brush with his leather pants on and grabbed the first one that tried to bite him."

"Madman. Is the camp readying itself to go?"

"Yes."

Something in her tone turned that into a *Yes, but . . .*

"What?" I asked.

She didn't want to meet my gaze. "We had an idea."

"What?"

"Shallia? Gulbuk? Jenina?" They joined us.

"The snakes are going to attack along the river bank," Jenina said. "As I said last night, our people will take to the water when that happens, return to the bank when it's clear."

"I understand."

"I'm sure that Daneeth will be watching. And he'll have many, many of his serpents there."

"Yes."

"So our Bardlings want to go to their Mother's citadel while Daneeth and the serpents are about it."

I looked at Shallia and Halleyne. "You're crazy."

Shallia shook her head. "Between us, we can sing the snakes to sleep. With two of us ... and a stronger song ... the vipers won't cluster so closely. But I want to see if we can sing their Mother back to sleep. From that habitation, which has to resonate with her presence and her energy."

"Shallia, no. Let's just leave. Go back to Fishtail and kill every serpent there. Let them do whatever they want here."

Halleyne said, "But Daneeth told us that their Mother was awakening. What will happen when she is fully awake? Another disaster like the one that befell the men here a long time ago? Or maybe the serpents will simply be directed by something with intelligence. Can we afford that?"

I looked between them. They'd already made up their minds.

"Just exactly when did I lose control of this mission?" I asked.

They smiled, and Shallia said, "When you brought the two Bards-in-training together."

"Of course."

I turned command of the exodus over to Viriat Axer. The party raiding the serpent habitat was to consist of me, Halleyne, Shallia, Nerrin, Jenina, and Gulbuk. Six against a mountain of snakes and their mother.

The people of Turtlehead packed, made sure their weapons were as sharp and ready as they could be, and prepared to go. The six of us did the same. As the mass of exiles headed off toward what we hoped was safety, the six of us accompanied them . . . then gradually slipped off to the side of the company and splashed out into the lake water. Soon we were standing up to our necks in water, holding our possessions (and Gulbuk holding his ridiculous leather pants) over our heads, concealed by the morning mist.

We waited there until Jenina decided by their sound that the main party was past the lake and headed out along the stream. "Let's go," she said. Then, pained, she looked at me.

"That's all right," I said. "You're not among enemies. You take charge of getting us there."

She nodded. "Let's go," she repeated, and suited action to words, wading back toward the bank.

At first, it was ridiculously easy. As stealthily as we could, we headed out along the main work trail from the encampment. The clinging morning mist helped. We didn't see our first serpent until we were nearly to Bucketfish Bay, and Gulbuk killed it without breaking stride.

We didn't see another until we were in the defile leading to Daneeth's hill. Then there was not just one, but several, crawling from burrows in a concerted effort to get to us.

Gulbuk stepped forward but Shallia restrained him. She began singing, the absurd lullaby about the watchful bird again, and Halleyne joined in.

And, one by one, as they neared us, the snakes lowered their heads to the soil and became still. We walked past.

Shallia and Halleyne kept the song up as we continued to Daneeth's hill. I can't count the number of times they repeated it, and I became so sick of hearing it that I swore no one would ever sing it in my presence again.

When we reached the base of that hill the serpents swarmed out at us in earnest. They came no closer than four paces before the song claimed them. Then, the most difficult trick was picking our way among their sleeping forms as we climbed the slope.

Jenina said, "I don't understand how there can be so many. I've seen no shortage of mits on the island. Wouldn't so many snakes clear out their prey, then die themselves?"

"You'd think so," I said.

"Then they must eat something else."

We reached the entrance to Daneeth's dig without incident. I used my flint and steel to light the torches we'd brought and we entered.

It was as we remembered it, except the snakes were not so numerous . . . and were asleep as soon as they came near. Our progress was slowed, though, by our need to use spears to shove the sleeping bodies aside; we did not trust the vipers to stay asleep if we stepped on them.

And then it was time to search the temples of the snake-mother.

Halleyne

Long before we entered the hill, I envied Shallia her vocal training. Oh, not because her singing was so much better qualitatively than mine—because it gave her

voice greater durability. I began to grow hoarse long
before she did. She squeezed my hand as encouragement, and I resolved that I'd keep singing long after
my voice was a rasp as harsh as a saw's edge.

We knew what lay down the hall where Kin and I
had been imprisoned, so we now poked our heads into
the doorways we hadn't previously explored, finding
empty chambers. One room was filled with trash,
mostly broken pottery, corroded bits of copper and
bronze, decayed cloth; I heard Kin propose that
Daneeth had gathered goods from the other rooms into
this one.

We went down the long hall we had not explored
during our escape. As we continued, more snakes
continued to emerge from holes in the floor—and walls,
and ceiling!—only to be quieted by our song.

And then I felt something, a pulse, the faintest touch
of recognition and awareness. From below. I looked at
Shallia. Her nervous glance told me she felt it too.

She gestured for me to continue with the lullaby, but
she made a smooth transition—to the ancient Terosai
hunter's song, the one meant to call animals to the kill.
I felt that pulse again, as though it were responding
to her song.

She poked her head into a doorway the men and
Jenina were already past, and slapped the wall there
to get their attention. She led us all inside.

The torches showed a featureless chamber with a
melthue-hide rug thrown carelessly in one corner. Or
perhaps not so carelessly; it moved and surged a little
as we approached.

Kin gulped. With great daring, at Shallia's gesture
he approached it, took hold of its corner, and backed
away, dragging it with him.

It concealed a large round hole . . . filled to the brim
with serpents, coiling, pulsing, hissing at us. As soon
as the cover was gone, the top layer of them fell asleep.

Shallia frowned, concentrating. Then she made another transition, this one into the song of the Bard Isbian. She gestured for me to join her, both in the song and beside the hole. I took the harmony while she held the melodic line.

As we approached, the plug of serpents retreated, lowering until we could see that there were steps carved into the living rock there. Kin and Jenina used their spears to sweep away the serpents we'd put to sleep. They looked at us, and at the steps . . . and, their faces ashen, descended before us.

We followed the retreating mass of serpent flesh down step after step, thirty-three of them before the floor levelled out . . . leaving us in a darkened chamber. The others moved out ahead of us, torches at the ready.

A stone chamber, not square like the temple chambers above; its ceiling was concave, as though it were a cave we were in. But the walls were plastered, painted over with a design I didn't look at immediately.

For it was the floor that drew my attention, the floor with its hundreds of symmetrical holes, each a handspan in diameter. The holes the serpents were retreating into, driven by our song.

I prayed the song would be enough to keep them at bay . . . for if it weren't, the snakes could leap at us from a hundred different places at once.

Kin's action, or lack of it, drew my eye; he stood stock-still with his torch high. I followed his gaze to the fresco on the wall.

The art was of a type I'd never seen, the figures almost more geometrical than realistic, though painted in bright and natural colors.

It showed a great mountain with a serpent curled round it three times. There were houses and temples and other buildings of dark stone, great organic clumps of them, built against the mountain slopes.

And where the serpent curled away from the mountain, where its underbelly showed, something clustered. I peered close to look.

More serpents. Tiny compared to the great one, they lay in hundreds by her side.

Suckling, like humans and beasts of the field.

I felt my gorge rise. I'd already been sick today, upon awakening, and my unsettled stomach threatened to empty itself again. I fought back the urge and looked again at Kin.

He seemed transfixed. He hadn't moved, not even the direction of his gaze, since I'd started to study the fresco.

The others—Shallia had her eyes closed as she maintained her song, but Jenina, Gulbuk, and Nerrin also seemed transfixed by the fresco.

Gently, I shook Kin. He started, looked at me, looked back at the fresco . . . and then forced himself to look away.

Together, we shook the other three awake. Then I gestured for them to go back up the stairs.

He shook his head. He didn't speak, fearing perhaps that words would upset the song.

I pointed again, more sternly. I wanted to tell him, *I think my song gives me protection from the power of the fresco. Stay here, and you may be enrapt again.* But I couldn't. I wanted to tell him, *I love you.* But I couldn't even do that, not while Shallia needed my help. I just gestured for them to leave, putting all the force of will I could in that gesture.

He looked at Gulbuk, who was already mesmerized again. He closed his eyes and nodded.

But they didn't leave immediately. He took from Gulbuk the skins of melthue oil the man was carrying and spilled those and his own across the floor. I watched the stuff trickle away down the holes. Nerrin joined him, pouring out his own supply. And only then, when the floor was awash in oil, save for a little dry path they left back to the stairs, did they shake Gulbuk awake and lead him forth.

Kin gave me one last look from the bottom of the stairs. I could read it like sheet music: A stern and loving warning that I'd best join him soon, or he'd come for me. Wherever I was.

Then he was gone.

Chapter Twenty-Two

Halleyne

At Shallia's signal we shifted back to the lullaby. This time I held the melody while Shallia experimented, explored.

She found a vocal pattern, an eerie trill, and while she sang it paint and plaster flaked away from the fresco. I thought that was good, but it wasn't what she wanted. She shook her head and kept at it.

Another in her endless variations caused another pulse—to me, it felt like dim awareness—from the force I felt deep below us. Again she shook her head. Not what she wanted . . . but it was affecting the right subject.

She experimented with that variation, singing it to create the pulse, then looking for another sequence to subdue it. Again and again she tried, with no luck, until I felt that by the very frequency of her attempts she was awakening what we were trying to put to sleep.

She left off singing for a while, signalling me to keep it up while she thought.

I saw serpents emerge from one of the more distant holes in the room. I sang directly at them and watched them fall asleep, sliding back down their holes. From then on, I slowly turned, bringing each part of the room into view every few moments.

Then Shallia's frantic gesture caught my eye. She signalled me to keep up the song . . . and then she launched into an entirely different melody.

I tried to make out what she was singing. A mistake; I felt my own song falter. More serpents slid up from below, this time only feet away. I clapped my hands over my ears and regained my melody.

The serpents drifted into sleep. Carefully, perhaps even daintily, I shoved them with my toe until they slipped back down their holes.

But deaf, I couldn't counterpose my song with Shallia's. I listened again, trying to hear only beat and measure while I interwove my song with hers.

Then I recognized it. "The Good Mother's Song."

A ghastly piece of music, written by some noxious male Terosai minstrel in honor of a long-dead Queen Dowager.

Sung from the old woman's point of view, it was a song of reflection as Death approaches. She recalls her children growing, achieving, having children of their own, as though their deeds were the only worthwhile things in her life. *Be content in your death, mother; your children have survived you.* I detested that song.

It was just what we needed.

For a short while, I switched to the tones she'd used to invoke the pulse . . . and there it came, flickering awareness from below.

Shallia's song smothered it.

I did it again, and this time she switched to a lower register, one more in keeping with the stone and somber manner of this place. And again the pulse was battered down, more effectively even than before.

The pulse came again, without my help. I could feel worry in it, desperation. And the serpents came crawling up from the holes mere feet away.

I returned to the main line of the lullaby and drew near Shallia, the better to concentrate my efforts and protect her. My voice was roughening, and I desperately needed something to drink.

Not so her. Her voice became stronger, surer. She gave herself up to that awful, smug song.

The pulse came again, more frantic, battering at us. She sang directly into it, her tones fusing with its silence, cancelling it.

The ground shook. More serpents emerged, one right beside my foot. It drew back to strike, but my song overwhelmed it and it fell over. Yet all around, they continued to emerge, driven by their mother's desperation.

But hers couldn't have been greater than my own desperation. I couldn't seem to put down all the vipers. Fear fueled my song, but more snakes emerged every moment . . .

I drew Shallia aside, to a spot left dry by Kin and Nerrin, and touched my torch to the floor. Fire flared up there and whipped out across the entire room. Serpents hissed, burned, blackened, fled back down whence they'd come.

Smoke began to fill the chamber. I drew Shallia down where the air was fresher.

And it hammered us, a pulse so strong that it threw us off our feet, an earth-tremble that kept us sprawling. My voice choked off.

Not Shallia's. While the pulse was alive, she could sing directly against it, and did, wrapping that blow up like a swordsmaster binding his opponent's blade.

A snake popped up to strike at her. I beat it with

my torch, hammering it away a handspan before it bit her neck. The lullaby came back to me and I sang again.

That pulse hung there in the air and Shallia skipped a stanza, final praises of vapid grandchildren who (no doubt) had grown up to be wastrels and idiots like their parents, and went straight to the last stanza, the touch of Death upon the old lady's shoulder.

The disarm. I felt her pull the pulse free from its source and release it into the air, where it dissipated.

The next snake emerged a foot from my leg and arched over to bite my calf. I felt its venom burn its way into my leg.

Kin

We waited at the top of the stairs while the sound of their song—songs—floated up to us.

Then the first dozen snakes, awake and hissing in fury, slid out of holes in the walls and ceilings and came at us.

We battered at them with stick and torch, but more were emerging behind them. "We have to get out of here," Jenina said.

"No!" That was me and Nerrin, simultaneously.

"Your lovers are protected by their song," she shouted. "We're not. Let them do what they have to do. If we stay, we die." So saying, she hammered the last snake before her and began moving toward the door.

Nerrin and I exchanged looks. She was right. Damn her.

I felt my heart tear as we abandoned our position and followed. Gulbuk brought up the rear, fearlessly stomping on serpents as they bit at his leather garment.

The hallway was worse. Vipers were swarming in. We

picked up the pace, lest we be trapped in the temple by the tidal wave of reptiles. Gulbuk took the forward position, stomping his way out with murderous fury as we followed.

Up the tunnel slope and we were out in the sunlight—and facing a hillside swarming with serpents. They climbed sinuously toward us . . . and among them came Daneeth, his face a mask of hate.

More vipers were swarming down from the hill summit. We were already surrounded by thousands.

Daneeth cried up, "I'm not going to make good children of you. You've made me too mad. They'll just bite you until you die. And then you'll serve us further."

I took my spear in one hand, my torch in the other, and struck at the nearest snake, piercing it through. Nerrin, to my right, struck at one near him. I heard Jenina grunt as she clubbed one of the vipers.

"I can feel them die, you know," Daneeth called. "That was three. But Mother will breed more. They suckle upon her and grow fast. She can replace them as fast as you can kill them."

Gulbuk hadn't taken any action. A serpent bit at him, its fangs foiled by his pants. He didn't even step on it; Jenina speared it. I asked, "Are you going to help?"

"Yes," he said. But he watched Daneeth and didn't move.

I felt a tremble from deep in the earth. I prayed that it was a good sign. I speared and burned more serpents, still keeping them back from the crude circle we were protecting. But they assembled in greater numbers, crawling at us. "Gulbuk," I said.

"A moment more."

Daneeth continued to climb. "The serpents caught every one of them. The men on the rafts. Those trying to join them."

"You're lying," I said.

"I'm not. They'll soon be here to help kill you."

I heard Gulbuk say, "Close enough."

He took three long steps into the sea of snakes, picking up speed as though he were running on a racetrack instead of a treacherous slope covered in living things. He launched himself into the air.

He flung himself so far out over the slope, and it dropped so precipitously, that he flew like a god-man taking wing.

But he wasn't. A mere man, he fell. Directly onto Daneeth, smashing the man into the stones with a hideous cracking noise like a cooked chicken being torn asunder.

They rolled through the sea of snakes, yard after yard, until they finally came to rest at the base of the hill.

Unmoving. I couldn't see their faces from this distance. I could see as serpents crawled over Gulbuk, striking him.

There was a last tremble in the earth.

Chapter Twenty-Three

Kin

Something changed in the serpents. Those nearest us still fought. Others crawled away, crawled toward us, crawled into holes in the ground, bit each other in vexation. We killed those that came at us and watched their numbers diminish.

Behind us, we heard a lullaby. Moments later, Shallia emerged, supporting Halleyne, who seemed dizzy. Both looked fatigued.

Nerrin clapped my arm and took over for me. I picked Halleyne up, cradling her.

"I was bitten," she said, sleepily.

Alarmed, I looked at Shallia. She broke off from her lullaby long enough to say, "No spirits. We've won." Then she resumed her song and joined her lover.

We made our way down the hill to where Gulbuk lay beside Daneeth Po.

Both were dead, smashed almost beyond recognition. Shallia and Halleyne wept for Gulbuk. I could not quite keep myself from joining them.

Jenina insisted we bury him until we made it clear

that we had nothing with which to dig. So we waited while she and Nerrin, ever mindful of snakes, rolled and placed stones atop the body until they were covered by a crude cairn.

Much later—and though I'd assured Halleyne that her weight was nothing, my arms were sore and weary—we found Viriat and his raft where we'd told him to meet us, on Bucketfish Bay. Casseyl and Eleyn were with him as rowers. They reported that all the rafts had put off safely, with only a few rescuees snakebitten.

We let them do the work as we pushed off from Turtlehead Island and put to sea.

"We'll reach home a day or two after the others," Viriat said.

"That's fine," I told him.

Some time later, I asked Shallia, "You're sure that thing is asleep?"

She nodded, almost asleep herself in Nerrin's arms. "I don't know how long it will last. But for now, she slumbers."

And some time after that, I asked Jenina, "Will you be joining us on Fishtail?"

She was a while in answering. "I think not. I think you're a bad ruler."

"I'm not. You just don't want to follow *anyone*, Jenina. But you've done so before. You might as well take the time, make the effort to find out what sort of townsman I really am."

She glared. "You hit me with a *club*."

"What?"

"In the fight on Fishtail. You hit me with a club."

"Well . . . yes."

"I don't like men who hit me with clubs."

I fell over laughing while she continued to glare. The others joined in with me. "It's not funny," she said.

"Yes, it is. Jenina, I'm sorry I hit you with a club. Will you come live among us again?"

She thought about it. "Very well."

And in one of the spells when she was awake and alert, Halleyne smiled at me. "There is someone new on Fishtail."

"Who?"

"A full Bard."

"Who? Shallia?" I looked at the sleeping singer.

"She confronted a goddess, Kin. She invoked powers greater than herself and wove them with her music. I saw her break through to the mastery that has always eluded her."

"She did amazing things," I agreed.

"So she's a Bard now."

"Very well." I kissed her nose. "But I'm not going to wake her up to tell her. Are you?"

"No. Let her sleep."

She slept for a day—I, for the better part of two. Halleyne recovered from the effects of the venom, only to relapse a month later. We were all frightened, I more than anyone because I could not face losing her. Still, so many bore the scars of the Gloriana vipers. But when Maydellan Ha closed the door behind himself and came out to tell me what he'd found, he was smiling.

"She's caught a child from you, Kin," he told me, and clapped me on the elbow. Had he been taller, I'm sure he would have slapped my back. "This has nothing to do with the damned serpents."

I wondered. There had been so many times for us after that first time. I had no reason to think she had caught child on the stone floor in that god-touched room. Until I had proof to the contrary, I would think otherwise. When I went in to her, I could see in her eyes a determination to believe as I did; that this child between us was a sign of hope and a promise for the future.

And that is how we came away from Turtlehead

Island: Battered, weary, drained, some of us poisoned . . . but with fear, for the time being, put to rest. We carried hope, that we had won and could win again. And we carried love, which made us strong and gave us wings.

Watch for *Wrath of the Princes*,
the next *Bard's Tale*™ novel
by Holly Lisle and Aaron Allston!

The following

is a preview of

SILVERLIGHT

The second book of

THE ARCANA

by

Morgan Llywelyn & Michael Scott

Available in bookstores

July 1996

Perhaps they were pilgrims, but the captain had her doubts. Misha had sailed the Island Sea for twenty cycles, eight of those as captain of her own vessel. She had carried warriors and traders, nobility and slaves, adjusting her prices and manners accordingly, and survived where so many others had failed because she knew how to read people. She could recognize those who would bargain and those who would fight, those who were desperate and those who did not care. She could tell it in their eyes, their voices, the way they moved.

These four so-called pilgrims were full of contradictions. They dressed like priests but walked like warriors; they shunned the company of others but Misha could detect no diffidence in their posture.

The ship's captain gazed with speculative eyes at the mysterious group now huddled on the foredeck. Each morning they spent a brief time there, leaning on the rail and examining sky and sea with an avidity more appropriate to sailors than to pilgrims. The four had taken passage in Sansen, where one young man did all the talking. In educated accents he had claimed they were making their way to the holy well at Tonne, supposedly the site of the lost city of Lowstone.

They were bundled in hooded cloaks, and masked and gloved in the manner of the lepers who sought the well's curative powers. But Misha had observed that their spokesman showed no sign of the disease. In fact none of them moved as though diseased, not the grossly fat, green-eyed one who made the deck creak when he walked, nor the burly man with shaggy blond hair escaping from beneath his hood who moved with such animal grace.

The fourth member of the party was undoubtedly female. Misha had glimpsed the outline of high, rounded breasts beneath her cloak, and a tumble of dark curls framed her masked face. She too seemed healthy enough on the brief occasions when she and her companions appeared on deck. Unlike the other passengers, these four seemed to prefer their cramped stinking cabin and spent most of their time below decks.

On more than one occasion Misha had heard sounds emanating from that cabin which should never have issued from human throats.

The wind shifted. When Misha looked up to check the sails, the long queue of hair depending from the back of her otherwise shaven skull slid across her shoulder like a crimson snake. There was a storm coming out of the north; she could smell ice in the wind. It might be what the Island peoples called a Shipkiller — a sudden gale whipping up huge seas that could take an unwary captain by surprise and dash a vessel to splinters on the serrated shore of one of the islands.

Misha turned to bark an order to Kupp, her First Mate, but he was already swinging the wheel, bringing the ship in toward the nearest island. They would ride out the storm in a sheltered bay.

Misha's gaze returned to the pilgrims. Pilgrims indeed! She hawked and spat over the side. They were no more pilgrims than she was. Fugitives, more like. Usually she would not have cared, so long as the passage was paid — in New Coin, in advance. She did not care what paying passengers called themselves, nor what crimes they might have committed.

But these four...

The young man, their spokesman, was making his way along the swaying deck toward her. He moved like a trained warrior, carrying all the balance in his hips. Through the slits of his mask his dark, piercing eyes could be seen constantly moving, watching.

"We've changed course," he said, pausing two full paces away from Misha. It was a statement, not a question.

Deliberately nonchalant, the captain canted her body sideways to lean one elbow on the rail. The salt-encrusted leather tunic she wore creaked with the motion. "There's a storm coming up," she said, pitching her voice so low it was barely audible above the snap of the sails and the slap of the sea. It was a tactic she often used to bring people nearer to her. She wanted a closer look at this pilgrim.

As he stepped closer to her, Misha felt a wave of intensity emanating from him that made her catch her breath in surprise. She had lived her life on the waves, attuned to the forces of nature: this man exuded an almost palpable energy.

"Where are we headed?" His voice was level, measured, the diction crisp and precise, but she could not place his accent.

"Straight ahead," she replied, pointing. "See that low island in the distance?"

The young man squinted. "Does it have a name?"

"There are countless islands in this sea, so many that only the Islanders themselves can tell you the names of most of them. I can identify some of the larger ones, but I'm not even sure this island has a name. It may not even be on the chart."

"How long will we need to stay there?"

Misha shrugged. "Until the storm passes over."

"And how long could that be?"

"A day, two, ten." She shrugged again. "Who knows? But which would you prefer: that we sail on and sink, or spend some time at anchor? At least this way you will reach your shrine alive. And which shrine is it again?" she asked abruptly, hoping to catch him off guard.

His voice remained calm. "The Holy Well at Tonne. Do you know it?"

"By reputation," Misha murmured.

The young man leaned toward her now, reading her as she had been reading him. Again she felt that wave of intensity. In spite of herself, her heart began to thud heavily, though whether with fear or attraction she could not have said. "Have you ever visited the well?" he asked her.

He was so close she could smell him, a mingled scent of cloth and flesh and sweat and...and metal? The mystery deepened. Misha tried to keep her voice casual as she replied, "I have never been to the well myself. But I once transported a group of pilgrims who had to be carried onto the island on litters, they were so crippled with disease. When they returned to my ship, they came walking." She made a gesture with her hand, index and thumb forming a circle, then flicking away evil spirits. "At night the sky above the island glows green and blue," she added, unexpectedly dodging to one side, trying to glimpse the man behind the mask. But she only had time to see that he was swarthy and strong-featured before he pulled the hood of his cloak around his face, hiding his broad forehead and thick dark hair. He moved too hastily, like someone with something to hide.

Misha grinned. "Do I frighten you?"

"My religion forbids contact with those not of my caste," the young man replied. He took a step backward, made a sketchy bow, then turned on his heel and hurried away. His heavy cloak could not conceal the tension in his posture.

The captain ran her hand across her shaved skull, adjusting the long plait of red hair as she watched him gather his companions and disappear below decks. She was stocky, muscular, with a heavy jaw, but she was a woman with a woman's instincts and the young man had disturbed her on many levels. His nervousness reassured her, however. He and his party were probably just another group of the hopeful and credulous, desperate for a cure. They hid some loathsome disease beneath their robes after all; a disfigurement he did not want her to see.

Misha bared her teeth in a humourless smile; putting them out of their misery would be a blessing.

The wide-bodied caravel found shelter in a small bay, where two wings of land protected the vessel like encircling arms. Once they entered the bay the wind dropped immediately, sails on the four masts cracking and snapping. Misha remained on the foredeck until the mainsail and the lateen sails were furled and made secure and the last of the crew went below. Then, after taking a final look around, the captain made her way to the safety of her own cabin.

Even though they were in the shelter of the bay, she knew what could happen to any living thing caught on deck. The Shipkiller drove a solid wall of sleet before it, razor-sharp needles of ice propelled with irresistible force. Such a storm could not only strip paint and tar and shred the sails — it could flay flesh from bone, turning a human being into bloody pulp in a matter of heartbeats. On some of the more primitive islands, criminals tied to stakes were put in the path of a Shipkiller. It was an effective method of execution and savage enough to provide a deterrent. What little remained after the storm passed was tossed into the sea.

The captain pulled a heavy wooden shutter across the polished horn porthole of her cabin just as the first spatters of ice struck the deck above. In moments the hail was drumming on the ship to such an extent it blotted out all other sound.

Misha reached under her bunk and pulled out a small hand-held crossbow, almost a miniature. It was Gallowan work, intricately detailed. She had found it among the possessions of a Gallowan mercenary taking the pilgrim trail in hopes of curing the disease that was slowly eating away his flesh. Misha had put him out of his misery, too. And very profitably.

Bracing the weapon against her broad leather belt, she armed the bow by fitting a tiny bolt into the groove. The pointed head of the crossbow bolt was coated with a mixture of fish oils; death would be swift and agonizing as the lungs froze. When she stepped out into the corridor, Kupp, the first mate, and two of the crew were waiting for her. The mate carried a cutlass; the crewmen had saw-toothed sea-shell daggers that tore flesh so badly it could never be stitched.

They did not speak to one another. Any sound they made could not be heard above the din of the storm anyway, Misha thought with satisfaction. Moving in easy unison — they had performed this task many times — they positioned themselves outside the door of the pilgrims' cabin. The two sailors stood on either side, the first mate crouched by the latch. Misha placed herself directly opposite the door.

When her men were in place, the captain bared her teeth in a savage grimace and nodded. Kupp lifted the latch with the tip of his cutlass. The door was weighted to swing silently inward. As Misha expected, the pilgrims were clustered at the porthole, staring out at the raging sea. She saw the young man turn, saw his mouth open to question...then she fired the poisoned crossbow bolt.

It took Misha several heartbeats to realize what had happened next.

Her tingling fingers reached up in disbelief to touch the arrow suddenly embedded in her own throat. Imprinted on her shocked brain was the image of the young man catching the poisoned bolt in mid-air, then sending it spinning back toward her.

Simultaneously the fat man whirled around, tossing his cloak aside. But he was not a fat man. The figure was that of a woman, unnaturally massive.

Kupp drove his knife into the woman's stomach, only to have the weapon shatter to powder against an impervious surface. The woman responded by pulping the first mate's head with one blow of her stony fist.

Meanwhile Misha felt her lungs closing down as the poison did its work. She writhed with pain; her knees buckled and she slid to the floor, clawing at her throat and screaming silently for air.

The two sailors shouldered their way into the cabin, one stepping over her body, but they were also doomed. The burly blond man lashed out with an animal-like agility to claw the face off the first sailor as effortlessly as the Shipkiller would have done.

At the same time, the dark young man who had caught and re-thrown the bolt from the crossbow stripped the glove from one of his hands. He chopped the chest of the last sailor, whose eyes rolled back in his head as his heart stopped. He was dead by the time he hit the floor.

Misha's dimming eyes informed her the fatal blow had been dealt...by a shining silver hand.

She knew them then, but it was too late.